ROUGH JUSTICE

Ralph Palmer

authorHOUSE®

AuthorHouse™ UK
1663 Liberty Drive
Bloomington, IN 47403 USA
www.authorhouse.co.uk
Phone: 0800.197.4150

Published by AuthorHouse 07/26/2016

ISBN: 978-1-5246-6118-2 (sc)
ISBN: 978-1-5246-6119-9 (hc)
ISBN: 978-1-5246-6120-5 (e)

Print information available on the last page.

This book is printed on acid-free paper.

Dedication

To my brother John, world traveller and ardent photographer, whose unwavering support and loyalty over the years is very special to me.

Ref 3

Acknowledgments

To numerous friends, who have devoted their time and energy to reduce the forest of errors, which grew out of the weeds of my original creation. In particular, I wish to thank Clare Jethwa, Wangu Wachira and Bena Shah, for their in depth examination. I also wish to record my thanks to Philip Horobin, Bismarck Durado, Vina Shah, and Rose Mitoko. Jacinta Salins, actually gave birth to a bouncing boy during the course of her examination of this text. I do not how-ever lay claim to inducing the shock that caused her happy event, but I do lay claim to the errors that have slipped through the net.

Also by Ralph Palmer

The Rainbow Addiction
Nukes Wild
Deadline
Code Orange

Prelude

The nimbus cumulus had been threatening the scene for days, but Kenya's Independence was planned six months after internal self-government, come rain, hail, snow, or high water. The climate was merely a blip in the calendar, and the mighty Raj was expected to roll back the clouds, because the short rains were never considered in the East African territories; Independence always dawned in December. Like Napoleon's march on Moscow and the German siege of Stalingrad, the elements were ignored and defeat had followed. The try and try again attitude of 'Bruce and the Spider' was a prominent feature in colonial times, but a second 'bite of the cherry' is never offered with Independence. Oh why couldn't they consider the weather just once and have a perfect day, before all was lost in a dwindling Empire?

So it rained and it rained and we all got wet, except for the privileged few. It was a good omen, the timing was perfect, and the crowds danced in the mud. An abundant harvest was bound to follow and the Africans proved they controlled the weather, or was it a masterstroke by the Almighty, to relieve the Government of famine, as they shaped the new nation?

Or perhaps after all, the wily British had planned the rain, as a farewell finale...

1

Lord Digby Banks was one of a rare breed; some forty years ago as Governor of a distant colony, he had stood in the rain with a stiff upper lip as the Union Flag was finally lowered. He was in the company of those who believed the past had bled their country dry, and such accusations from newly elected leaders were expected in international circles, and on occasions justified. But, to cry foul, to hide bad governance beyond the twenty-year period, was 'a bit off' in the words of Lord Digby. So he wanted to know if the ugly rumours were true, and what exactly was happening in 'his' last outpost of the British Empire.

Dozing in his hereditary seat that afternoon, he recalled happier times and happy people prior to the granting of Independence to Kenya. He still talked to many of the 'boys' who had become the governing elite; but now for some reason he found difficult to explain, he was losing sight of their earlier good governance. The confidential report from the Foreign Office of 2008, concerning the cessation of British aid to the African Continent had made disastrous reading, and cut him to the quick. It described his pet country as being run by a bunch of thieves with an endless list of transgressions, and the 'Times' newspaper cutting he had in his pocket confirmed just that. Enough was enough, he had to take a stand and put things back on track, and make up for the mistakes in his past. He had earnestly believed the masses were about to prosper with the birth of the new nation, but this ideal had failed because of the greedy few.

Collecting his thoughts to find a solution, he concluded he needed a partner… and who better to ask than his fellow peer, an ex-governor himself, in the personage of the Honourable Lord Rupert Crook-Smith. Whom, much to his chagrin on occasion, Digby addressed as Rupert Crook, if not more endearingly as Crooky, as his classmates called him at Eton. Despite this unusual quirk of name, he was in Digby's opinion, the right man to be interested in such affairs, and would be able to verify or rebut the horrific position. There and then, Digby decided to stay over at the weekend, in the knowledge that Crooky would be at their club off Horse Guards Parade.

"Evening Diggers," came the call from behind the 'Times' that was lowered to reveal the owner of the voice, recognised by Digby, even before the face appeared.

"Surprise, surprise, old boy," Crooky continued. "Thought you went down to the country weekends?"

"Quite right, but I have important business that just couldn't wait; in fact…" he paused, rattled his thoughts, and came straight to the point. "It concerns you."

"Oh!" A bushy eyebrow was raised in disbelief. "Sounds interesting Diggers, but the last time you consulted me on something... can't remember for the life of me what it was, but I do distinctly recall you didn't take my advice. Are you having Tiffin?"

"Yes, with you I hope, and it's on my account."

"That's damned civil of you. How'd you know I'd accept?" Even as he questioned Digby's invitation he was drooling at the thought of the succulent lobster he had in mind to order, and he wasn't footing the bill. "No matter, Diggers; always pleased to be of service, even if you didn't take my advice before."

"Shall we go in?" Digby motioned with his hand toward the dining room, and waited for Rupert to ease his lengthy body to the edge of his chair and stand up.

"Can hardly wait to hear what kept you up from the country; must be hellish important. C'mon Diggers, what are you holding in your hand; is that it? Is that what this evening's all about?"

"Could be" Digby admitted sparingly.

"So?"

"So, why don't we eat first, and then digest this with a good Napoleon." He pocketed the piece of paper he held in support of his good meal first suggestion, and Rupert accepted without his usual, 'steady on man'.

They entered the blue room, as the dining room was popularly called, and were escorted by the maitre d' to their corner table. In Digby's belief the room was named after the royal blue carpet, but for the sake of contention, Rupert said it was named after the pale blue walls. This subject of naming was usually raised again and again as an evening wore on, if they had nothing better to discuss, and nothing ever came of it. But whatever the odds, and whatever the colour, they agreed that the dining room was a splendid place. Oil paintings in heavy gilt frames, depicting some of England's finest seafarers, Nelson, Rodney, Grenville, and Raleigh, monopolized two walls, and the finer details of their warships discharging broadsides were impressive; but they tended to fade into insignificance as other attributes took over. Chandeliers, blue velvet drapes from brass rails, and well-preserved plaster moldings from a Victorian era.

The white tablecloths were made from the finest damask to flatter the crested silver, and the sparkling wine glasses seemed to stand tall, out of respect for the Chateaux to come. As impeccable as ever, the waiters draped napkins across their laps, and Digby tasted the wine with a practiced rinse to pronounce it fit to fill Rupert's glass, and then his own. By habit, they knew exactly what they would order, and so did the staff. The lobster tails in white wine sauce was their favorite when they dined together, and the entrée dish bearing their choice never failed to inspire a deep sniffing, and a certain amount of salivation, as the sweet aroma foretold of the succulent taste to follow.

"Thank you Diggers," Rupert wiped his lips with his napkin, "you can't beat the grub at this club—first class I say; no roaches in our kitchens, eh?" He was thinking of the scandal next door at the Café Royale, some years back, when their resident roaches had become the darlings of the tabloid press. Finally, napkins were left unfolded on the table as they pushed back their chairs assisted by indulgent waiters, whose job in life it was, to look after codgers, such as they.

"Cigar?" Digby extended a leather case towards Rupert; it held two medium sized Havanas.

"Don't mind if I do." Rupert reached forward and took one, slipped the gold embossed label off the body, and leisurely rolled the leaf between his thumb and forefinger listening to the crackle, before he sniffed it, to seek a second sensual opinion. It was then precisely clipped, conveyed to his mouth, and the flame from the Swan Vesta match brought the ceremony to an end.

"Now Diggers, let's see that bit of paper." Rupert held out his hand in expectation.

Diggers calmly dipped into his jacket pocket, withdrew his precious press cutting, and reached with it through the smoke to his puffing friend, who was still in the process of getting his cigar to glow. He then eased back into the adjoining chair, drew on his own cigar, and enjoyed the taste of the leaf on his brandied tongue as he waited for Rupert to finish. Eventually, Rupert returned his spectacles to their case, and snapped it shut to shout completion.

"Mmm…fascinating," was his first reaction. "So what's new? They're stealing the family silver. You may ask why, and they'll tell you everyone's doing it; and if they stop someone else will take their place in the queue."

"Rupert, theft is theft, and there's no way to justify it. It's against the laws of the country. They should be prosecuted and go to jail."

"Grow up, Diggers. Get real. The Judiciary is rotten and they're all scratching each other's backs. No one ever goes to jail, and nothing ever comes of these numerous commissions. Smoke screens…bloody smoke screens I tell you, that's what they are."

"I don't accept that nothing can be done. It's outrageous!" He got carried away as he shouted 'outrageous', and then looked around the room to see if anyone had heard him. Only the barman was present.

"I didn't help educate some of these lovely people to turn them into high-class thieves. I feel my efforts over the years have been wasted."

"So what?"

"What do you mean, so what? I intend to do something about it, and I want you to advise me… and perhaps help me?" he added 'help me 'to build Rupert's ego.

"Diggers, listen to me. At our age we have to be realistic—look at yourself in the mirror and what do you see? An elegant old man, who's thin on top, with a bulbous bucolic nose that lights up when he's angry. It's true, you've covered up the spider lines on your upper lip with a soup-strainer moustache, and today, by coincidence, it needs trimming. But that's a point in your favor, covering up the lines and all that. Your big brown eyes, staring at me in disbelief of what I'm saying are another good feature you have, and about which I know to my cost, when you charmed my filly into the sack many years ago.

"Do you mind? Have you quite finished with your insults Rupert Crook?" He used 'Crook' to show his displeasure. "I hope you're not going to bring up that Doris, business again. It was a terrible mistake when *I did for her*, and how was I to know she was your girl at the time. It just happened on the spur of the moment—after a boozy night out on the tiles."

"To hell with Doris. The last I heard of her she had six kids and I had a lucky escape, for which I'm obliged to you."

"Crooky," Digby's nose had returned to a light shade of pink in tune with his pressure, "my 'full head' of white hair, wavy at that-- still gives me a bit of an edge over you with the ladies. And, I can tell you this much; you're never going to charm the 'birds' out of the trees with your sideburns, and that excuse for a moustache you wear to make up for the vacant 'plot' on top of your head. For all intents and purposes, you're practically hairless, and it's not a bad thing-- you're missing hair and all that-- if we're to avoid being called the twins by the riffraff in the House. You may well claim an aquiline nose as you choose to describe it, and tell me it doesn't turn red like mine when you're angry, but you're forgetting that yours turns permanently blue during winter, and matches our dining room walls. Ruddy looks, burned into our faces by the African sun in our youth, I'll concede, we both have. And as much I detest it, that extra inch in your height at six one you keep bragging about, is hardly noticeable. I have an idea for you to chew on Rupert Crook-- one of us should give up wearing his paisley waistcoat; that's my suggestion to you. What about it?" Digby used Rupert's derogatory name again to show his displeasure, of the transparent truths they'd just traded.

"Diggers, 'young' man," he smiled, and tempers quickly returned to normal. Their friendship ran deeper than name-calling, and each, always believed they'd got the better of the other, before shifting to common ground. "I still say, this is not our time in life to save the world, and take a stand against corruption by using powerful words that no one ever listens to. And quite honestly the alternative, physical action is out of the question."

"What about it Rupert; will you help me if I come up with a physical plan of action?"

"I don't believe what I'm hearing, but for what it's worth, if you come up with a physical plan to sort out the dishonesty of the world, it'll have to be radical, and you'll need all the help you can get. But quite frankly, I think you're dreaming."

"Well, if I'm prepared to try, will you help me? And so that you don't think I'm labouring under any misapprehension, I state here and now, I'm aware I'll have to meet evil with evil and people are going to die. But hear you this, my conscience will be absolutely clear when I think of the starving masses, I'll save by my ruthless acts."

2

The advertisement on the Internet was unusual. It begged the question. 'Who are these people and what are they planning?'

Wanted – Personnel – Terminally ill. Must have military training and a desire to leave a legacy. Indigenous Africans only, need apply.

It was placed on the Net on Friday afternoon and the application list closed Sunday night. At the time of drafting the solicitation, Digby had failed to comprehend the hundreds of people out there who fitted the description, and the torrent of applicants had suddenly changed the simplicity of the project into something too big to handle.

He fixed himself a whiskey, settled down in front of the fire, and picked up the phone. "Crooky! Diggers here!" he bellowed down 'the blower' to compensate for his deafness. He reckoned the whole world was whispering these days, because he was too stubborn to admit he was going deaf; besides which, an 'earplug' as he termed it, was 'damned demeaning'. "I must see you tomorrow about this business we discussed. Are you in town?"

"Can be, if it's important," Rupert, warmed to another free meal.

"Lunch at the club suit you?"

"See you then Diggers, about twelve for a G & T."

That night, Digby set the alarm to ensure he was on time for the 6 AM morning dash to London; he had a lot of ground to cover on other matters before the mid-day deadline with Rupert. Last evening had been spent choosing names from over 500 applicants with the assistance of his secretary Jean Brown, his guide to the Internet

World, that he had abandoned as so much twaddle many years ago. She had used the new laser printer to make short work of the final pages he eventually stashed in his briefcase. Jean was perfection, and after Rupert's input she would know what to do with their analysis; the short list they were about to compile at the club.

He still hadn't decided the number of people he wanted to recruit, and what method he would use to maintain ambiguity. Anyway, Rupert would know; Rupert always knew what to do and could advise him over lunch. But one thing that stood out a mile... recruits, had to be distanced from their controllers in the interests of security, and the histories of those on the short list required scrutiny by a deep-seated friend specialised in such matters.

The Express from the West Country slid into Waterloo station at precisely eight, and by noon with numerous tasks behind him, Digby entered the club for lunch, bearing his list for Rupert's inspection.

"By gad, Crooky, the pungent taste of this red bean soup opens up a chest of memories; takes me back forty years; nothing like chili pepper and the tang of tomatoes to drown the beans into submission. Just the smell of this soup regenerates the bellowing voice of my ADC, shouting, 'funga safari', to ring in my ears. My escorts then echoed the call again, as they clambered aboard our safari-built trucks. Real men in those days Crooky; dressed in red pillbox hats, blue jerseys, puttees and boots, each with a 303 Enfield. The scene as we lumbered down State House Road was an act in itself, never left anything to chance you know. Nearer to nature in those days… we could actually stop for a leak with no one in sight. God only knows, from where the chef got the African beans to cook up this soup today." He chuckled, sighed, and continued to reminisce. "You know, I can just see the sunsets now, with thorn trees silhouetted on Maasai Plains, and I hear those damned frogs, crickets, or whatever they were in the background. Always started their racket as soon as the birds stopped chirping..."

"I don't know about the East, Diggers, but I also had my times on the West Coast with my travels in the northern deserts. Those harsh barren landscapes that possessed their own extraordinary beauty, created indelible scenes I'll take with me to my grave." His eyes glazed over, as he too, dug into the past. The roast beef, which was the next in line on the menu, didn't particularly strike a memorable chord, and the fancy ice cream that followed was almost impossible for any Governor's Camp to create in those days.

Digby and Rupert were always sparring to outdo each other as they reminisced about their African adventures, recalling their fashionable Bombay Bowlers made of cork, and their aching feet and sweating brows they shared in common, as they trudged over hostile territory to administer the Continent. The hand-made leather boots they wore to accomplish such feats were laced up to their calves, and as time drew on, they became prized possessions. On rare occasions, such relics could even be dragged, protesting into the light, after nearly half a century in musty cupboards, when laughing children doubted the stories that flowed from Grandpa's lips of a winter's night, as they snuggled up around the fire. Neither Rupert nor Digby, really challenged the other as to whose experiences were the better, but by painting intriguing pictures of safari treks over mountain ridges, dried up riverbeds and deserts, they somehow showed the flag and their mettle, reliving exciting memories as young District Officers in the field. The Lords, career administrators, they were not; but the years in the African bush in their youth before taking up work in the City of London, was a plus in their favour, when they applied through family connections to be the last Governors of the countries they loved and knew, in the final run up to independence.

The human train of porters always traveled in single file on foot safaris, with the Bwana in the lead and his gun bearer close behind, just incase, a charging animal had to be felled. More often than not the porters, locally hired, were lean of limb, and wrapped in colored kikois with shirts hanging free. They wore sandals strapped to their hardened feet that were more than a match for the rock-strewn paths they trampled without complaint. Each man, carried a load on his turbaned head of 56lbs, which was the imperial weight or thereabouts, of a commodity sack in their day. Sacks of rice, sugar, wheat, folded canvas chairs, water, crates of beer, and camping equipment; were all the necessities of safari life. Transported by human endeavor-- it was called adventure, and enjoyed as a sinecure by those with masochistic tendencies. And as the supplies dwindled, the head-loads were transformed into single elephant tusks, hacked from rotting flesh that swarmed with noisy black flies and bloated white maggots-- the location of which was traced by circling vultures and the stench that poisoned the air. The tales of sweating to administer the natives were riveting when heard by strangers for the very first time, and even when retold, they bewitched the same listeners with different detail, forgotten from a previous telling. 'Hands on administration', as Digby called it, was his answer to good governance. And if Rupert were there, as Digby reminisced about bleached bones and human skulls he had poked with his walking stick without much reverence; he too would add his extra spices, to the meat of the story in hand. Not often, would they jointly portray such magic, but when they did, their listeners were spellbound, and 'Super-glued' to their chairs. Alas, the stories always ended far too soon, and such memories only sprang to life when the occasional mood took hold, and then died, almost as quickly.

"Diggers, tell me, how many answers did you get in response to your ad?"

"Over 500."

"Impossible."

"You asked me the question; I'm giving you the answer. Why do you think it's impossible?"

"Well, to me, it seems unlikely that so many people would fit your specification. Can there be that many terminally ill people on our doorstep?"

"The advert went worldwide. Does that answer your question?"

"I still want to see the printout." He didn't want to let go, even though he now conceded that the worldwide figure in excess of 500 made good sense. Digby opened his case and handed over the printout compiled by Jean from the computer. Rupert glanced at the columns, and without hesitation proposed a solution.

"Colonel Jesse Holt's our man," he declared.

"Never heard of him," Digby responded.

"I've known him for years; he's much younger than us. Come to think of it, who isn't much younger than us?" he laughed. "He fagged for my younger brother at Eton and they became good friends; used to come home weekends."

"You're telling me that we need this chap because he fagged for your brother at Eton?"

"No, no, no! I'm telling you we need him because he was second-in-command of Special Air Services at the time of that Gibraltar operation. He'll organise us. He's one of us. I'd trust him with my life. That Gib. show was a great success, even if human rights activists didn't think so. I'm sure you recall the event. His team shot those Irish bastards with the bombs, and I say good riddance to them too. Your thoughts Diggers— let's have em?" He drew on his cigar and waited.

"Well, what do you think?" Rupert asked again.

"I'm thinking." Digby massaged his chin.

"Have you got a better idea?" Rupert pushed for a reply.

"No," Digby admitted.

"So we try mine?" He held out a hand in askance. "But if you don't feel comfortable with my suggestion...?"

"Rupert, I know what you're going to say-- I never take your advice. But this time it's different, since I don't have any better ideas of my own. And again, I really believe yours will serve our purpose."

The first item on the shopping list was then crossed off by mutual agreement. One retired, Colonel Jesse Holt, was to be put on notice with immediate effect, and Rupert was delegated to 'flush' him out. A cash-stash, of about a million dollars from different sources to back the mission became the next hurdle. A tedious task by any reckoning, but it had to be done over a period of time, to avoid money-laundering restraints.

"Hallo?" Rupert recognised the single word of greeting from Colonel Holt, who answered the phone, but enquired in case his memory was faulty. "Is that you Jesse?"

"Croooky..." came back a stretched version of his name. It was Jesse all right, and he was sure of Rupert's identity.

"How nice to hear from you; it must be a couple of years. So what's the problem?"

"Problem— who said there was a problem?" Rupert innocently answered.

"Croooky, the last time we spoke you had a problem; has anything changed?"

"Well, not exactly," he hesitated, "but this time I want to offer you a job. Interested?"

"Try me."

"Well," Rupert was pleased to have detected some interest, which was more than the last time he'd spoken to him, but on that occasion he wasn't offering a job. "It isn't as simple as that. We have to meet and discuss it."

"Your place or mine?" Jesse shot back.

"You're still in Richmond, same address?"

"Sure..."

"Okay, give me a time and I'll come over. We'll enjoy the drive through the park at this time of the year." He had just renewed his license for the next three years.

"Seven tomorrow evening suit you?"

"Perfect. So until then I'll bid you good night. Oh, there is something I almost forgot; I'll have a friend with me."

"Hope she's sexy!" He hung up instantly and missed the splutter on the end of the line.

"Bloody fellow," Rupert mumbled. "Who the hell does he think I am at my age, sexy-- be damned! It's shrinking by the day."

3

Rupert and Digby walked from the Old Deer Park across Richmond Green to where Jesse lived in one of the more expensive dwellings. For a change, they were in total harmony as they discussed the brick façade of Richmond Theatre, and declared it worthy of heritage status, which in fact it already had. The bell-pull on number nine was an imitation antique, and the chimes were clearly audible from the steps.

"Croooky, come in, come in. So this is your beautiful lady!" Jesse peered at Digby and thrust out his hand.

"Take no notice of him, he's always joking," Rupert came to the rescue, as Digby felt Jesse's firm grip for the very first time. The living room they entered was not remarkable in any way, except for the size of the glass-cabinet that covered the back wall and faced the bay window. It was at least twenty feet wide and six feet tall, and the curved glass doors on either end, nicely rounded it off.

Colonel Jesse Holt was retired, lived on his own, and was ably assisted by a housekeeper to keep the place tidy for the occasional visitor. Maria, his wife, had left him after only five years of army life, finding it difficult to keep up with the SAS that was constantly on the move. At seventy-one, he looked younger than his years, and it was not because Maria had left him after only five… his standing joke, but mainly due to his active outdoor life.

However, time eventually catches up with every career, and in the army it's sooner than most if you hadn't reached the heady-heights of General. In Crooky's opinion, Jesse was retired by his Commanding

Officer far too early, and for this reason alone it made him a suitable candidate. His full head of sandy hair with strands of grey matched his bushy brows, and balanced the piecing blue eyes that stung Digby the first time they met. Full lips below a pugilistic nose hinted of humour, and he rarely disappointed his friends with his dryness and subtlety, which was difficult to follow if you didn't know him well. To Rupert's secret delight, Digby had been the butt of one of Jesse's remarks on their first encounter.

"Do you mind if I have a look?" Rupert walked toward the glass cabinet when asking the question.

"Help yourself," Jesse invited.

"It's a hobby I took up on retirement, and I'm still collecting; I suppose you could say I'm just getting into my stride. Some of my latest finds come from a collector friend of mine, who was on the Afghan border at the time of the Russian occupation." He turned the key in the glass door and reached inside. "Look at this magnificent barrel, part of a threaded sniper rifle; drilled out by Pathan craftsmen... 0.388 mm. It's unique, handmade, and takes the Rolls Royce of ammo." He picked it up with loving care and caressed the gunmetal, using a tender touch one would normally reserved for the inner thighs of a lover. Digby looked over Rupert's shoulder, putting distance between him and his new acquaintance, of whom he remained wary, after the banter of the 'beautiful lady'.

"Where did all this stuff come from?" Rupert enquired as he peered into the 'Aladdin's cave' of specimens.

"I've always been interested in the exotic and the unusual, a bit here and a bit there, and after every war someone always has a souvenir to sell. Mind you, they have no pins, but all that could change if war broke out on the London streets." He laughed. "Specialist ammunition might prove more of a problem if the truth were known," he laughed again.

"Will you open the subject or should I?" Rupert asked Digby as they settled themselves on the Chesterfield couch.

"I will," Digby almost demanded. After all, it was his show and Rupert was the invited partner, being a reliable sort of chap who always offered a second opinion, requested or not.

"No problem, we both know the score." Rupert graciously acceded to Digby's centre stage attitude and was content to sit mum, even though Jesse was his man. Digby produced a notebook to act as a prompt and leaned toward Jesse, while Rupert rested his arms along the top of the couch.

"The law is an ass," Digby declared, and paused for his statement to gain momentum..

"Why?" Jesse was not impressed by the drama and the statement didn't gain weight, but he kept any cutting remarks to himself.

"I won't go into the nitty-gritty of the matter," Digby said, and Rupert sighed with relief. "But it's like this...Rupert and I are tired of Third World corruption in our Colonies."

"Colonies?"

"Well, they aren't our colonies now; so I'll rephrase that and call them our late possessions, but when Crooky and I were out there on the ground they were called our colonies, and that's the crux of the matter. We left them in a good state of repair, so to speak. I admit we looted their minerals and grabbed their land, but their financial reserves were in the black when we left... and now the bloody places are falling apart."

"So?"

"So we want to do something about it; and we need your assistance." He looked at Rupert and received a nod of encouragement.

"And how can I help you from my position as a retired army man and a collector of odd weapons? I'm a bit like a toothless tiger..."

"Not really...let me explain how we see it." Rupert gave Digby the nod to continue. "You have the expertise and experience to execute our plan, which is not unique in itself because it's been done before. In fact, the only aspect of variation compared to other programmes is probably the reasoning behind it, the area of operation, and perhaps our self-righteous assessment of the morals of those involved." Rupert held up his hand to forestall a full-blown explanation he felt was about to follow.

"May I stop you there, Digby?" Rupert knew Jesse could do without the justification spiel and further explanation was irrelevant. What he needed to know was the object, and the task to be performed. The basics-- was as simple as that.

"I'll brief it up, if you'll permit me." Rupert chipped in. "In Africa, it seems there are greedy people stealing from the poor. Occasionally they are arraigned in court, but their lawyers make an ass out of the law with technicalities, so they continue to enjoy their stolen millions while most of the population lives in abject poverty. It's the wish of Digby and me to put the fear of God into such people and stop the looting."

"We think," he indicated Digby and himself as one with a wave of his hand, "if a few of these thieves are assassinated, it will act as a deterrent and send a message to those still alive that corruption's bad business, which in turn will cower them into making confessions, and return their assets to the exchequer. It may sound a bit far fetched to you as I explain it today, but a simple Treasury receipt could be their salvation. They could even live to see their grand-children grow up."

"Now the twist in the tail is this," Digby took over. "Compound interest from the date of theft will be calculated, and receipts from properties sold will include the appreciation value and rent collected during their spurious ownership."

"Is that all?" Jesse still had to come to terms with the plan. "It sounds ambitious, but I suppose given the will... How many of these people are there?"

"Several thousand I fear, but in all truth, we really don't know."

"What!" The size of the figure had triggered his response.

"It won't come to that," Digby reassured him.

"These people are such cowards when they can't hide behind the law; so it's merely a case of hitting two or three, and I promise you, the rest will find a way to save their skins. At best we could reach a dozen in each country before they get the message; who knows? But whatever the outcome, I say we're doing Africa a good turn. And when things begin to hot up, we envisage a settling of personal vendettas among the thieves, followed by political rhetoric and finger pointing, but in the end such attempts at deflection will fail. They know exactly who and what they are, and their deeds will come home to roost. Now, to put you in the picture about what is happening in my ex-colony, I suggest you read the National Daily on the Internet for a couple of weeks, and observe the frightening pattern of criminality. I earnestly believe, it can only serve to support your resolve that we're doing the right thing."

"So you want me to light the match and burn a sample for the many."

"Well put. That's about it." Rupert agreed.

"Okay Rupert, now let me continue... Rupert and I will get you details and pictures of some of the Biggies from press cuttings in my favourite country to get the ball rolling; I'll finance the operation. However, there's something I must confess before we go any further, and I hope it won't create any difficulties. I naively advertised on the Internet and received this response." He opened his document case and produced the same papers he'd previously shown to Rupert.

After a couple of minutes of sifting, Jesse had a grip on the situation. "Don't worry, let these applicants go," he smiled reassuringly, "but let me keep these papers just the same. I'll do it in another way in spite of my liking for the terminally ill touch, which I'll definitely keep in mind." He bit his lower lip in thought, and his vacant eyes seemed to concentrate for a moment on the shiny surface of the table, before he looked up and asked. "How much money do I have to play with?"

"Up to a million US." Such a figure had already been agreed the two, because it had to be one of the first questions from any serious recruit.

"Do I get some up front?"

"To tell you the truth Jesse, we're still collecting the cash little by little, to avoid awkward questions from nosey bank managers... I'm sure you follow our caution?"

"Good thinking on your part," he was tapping the table to contain his excitement. "So, assuming I accept your offer; what do I do in the meantime?"

"Well, by the end of the month our tedious business of visiting Thomas Cook branches and other cash sources will be completed, and we'll have all the money you need, but until then I really don't know, any suggestions?"

"I suppose I could finance my own trip to Pakistan to check out the weaponry and source a few other items." He had a plan already. "It isn't as though you'll be leaving the country and I'll lose my investment, is it?" He burst out laughing, slapped his thigh, and his visitors joined in with rather less gusto.

"We'll lodge our passports with you if you insist." Rupert in turn slapped his thigh and laughed at his own joke, forcing Jesse to grimace and stand up rather abruptly to indicate the meeting was over, his visitors should be on their feet. Inwardly, he could hardly contain his excitement; he wanted to get on with the job.

It was his first time not to be over-shadowed by a commanding general whose strings were being jerked by Westminster, so he was ready to get on with the job, with or without the provision of finance. As his training over the years kicked in, he already sensed the cool air on his cheeks sweeping down from the Khyber Pass.

4

The temperature was -5 c without the wind-chill factor as Jesse and colleague debussed at Peshawar, the last frontier town of any size before the Afghan border an hour away. The single street with lean-tos of corrugated iron construction and porches was not an unusual set-up in the North Eastern territories. Dara-adam-khel, the particular area they sought, was in the old part of town across the railway line, where the age of the structures was only surpassed by the snow capped mountains, and perhaps a couple of mosques and forts that were noticeably worn. The only concession to change in recent years was the influx of motor-vehicle traffic, from the time the Taliban had lifted their skirts and fled from the Bush invasion. Donkey carts were definitely in decline.

Brian Stewart, knew exactly what he was looking for, and in spite of his absence of years, the dilapidated building had remained unchanged. The iron gates might have had an additional layer of rust, but they were the same ones with a small door inset for visitors on foot, and told him the manufacturer of the gun barrels in Richmond was just across the yard.

It was Jesse's intention to build three complete rifles using the threaded barrels in his present collection, and to keep them for himself after use, with the upgrades to add to his collection. He was also filling in his time as he waited for the cash injection from Crooky, and 'Diggers' as he now called him. Having heard 'Diggers' used so often by Crooky, he'd become accustomed to the old boy jargon when thinking of them as a team. He chuckled in spite of the biting wind, as he recalled his opening remarks and Digger's indignation when he met him for the first time.

The door with the observation grid opened before they could announce their arrival by a tap on its rusty exterior. The same guard who had been there for eons, recalled the unremarkable face of Stewart without too much difficulty, and flashed a betel-nut smile as he stood with his back to the warmth of the brazier. Stewart's credibility leaped to new highs.

"You'll want the office at the back, Sahib?" He attempted a knowing wink of sorts, since the office at the back meant nefarious business.

"Yes," replied Stewart, before he received the 'follow me, Sahib,' and they were led to where the 'nefarious business' was about to unfold.

The office they entered bore no resemblance to the ramshackle building in which it was housed, and only a slight smell of oil permeated the air as the man behind the desk stood up to welcome his honoured visitors. He smiled and reached forward across the desk extending his hand in western style; a brief handshake followed, and he gestured toward the two vacant seats in front of his desk. "Please gentlemen; now what can I offer you to drink?"

With the first sip of the steaming milky tea, thoroughly laced with sugar, the meeting got under way. They had rather expected Kawa green tea when they were asked, but it wasn't to be the case. Jesse handed his drawings across the desk to the naturally gifted craftsman, who had been in the business of hand-made weapons as his father's son, who in turn had learned the trade from his father before him. No explanation was necessary; Jesse's homework had been precise, and the unusual barrel was easily identified from the micro-digital photographs offered to back up the articulate drawings. "Hmm…" the gifted craftsman was suitably impressed, and continued to pore over the detail long after he had formed an opinion, more in self-admiration of his own work than anything else.

"Gentlemen, I recognise my work; so how can I be helping you?" He wobbled his head from side to side.

"I have three threaded barrels identical to the one you see in the drawing. I want to make use of them if you can supply triggers, bolt actions, and light aluminium clip-on butts with thick rubber to absorb the high-recoil 338-magnum ammunition. I shall also require sight mounting brackets for the scope and the infrared rangefinder, plus a couple of hundred rounds of Lapua. Is it possible?"

"It is possible, yes. But I don't recommend it."

"Why?"

"For, many many reasons, Sahib… and the first one is you want it to work."

"Well, of course I want it to work."

"You want reliability, yes? You want accuracy? I'm thinking for you, Sahib." In his wisdom, he never asked the purpose of acquiring such weapons. He had clients worldwide, and would go out of business if he did.

"Of course I do, reliability and accuracy up to 600 yards, sums it up exactly."

"So, I'm telling you Sahib, forget the old barrels you already have, and we start again using the latest light alloys from the American military base, just over the border. Can't fit new parts to old in sniper business; not with a twenty year gap… like putting new wine into old bottles; just won't go, Sahib. Cheaper price for what you ask, but..." he shook his head, "when your weapon breaks down, big mess-- you understand." His argument seemed sound, and his advice was surely as valuable as the extra premium it was about to cost. Jesse asked himself; did the old men in Westminster want the mission to succeed? To which the answer was yes-- in excess of a million dollars.

"I'll accept your advice, Mr Khan." Jesse read Umar Khan from the nameplate on the desk, but preferred to leave Umar to the more enlightened for the present.

"It will be more expensive," Umar confirmed his suspicion, "but satisfaction guaranteed." Umar's smile engulfed his face, aware that Jesse must go for the all-new option. "Satisfaction guaranteed," he repeated.

"More tea," he offered, and Stewart accepted. In the meantime the decision to select the best equipment was left to Jesse as the servant was summoned, and the room fell silent until he left. Conversation then resumed, and the cooling etiquette began all over again. Umar poured the tea from his cup into his saucer and blew across the surface, whereas Stewart and Jesse used a spoon to clear the skin from the surface, before they started their own blowing process with the tea still in the cup. As the ceremony progressed, Jesse pondered his options, well aware that cash, diamonds, gold, uranium, and any other hard tangible assets, of which he had none, fueled the arms business, and he wanted the work to commence. So, a deal of sorts, had to be struck.

"Have a look at this..." Jesse had hoped it wouldn't be necessary to show his plans prepared in advance to cover a whole new weapon, which somehow exonerated Umar's declaration, about matching new parts to old. It was a first in Jesse's life, to design a weapon to meet his own tough specifications, irrespective of cost. His dream-piece, was now in the making at someone else's expense, and about to become a reality; though he doubted he would be using it himself, it could well become part of his Richmond collection. He passed a new sheet of paper across the grubby desk, avoiding the pieces of metal that littered the landscape, and Umar's appreciation quickly followed.

"Ah, Sahib, you be knowing all the time we must make new weapon...yes?" He pawed over Jess's proposal.

"You're right of course," Jesse admitted, "but my Mother, God rest her soul, always taught me to make do and mend," he joked.

"I understand, Sahib," he wobbled his head from side to side for the umpteenth time. "But with guns it can't work, and I think you are agreeing with me Sahib; or I wouldn't be looking at this..." His dirty fingernail tapped Jesse's new design; actually all his fingernails were equally dirty, and this was the first time Jesse had noticed.

"Mr. Khan, that's what I need," Jesse referred to his drawing. "Three pieces, each one packed in a black fibre-light suitcase with all the accessories...so let's talk money."

At the mention of money, Umar's eyes lit up like a fruit machine showing three bells and his expression changed completely. Jesse, however, offered no such illumination; his poker face portrayed a tight-fisted client on the outside, and he secretly laughed within at the progress he was surely making.

"Let's talk money," he deliberately repeated, to witness another performance of delight from Umar on hearing the word, 'money'.

"Well, Sahib, these weapons will be custom-made to my highest standards, using expensive new alloys," Umar attempted to justify the high price he was about to ask, "and I'll add my personal modifications to the specialised ordinance from the American base, which will leave you breathless Sahib, when you see my magnificent creations." He raised his hand as high as his head to make his point. "Imagine Sahib, light as a fiddle with the new alloys." 'Light as a fiddle', was a new expression, recently picked up by Umar from another client, and Jesse was suitably impressed by his use of the phrase. He was a likeable rogue, and continued to amaze him, as his presentation unfolded to garner the best possible price.

"Mr. Khan, you mentioned specialised ordinance from the American base. Now let me explain exactly what I want... You know Leupold scopes?"

"I'm in the business; just tell me the mark and I'll get it, and I'll make the attachment lugs on the barrels."

"I favour the Mark IV ultra scope 16 x - power; excellent for lower light capabilities... I think you'll agree?"

"I do Sahib. I have fitted them before for connoisseurs like yourself."

"And as I have already mentioned; I will also require infrared detection aids, with an illuminated range finder reticle effective in daylight, against point targets. Now take your time and give me your price, but remember I'm acting as an agent; so if it's beyond my reach I'll have to go back to my sponsors. I have my limits you know," he lied.

"Ah...so what are your limits?" Umar smiled, but didn't expect an answer.

"What is your price?" Jesse, fired back; and the sparkle in Umar's eyes began to fade in the knowledge that the business was not going to be the pushover, he once thought. He knew he had to get his figures more or less right the first time, and be below the limit whatever that was; and that in turn, could hurt his profits, if he opened too low. Alternatively, if he added extras at a later date he could gradually increase the prices, to a limit he judged acceptable, before renegotiation was threatened.

"What would you say to about $3000 per unit…including all the accessories and special ammunition?" he enquired, with an inflection of humility to lessen the sting if his prices appeared outrageous; neither of them wanted the hassle of consultations with sponsors.

"Is that the price you're offering me?" Jesse asked with no sign of humour in his eyes, which Umar tried in vain to read before he answered. He knew there were other gunsmiths in town that could also do a reasonable job.

"It's a very good price I assure you Sahib, and it carries my very personal guarantee for a life-time of service, and of course, an offer of absolute secrecy to protect your honour from snoopers." *Providing the price I'm offered, to divulge the information is not too generous, the thought automatically crossed his mind.*

Jesse said nothing; he was in a difficult position without money and wanted to hold onto all the guarantees offered.

"Mr. Khan…?"

"Yes?"

"I have a ready-cash problem at the moment, but I want you to start work on my order."

"But Sahib, you know the armaments industry; it's a cash only business." Umar now wondered, what he was about to be offered to get the work underway, knowing his price was more than acceptable if payment wasn't to be immediate cash.

"I'll give you my personal cheque on Coutts Bank in London to hold, until my associate comes back with the cash. What do you think, Brian?"

"It's okay by me." Brian accepted the challenge

"A Coutts cheque is really as good as cash," he assured Umar, "and I'll also agree to your price of $9000 if you'll accept my cheque until I exchange it for cash. One more thing... I'll need to see evidence that you're working on my project and can deliver within the month; so either my friend or I, will return here in a couple of weeks to monitor progress. If production is on schedule at that time my cheque will be exchanged for cash…have we a deal?"

Umar breathed a sigh of relief; in his experience Brits were basically honest, and it wasn't his first time to take a cheque from a Brit. "I agree…" he said, with a hesitant slowness calculated to hide his desire to wrap up the matter quickly, and at the same time, not to appear too grasping.

"I'll also need to check accuracy up to a thousand yards before we completely finalise," Jesse added.

"I would insist, Sahib." Umar said, as he pushed back his modified chair from a luxury bus seat, and reached across the desk to shake Jesse's hand, and then that of Stewart, who was responsible for their meeting. It had crossed his mind from the beginning, that Stewart might ask for an introductory fee, which he had included in the price, but these Brits were usually beyond reproach; his profits looked good in such light.

The flight home was uneventful; Brian Stewart had enjoyed reliving his past and was looking forward to the prospect of another visit within the next two weeks to examine Umar's progress, recover Jesse's cheque, and make the cash-payment. And his own emoluments that Jesse had generously offered without any nudging from him, had served to lift him out of the counting trap when he visited restaurants.

Catching the underground train from the airport had been a bit of a let down, but until the next trip, he had all the time in the world to catch up on the TV soaps.

5

The granite walls of the bank's exterior, embellished with black glass doors and large brass handles were there to impress. It was the first time for him to receive a welcoming salute from a doorman, or from anyone else for that matter, that clinched the deal for the Rocky Bank, to handle Kariuki's affairs. The banking hall also impressed him, and the power of its chandelier that lit the interior made him feel secure; he was convinced his money was in the right hands and was safe at 12 %, four points above the market average.

Johnson Blackstone Kariuki, had just retired from his lowly government job after thirty-five years of loyal service, and his pension was calculated on his last salary of 12000 shillings a month. He was ready and waiting for a laid-back life, and the only problem that remained was the education of his last-born daughters, which had left him no option but to retire to his farm where the cost of living was cheaper. For a couple of reasons he could no longer occupy his government quarter in the city; the first being retirement, which was quite understandable, and the second, about which he was not so convinced, was the sale of the block at a knockdown price to his Permanent Secretary. So in a reverse of roles, his wife was going to stay in Nairobi, and continue with her job to see the children through school, though the room she rented was far too small for him to join her on a regular basis.

Many visits to the National Social Security Fund had at last yielded his entitlement of 125,000 shillings after he'd parted with 5,000 shillings to the clerk, who was forever hanging onto his cheque with the same story each week, to come back the following Monday. Luckily, he'd been informed by a man in the queue of a person just like himself, whose file had got lost for over a year until he'd coughed 'chai' (tea money) for it to appear. Johnson, was mentally sick, but strangely elated, as he clutched the results of his 'chai' and descended the stairs of a building he prayed was behind him forever. In total, he now had 125,000 shillings less the 5,000 it had cost his wife, who had taken an advance for him to get hold of his cheque; plus funds from his pension commutation and some recent harvest receipts, which in total, yielded the magnificent sum of 500,000 shillings.

As the chosen custodian of his life savings at 12 % per annum, the Rocky Bank was about to receive his cash injection. In fact, the experts at the time of making his arrangement had told him his yield was fractionally more than 12 %, because he was drawing interest each month instead of at the end of the year. He pushed three cheques toward the cashier with a sigh of relief, and to his surprise the cashier showed no emotion as he handled the large amounts; he merely channelled them through the machine and handed over a printed receipt.

So with the responsibility of his daughter's school fees allocated to his wife, Kariuki was now looking forward to a well-earned rest on his farm, as his income rolled in, and his wife took charge of the girls in the city. His age-mates had also made similar investments of half-a-million on his recommendation, and were happy with their monthly collections.

However, there was always someone who stepped outside the circle of the retired, and his friend Kamau did just that. He took on a new young wife, and paid her father with five of his older cows after her impregnation began to show. His first wife was far from pleased but held her peace, as she sought allies against the new woman to make her life as unpleasant as possible. But retribution from the new wife wasn't long in coming, and she gave birth to a son. Mama's boys then turned on their father cursing his pleasure, and prayed for his impotence as their inheritance dwindled. Now Johnson Kariuki was also a man with a wandering eye who liked a bit on the side, but he wasn't prepared to go as far as Kamau, whose very shadow kept him in check and curbed his wayward ideas.

In the course of time, six months had elapsed since their first deposit, and the investors were calculating how long before their capital was returned 100 %; an enjoyable thought indeed. It was the end of the month, and Kariuki as usual prepared for his visit to Nairobi with a squeezed overnight stay at his wife's. He felt good at the thought as he boarded the bus in Nyeri and shot a 500 note in the direction of the *manamba*, projecting the air of a successful farmer travelling on important business. Alighting at Machakos Airport Bus Terminus, he made his way toward his bank on a corner close to the Globe roundabout, paying particular attention to the security of his pockets as he sauntered down River Road. The gold lettering in the distance as he approached declared the presence of the ROCKY BANK, and shone confidently in the low morning sunlight. The black-glass doors beckoned him on. Strange he thought, even at the end of the month, I've never seen such a crowd assembled at the entrance to my bank.

"What's happening?" he asked a jostling man, whose elbow was painfully planted in his ribs.

"I don't know;" he shouted above the noise of the crowd "Ask the *askari*!" Johnson forced his way to the front of the crowd, used his hand to shade the black glass, and flattened his nose against the surface to see what was happening inside. The blow from the truncheon came quite unexpectedly, and was followed by a blackout and the appearance of a painful lump on top of his head that he gingerly felt, as he face a hail of stones from the angry crowd. Still in a daze, he was rescued by a good 'Samaritan', who helped him up and guided him toward a vehicle. He was then bundled inside and the door locked behind him; the good 'Samaritan' had made an arrest. Ten minutes later, still in a state of shock, he was helped yet again by the 'arm of the law' into a cell. His shoes, his mobile, and anything else that could make his stay more comfortable were taken away.

The prospect of 24 hours of dehumanizing captivity behind bars was a humbling experience for Kariuki, and he could do little about it until Wanjiru posted bail for him to appear in court. In the meantime, the stench in the cell that groaned with humanity showed positive signs of strain on the system, and some of the penniless devils he met, had been on remand for weeks.

Out on bail and among friends next evening, thanks to Wanjiru, and consuming what might be his last bottle for a considerable time if he went to jail, he was earnestly advised by those who had experience of similar treatment, to make sure his wife was in court to pay the fine, or he could be out of circulation for months. They also expressed with glee, the hope that he was on good terms with Wanjiru, and taunted him with a case where the wife had failed to turn up and the husband had been sent down for three months, and she had slept all over town in his absence. The raucous laughter that followed was deafening.

"But I haven't done anything," he protested his innocence.

"It doesn't matter whether you've done anything or not, the police enjoy beating their customers' heads." His friends laughed at his naivety.

"And plead guilty, whatever you do! Because if you don't," his advisor advised him, "you'll be remanded for a month and then month after that, until the magistrate comes to work on time!" Another round of beers arrived, and someone else took up the theme to relate his own grisly story at the hands of the police.

"Yeah, that's how it is," he confirmed with a slur. "I've got a police record!" he proudly shouted for all those present to hear.

"It's a long story, but I'll tell you briefly what happened... on the day I forgot my wallet at home, and became a vagrant after only three hours at large in the city..." he lost the thread of his story, picked up his beer, and drained it.

"Where was I?" he mumbled.

"You were just about to become a vagrant," someone who was less drunk than he was, volunteered.

"Ah yes, I was on the edge of the precipice walking home with empty pockets, when this policeman pounced from the shadows and demanded money. *Ateriri!* I didn't even have a five-bob banana to stick up, you know where, and in the end it cost me 3000 bob and I was out of circulation for a couple of days. So now with my police record, I use my cousin's passport to collect my benefits in the UK!"

Johnson's friends proved right, and twenty-four hours later he was a free man and his wife was the poorer by 3000 bob. It was the unsympathetic women on the bench he had addressed as 'your honour' to placate her extortion, that he blamed. She had a heart of stone, had ignored his pleading, and had insisted on grabbing his pennies to pay for the new MP's allowances and pensions, that were about to cost the nation billions.

He had now lost 8000 bob to the system in the last six months, or rather Wanjiru had, and his morale had reached a new low as he boarded the homeward bus to recover from his latest ordeal. No matter, he comforted himself; he would collect twice the interest from his bank on his next Nairobi visit.

6

"Wake up! Wake up! *Amka, Amka,* Kariuki!" It was Kamau, his non-conformist childhood friend with the two wives, who lived on the farm next door. He was shouting his head off. They had served together in government and had virtually retired on the same day, and what's more they both banked at Rocky Bank. Sometimes, they even made the trip together from Nyeri to withdraw their interest at the end of the month.

"Wake up! Wake up!" Kamau banged on Kariuki's door for the umpteenth time. "What's up with you, can't you sleep?" came the groggy voice of Johnson Blackstone Kariuki from within, as he staggered to the door and shot back the numerous bolts.

"Come in, come in, and don't make so much noise; even the cows have to sleep if I want good milk. What's all the *kelele* about?"

"Our bank has stolen our money!"

"Talk sense, what are you saying?"

"It's all here," Kamau flourished a copy of the Daily National for Johnson to see the front page. "ROCKY BANK COLLAPSES"

"Give me that!" Johnson grabbed it, and stared in shock at what he read.

"Are you sure it's ours?"

"Read it again!"

"Aeeh! We're ruined! We're ruined!" Johnson collapsed in a chair; the paper fell to the floor and he buried his head in his hands in despair. Kamau, who was also affected, stood stock-still in a state of shock reflecting on the seriousness of his own situation, questioning the steps he could take to recover his fortune. His expenses with two wives and the newborn son to support were far greater than those of his friend Kariuki.

Johnson, as yet, wasn't tuned to recovery. He was on another track completely as he snapped out of his trauma, and his mind turned to hate; a hate so deep he was prepared to kill. Corruption, he was convinced, had caused this disaster, but who was responsible for the evil of this act? He check through the news item word by word, and his view of the beautiful world into which he had retired changed; it was no longer a rosy place to live in. He sank into a gloominess seeking revenge without consequential thought, and eyed his trusty panga that was usually by his side to fight off thieves in the night. It was never far from his grasp, and its presence somehow helped to assuage his thoughts to deal with the villains in the bank, who would be made to pay for his loss…the time had come to fight back.

The search for the welcoming letter from the Chairman of Rocky Bank to new depositors had occupied Kariuki for most of the morning. In particular, he wanted to examine the names of the directors printed at the foot of the page. He recalled, the contents had portrayed Rocky Bank as a caring institution compared to the Internationals that only dealt with millionaires, and it had been aimed at the little depositors to swell their hearts with pride. Kariuki had proudly shown it to Wanjiru at the time, and she must have put it in a safe place; so there was nothing he could do to formulate a plan until she came home at the weekend to collect vegetables for the girls. He recalled his pride; the Chairman had addressed him as 'Dear Mister Kariuki,' and welcomed him into the close-knit family circle of depositors at his bank.

Kariuki had known Kamau all his life and was warned by his close association with him, that he wouldn't be a suitable partner to lead an attack on the banking community. He was a nice enough guy when sober, and had also lost money like he had, but unfortunately he was one of those who shouted his business from Nyeri town to Sagana after a couple of *muratina*. He was therefore on his own if he wasn't to get caught by the dreaded police, in whose cells he had recently spent a short time. True, the torture chambers in the basement of Nyayo House had been closed without recrimination, but scandal-mongers continued to spread nasty rumours of alternative places, and that made him nervous, should he plan an assault on a powerful Bank Chairman, which could end in his torture, if he wasn't gunned down as a *mungiki* suspect sooner.

Eventually, it was the elusive letter found by Wanjiru that gave him the lead he sought to work out the plan maturing in his head. Sure enough, Ambassador Professor Isaiah Opugi was the Chairman of the bank. Now he knew for sure, according to his messenger friend in Foreign Affairs, that Opugi wasn't a real Ambassador, or High Commissioner if it came to that, and such a title was bogus if you were not representing your country overseas. It was only used locally as an ego building exercise, and was of no consequence, but the professor title was another dimension and was probably real, which gave Opugi learning status, and demanded he be approached with caution. Another point, Opugi led the string of names at the bottom of the welcoming letter, which made him doubly responsible for his loss, when he saw he had signed the actual letter to him. This was precisely the information Kariuki sought to give him direction, and he reasoned the Chairman shouldn't be too hard to find.

7

There he was again, Chairman Opugi, hitting the headlines as a benevolent pillar of the community handing out corrugated-iron sheets to the needy. Kariuki avidly read the article in the National Daily, and confirmed Opugi was the one and same crook from his bank, who was apparently massaging his ego at knock down prices in the company of his brother, the Honorable Tamaa, Member for Zita.

Location, location, was his aim as he re-examined the article searching for the area of Opugi's generosity, and picked out the name of a slum in the Kiambu area, in Tama's constituency. He noted the details, and was about to ask the Constituency Development Fund to unwittingly help him track down Opugi.

The replicated wrought iron gates of Buckingham Palace came into view as he rounded the bend in the rusty, dusty, red murram road, up which he had trudged from the junction. He joined the queue of hopefuls at the gates looking for casual employment, feeling a bit like James Bond, African Style. He was wearing his scruffiest clothes and had dyed his hair black to disguise his age. They were recruiting in large numbers, and he was selected almost immediately for a twelve-hour shift. On the way to the coffee factory, he wisely observed the razor-wire fence from the shadow of his hat as he walked down the path in the company of his new-found-friends; he might have to escape in a hurry. His ultimate aim, to access the main house in a menial capacity was still in the future, and his present employment was but a small step in the right direction. He had now to impress his supervisor to gain promotion within the Opugi Empire, if he was to achieve his final objective, to lay hands on the big man, and put all his troubles behind him—close the book on his losses, chapter and verse.

On the other side of the coin, Kamau's imagination was running wild back home, and with every recount, and every beer, the size of his losses increased as he drowned his sorrows, and uttered vociferous intentions to slay the bank that had robbed him.

But it was Kariuki's action rather than Kamau's dreams, that were coming together rather nicely as the month drew to a close, and he accepted accommodation status on the farm, in one of the rondavels on the outer perimeter, miles from the main house. His objective, to transfer from the coffee factory to wash the luxurious cars squeezed into the Opugi stable, had already been accepted in principle by his boss. In his estimation, the time was now ripe for a few days' leave to scotch any rumours flying around back home regarding his disappearance. He knew his relatives well, and they might even have declared him dead in his absence; the dear fellows were jealous and always looking for ways to get their hands on his wife and property. So under the circumstances, it was important for him to dispel such thoughts from ill-wishing people, before they got out of hand.

"Kariuki!" Kamau shouted, as he peered through the unwelcome hole he had made in the hedge dividing their shambas. "I thought you were dead!"

Typical, Kariuki thought. I go off for a month and the hyenas are sniffing at my door. Thank God Wanjiru obeyed my warning not to discuss my business with Kamau, or anyone else, as she made her regular visits. In any case, his explanation to her when he'd left for the first time hadn't been that informative. He'd only said he was going 'undercover', using an expression he liked; to sort out family affairs, and she shouldn't be worried. So when he set off again to return to his project she hadn't asked questions, since she didn't want him brooding during his absence, of her forgetting her wifely position, which could earn her a slap in the future when he came home drunk, with evil thoughts in his head.

"Is that your ghost Kamau?" he shouted back. "I came especially from Mombasa to bury you, and it appears you're stinking more alive in this heat, than if you were dead!" he enjoyed his insult, and his crafty deception, as he slipped Mombasa into his tirade.

"See you tonight!" Kamau laughed, impervious to the insults.

It was early evening and the 'Kazi Kubwa Day & Night Club' was packed to capacity. Kariuki eventually spotted Kamau in a corner of their local drinking well.

"Why did you go to Mombasa?" he demanded; the beer in his belly was already posing a question.

"What's it to you?" Kariuki was stone cold sober.

"I was worried."

"Liar!

"You want a beer?" Kamau offered.

"Gimme cold White-cap…gimme two!" Kariuki upped his demand. Kamau obviously wanted something or he wouldn't be buying a beer in the first place, so it had to be good tactics to raise the stakes.

"Shiko, four beers!" Kamau roared at the over-worked slip of a girl. He would also have two, and make sure he got both of them back from Kariuki before the evening was out. The custom of buying for the whole evening had died long ago with the hiking of taxes.

"*Maisha mrefu,* long life!" Kariuki saluted Kamau.

Three hours later, Kamau had recovered his two beers and a few more besides, and was asleep on the floor in the shade of a cheap plastic tablecloth. And Kariuki, to cover up his shame, had by then resorted to informing patrons that the body on the floor, was merely, 'looking for something', though the upturned shoes indicated, he was flat on his back and out for the count. Kamau never did get around to the questions Kariuki was expected to answer in payment for the two beers. He had started off on his usual subject of thieves, robbers and bank managers, and Kariuki had become a good listener.

8

Kariuki acknowledged the trip back home had been a success, and he actually felt invigorated until reality struck the following morning. "It's these bloody chickens; chickens, cocks, what the hell," he muttered under his breath as he woke to their call and dragged his leaden body out of a rickety bed. The morning was cold, the mist was always there on a coffee estate, and it was dark outside. The pit latrine seemed miles away, cold too; and if it hadn't been 'serious business' he would have used the tree, but two yards from his door. Systematically, he examined the hole by torchlight to make sure there were no nasty shocks lurking inside before he sat down; the last thing he wanted was a bite from an irate snake to complicate his undercover operation.

Damp cold clothes and musty smelling gumboots embraced his whole being as he trudged in the direction of the garage, dreading the prospects of the icy- water into which he would plunge his hands to splash down the luxury cars. According to his co-workers, hoses weren't supplied, because the bosses said they wasted water; whether 'they' was the hoses or them he wasn't quite sure, but it wasn't all bad news; he had his break to look forward to at ten. Tea and milk with loads of sugar, and a chunk of bread with Blue-Band was provided by the estate in the new canteen built by the mighty Opugi, to comply with regulations, even he found difficult to ignore. Whatever the outcome he was philosophical; the job was temporary and a rest from the beer would be good for his health.

He had been labouring at the garage facilities for the past two weeks, and was about to give up on his plan to gain access to the main house as one of the more favoured staff; not because he wanted a full stomach twenty-four hours a day, but because it was part of his plan to get close to the big man. Unfortunately, his only contact had been the lowly kitchen boy who sorted the garbage for feeding the pigs; they had talked as he dumped the trash at the back of the house, where the door was kept locked to keep out thieves. On another occasion the cook with a tall fancy hat had crossed his path, but had failed to return his greetings, so further progress in this direction seemed almost impossible.

But to those who knew Kariuki, even if his eyes reflected torment, he was not the type to assault his prey in a fit of frenzy. When eventually, he did what he had to do, he would make sure it was devious and remained unsolvable; and if the present police performance was anything to go by, he stood every chance of success.

Poison, delivered in food to the house, was an option he had considered and abandoned almost immediately, because of the hit and miss action that might kill innocent people. Parking a farm tractor at a bend in the road, where he knew the big man's car would pass at speed was another idea, not without charm. He had noted the plume of dust as the car sped toward the house, and it wouldn't be the first time such an accident had been staged to write off a worthless creature.

Another method that had crossed his mind was the basic use of a *panga*, his all purpose knife, but with the tight security on the estate he had trashed the thought almost immediately. It was far too risky, and his freedom was worth much more to him. Reflection, more reflection was needed, and his problem was-- he couldn't confide in anyone.

9

"Diggers, can we meet?" Jesse's enquiry was curt. One couldn't be too careful since Blair, who in his estimation had been a good man in his time, had introduced eavesdropping after he was hijacked by Bush to wage war. Ironically, Jesse as a professional soldier would have liked to serve in the Gulf, but his luck ran out with demobilization, and in retrospect perhaps he was better off out of the game of poison gas and radiation, and the shocking way in which governments rejected the newfound medical syndromes-- as if they didn't exist.

"Catch the Falmouth train on Friday and I'll meet you. It'll take me ten minutes to pick you up if you flash me on arrival." The conversation cut without so much as 'Cheers!' or 'See you!'

The black E240 Kompressor was sleek; he recognised the shadow of Digby behind the wheel as it approached him head-on and he waived it into the curbside. "Good to see you!" was Digby's first remark, as the window slipped to the sill.

"Jump in. How was the trip?"

"I take it you mean Pakistan, good—but it could have been better if I'd money to pay the bills."

"Well, now that's all behind us-- we've finished collecting." He was referring to the efforts of Rupert and himself.

"That's just what I wanted to hear. What else happened in my absence?"

"Hang on a minute Jesse, you're talking to an old codger; not so fast." He grinned and continued to concentrate on his driving.

"We're having dinner at the 'Crown' in the village before a session back at the house. Is that all you brought?" Digby glanced at the Samsonite briefcase in the passenger foot-well.

"It's only one night; I've a fresh shirt, toothbrush, and I'll sleep in my skin if that's okay with you?" he chuckled.

"Well, if you're short of anything just ask." He turned left into a country lane with a dimly lit pub sign; only visible to those who knew it was there.

"We've arrived," he announced, as though he doubted his navigational skills. Jesse had years to go before he reached Digby's age, but never ceased to wonder if he would fend off the ravages of time like these grand old men he'd come to meet. He recalled the words of his grandmother at the age of ninety; 'it's all in the genes', and it seemed she was right.

"Good to see you Jesse," Rupert offered his hand. "You're looking tanned from your trip," he joked, knowing well, the temperature in Pakistan had been sub-zero.

"Brass monkeys to you too Crooky, anyway, I'm sending someone else back there to collect the bits and pieces..."

"What's your poison?"

"Give me a pint of that," he pointed to one of the shields lined up on the bar.

"Good choice...I'm drinking the same."

"Cheers!" he lifted his tankard and quaffed a large mouthful, before he returned it to the table and reached for the onion and garlic crisps. Food followed, and they finally ended the evening in the Baronial Hall by ten, feeling comfortably mellow with whiskeys in hand; the roasted pheasant had proved a good choice.

"Now tell us about the trip?" Digby opened the subject, and Rupert's ears began to tingle...

"Well," Jesse began. "I went with my friend Brian Stewart, since he was the guy from whom I got those gun-barrels in the first place and he knew the manufacturer. You see, I wanted to reconstruct the weapons using the old barrels, but until I knew it was possible I couldn't make any plans. I made drawings and used my digital camera to illustrate further, which was just as well, because Umar the original manufacturer convinced me, it was better to have all new weapons using the latest alloys, at a cost of 9000 dollars for three pieces; on top of which you owe me another three for travelling."

"Sorry about that Jesse, but you know I don't have a problem with the cost; it was the cash laundering business that was screwing us up. What I really want to know now, is the delivery time for the weapons, to arrange their shipment."

"Well, if everything goes according to plan, it'll be by the end of the month. Brian returns to Peshawar in a couple of weeks to check out progress, and if Umar's on schedule he'll pay him cash, and redeem the personal cheque I issued to get business under way. Cheques, tell too many tales."

"Again Jesse, I do apologise about the cheque business, but whatever happens I'll make sure you don't lose financially. Now listen up-- the destination of the weapons will be Mogadishu. Which means, you'll have to devise your own tactics to enter Kenya within the next few weeks-- from the time the ship docks it's your show entirely." Jesse's eyebrows lifted fractionally as Digby broke the news. "I see from your expression, you haven't yet read the Daily National on which we've decided to base our selection policy. Rupert and I are unanimous; we want to deliver our first wake-up call to my part of our beloved continent; East Africa to be precise. And after, that we can fan out toward the West Coast, through the diamond and gold fields of the Congo, to the oil, gold, and diamonds of Ghana, Ivory Coast and Nigeria-- followed by States to the north and south, if they haven't caught a chill by then from our operations to make them behave, and consider the poor. Our aims and objects are, to make terminal examples of the corrupt officials who flout laws with impunity. Those types, who use skilled lawyers to make an ass out of the law: Rupert, have I left anything out?"

"No. That's about it, but I think you should have told Jesse, that we don't think it will go as far as that, because well before then the thieves in big business and Government will know their days are numbered-- bad news travels fast; and we doubt we'll have to invade the whole continent. We are dealing with intelligent thieves, and one thing they love beyond money is life. We're just going to change their lives—if they're left living?"

"Well said Rupert." Digby pursed his lips in a belligerent fashion, and Jesse's face remained passive. Digby finally broke the silence.

"Jesse relax-- and don't worry about the shipping to Mog. I'll handle that using the UN food relief out of Karachi; we'll pay-off a few officials here and there, and the UN people aren't too greedy."

"Hey! Isn't that against your principles?" Jesse asked.

"Err...yes, that's true, but principles sometimes have to be weighed in favour of the bigger issue; and I suppose you could call this a typical case of a 'bigger issue'... right Rupert?"

"Right Diggers."

"Let's see if I got this straight?" Jesse wanted to be absolutely sure. "My people collect the means to do the job from the workshop in Peshawar and hand them over in Karachi for shipment to Mogadishu; from where we collect them, and then transport them across the southern border into Northern Kenya. And by then of course, the targeted list of 'biggies' will have been selected for my teams to get on with the job. Correct?"

"Correct," Digby confirmed. "So the next thing we expect from you is the date when the weapons and ammunition will be ready for shipment from Karachi. Now, as for money, you'll receive a hundred grand this evening; actually it's on that desk over there in the brown paper parcel. And don't hesitate to ask for more, when it's about to run out, but do that well in advance, since I have to go to my deposit box in the bank. Do I make myself clear?"

"Absolutely, and I'm dying to proceed-- perhaps I shouldn't say dying?" he laughed, showing nervousness and then relief. His orders were clear, and one thing was certain; as a mercenary directing the mission from home he would continue to sleep soundly at night—unlike, the hands on battle experience, in his heyday.

10

The team was gelling nicely; Brian Stewart and Jesse had recruited the skills of a Kikuyu, Joseph Wainaina, and a Somali of Kenyan origin, Abdi Suleman, both of whom were known to Jesse from his SAS instructor days at Hereford. In their time they had been top performers, but were now reduced to asylum status guarding buildings in London; nevertheless, they counted themselves lucky to have escaped with their lives from failed intrigues back home. Strange though it may seem, they had kept in touch over the years, and were now being offered a helping hand to return with a fistful of dollars. And their first assignment, to assemble the teams in Mogadishu to meet the ship from Karachi, was but the first step in their homeward journey. A bogus UN truck fitted out by Jesse for that purpose was already in Mogadishu, and had been delivered through a network of Warlords from Baraawe in the south. It was now on stand-by in the shadows of a cavernous warehouse waiting for the ship to dock with a load of grain for Kenya, as part of the UN relief programme.

Recruitment of six marksmen became urgent business. Two per weapon, able to shoot without compassion, and aware only of the specifications of those they were detailed to kill. Jesse had actually admired some of the terms put forward by the Lords in their original one-liner. The terminally ill qualification and the leaving of a legacy was a bit theatrical, but of black African origin was paramount; to which he mentally added, knowledge of the theatre of operation and local dialects, in addition to a seasoned military career.

It had been madness beyond belief for the Lords to advertise a covert operation on the Internet, and Jesse had purposely said nothing at the time of Digby's disclosure. But it was now up to him to change tactics beyond recognition before curious surfers exposed their intentions. Thank God, they hadn't done anything more to promote their ill-gotten ideas by the time he was next contacted by Crooky. Even so, the hi-tech recruitment was scrapped in favour of a personal contact programme using insiders; ex-regiment personnel recommended by those who knew them through and through, and in whose company they had lived on the brink of stressful action; above all, they must blend into the background.

"Brian, meet me tonight, our usual bar, same time."

"We have a problem," Jesse confided, as he carefully eased his huge frame into the corner chair-- not wishing to spill a drop from his brimming jug.

"Problem?" Brian queried.

"You heard me?"

"Do you want to share it, or is it a secret?"

"Of course I want to share it, why else are we here?"

"So share it." Brian wanted to know.

"Recruitment's too slow and I'm running out of ideas. I need your input. What it really boils down to is this, whom do we know who can trace the military personnel who sought asylum from East Africa at the time the Lanet coup was put down by the British. And where is the residue of the rebellious soldiers from Kolito barracks, who scared the shit out of Nyerere."

"Surely they're too old for our purpose."

"I'm not considering them in that context; it's their relatives we seek... those who are likely to be sympathetic to our cause and made the army a family-generation career, father to son. What about British Legion contacts? Ideally, we need talent on the spot down there in East Africa, if you follow my thinking."

"Loud and clear; but why do that when the British army has personnel records on everyone they trained over here, and I have a little girl in the right department," he winked, "who I know can be persuaded to help out, if we offer her a little something."

"You're pulling my leg."

"I'm not."

"Here we are, Knights in shining armour, trying to rid the world of corruption, and you're suggesting we bribe a secretary in the Ministry of Defence, to hand over classified information—when do we start?" he smiled and looked behind him, to flavor the plot.

"Well...it's all a case of priorities, and price of course." Brian recalled the story from Jesse about the UN shipment out of Karachi, mentioned as a priority by the Lords to justify bribery, "we can't get one without the other."

"And what will our sponsors think?" Jesse asked.

"Stop playing games Jesse; why tell them? It's an excellent way forward with only a tinge of corruption, compared to what we'll 'kill-off' with the information."

"Tinge, call it what you like, has nothing to do with it. It's the principle. On the other hand, if we have no option," he wavered, "it might not be a bad idea for you to tell me how much a little something's going to cost?"

"Well, as a matter of fact I know what she wants, because she's always crowing about it."

"Can you be more specific?"

"I suppose it all comes down to what we think the information is worth."

"Please…?" Jesse coaxed

"Well, it's about twice the price of the weapons from Paki."

"What! What the hell is it…?"

"Hmm… you really want to know?" Brian was enjoying Jesse's torment.

"Okay, okay, you win, I give up! What is it?"

"A red mini-minor with a white roof, and white stripes painted down the bonnet."

"Only a mini, I'm surprised she doesn't want the moon. She must have some Kikuyu blood in her veins... I think I'm quoting the right tribe?" Jesse was temporarily winded by the size of the 'little' something.

"I know you think it's a lot, but compared to our footwork to get the information from other sources it seems quite reasonable to me. What's more, I confirm her mother's not Kikuyu...I rather think she could be Scottish." Brian failed to hide his smile.

"Okay," Jesse smiled his agreement. "Go ahead, but be careful. I'm certainly not planning to go to jail at my time in life, and neither should you be; and it's on your head to make it work. So if you're prepared to accept the responsibility I'll give you the cash, but I don't want to know about the details. Just get twenty contacts under thirty years old."

"Have the other half, Brian?" He lifted his glass as he offered.

"Don't mind if I do.... Thanks."

"It's red with a white roof," were Brian's opening remarks, as they positioned themselves in their usual corner.

"I don't want to know."

"Don't you want the list?"

"Yes, it cost enough!" He snapped.

"Here, take it!" Brian thrust forward a typewritten sheet and all conversation ceased. Jesse ran his finger down the names and mentally fitted them into their home areas, even though he was aware that most of the killings would be in the Nairobi vicinity. His local knowledge from a brief stay in Kenya some years ago told him Njoroge had to be central Kenya, but Nyongo could be either Kenya or Tanzania.

"And the addresses?" Jesse held out his hand.

"Here; they're on this separate piece of paper; that's how the girl produced them. By the way... she says thanks for the mini, whoever you are?"

"I see from this list, nearly all of them are working in England, in the usual demob specialist trade of security. Interestingly enough, some are actually in hi-tech jobs to fit their qualifications, but the majorities are wasting their talents in ordinary run-of-the-mill occupations, guarding office doors etc. Let's face it, there's nothing for them back home, and there're no prospects for them over here as they join the ranks of remitters to their families, scratching a living from the soil in distant lands. It's a hard life," he sighed, "but this is a good chance to lift six talented people out of the poverty trap, and at the same time they can be of good service to their country. What say you, Brian?"

"I like it, but it's a pity they are not already on the ground out there."

"That I don't deny, but we can't have everything laid on, can we? Let them fly out to Mogadishu; that town's wide open, and Suleman knows the warlord controlling the airport. Anyway, the interviews will be a lot easier over here, and Suleman and Wainaina can help selection as the operation team leaders. I'll go through this lot tonight and mark a few names-- and you do the same on your copies. I take it you have a second set?"

"Sure..."

11

Digby was the weekend host, and Jean Brown his secretary had been persuaded to stay over in case her office skills were needed; not to mention the special favour asked of her to help Mrs. Catchpole with the catering. It was an all-man affair to test the cunning of the pheasants about to fly into harm's way. The shotguns locked in the steel cabinet behind the study had been specially cleaned for the occasion by Sam, a junior from the village garage with a fascination for guns. Digby was quite looking forward to the event; it would open the season without too much fanfare, and lead easily into the operational planning that was the main point of their meeting.

They arrived two by two except for Crooky, who came in his classic green Bentley built in the early years after the war. Brian was with Jesse in his red Mercedes Kompressor, and project workers Abdi Suleman and Joseph Wainaina enjoyed the confines of their yellow 'BM' as they peeled off the motorway in hot pursuit of their lead.

In the lounge that same evening after a satisfying day with plenty to shoot at, they at last got down to the business they had come to conduct. Comfortably seated in front of the usual log fire, Digby opened the discussions; it was after all his brainchild and his mansion, so he got to preside.

"Gentlemen, before I go any further, I must congratulate Wainaina for bagging the most birds, and at the same time thank God there isn't a marathon coming up, or he'd win that too," the clapping died down. "We're here this evening to formulate a means of communication, to be used on the Internet to notify selected targets.

Jesse and I have been working on the code for the past week, and now I believe we have a winner."

"Jesse, please take over?"

"Thank you, Diggers," Jesse acknowledged the chair and then switched his glanced to the block of notes in front of him. "We will be using the media to identify our targets. Instructions will be issued in code, using numbers and letters to identify persons in newspaper articles, available to you on the Internet. I can best describe it as a loose-form of cross-referencing. I'll give you an example." He held up a copy of the National Daily of the 23rd of December 2002. If we look at page three, what do we see? Two articles; in column one 'Matatus Seat-belts Stolen', and now concentrate on column two – 'Rocky Bank rocks away', and there is a picture of the Managing Director with two of his cohorts. All of them ex-civil servants living in luxury, with their court prosecution bogged down by legalities, cleverly devised by their lawyers to cripple the justice system. These three people, according to the paper, have jointly cheated their small depositors out of their life savings, and at the same time they have stolen millions from the government by misusing their positions of trust.

Isaiah Opugi, the Managing Director, is to be one of our prime targets. He's typical of the many still at large enjoying their stolen millions. Are you with me?" A murmur of agreement followed.

"So the instructions in the email will read like this.... N23M120232. N is for National, 23 the Date, M12 is December, 02 is the year, next number 3 is the page, and the final 2 is the column on page 3, on which there is a photograph of the targeted persons. Abdi, Joseph, do you think you can work this? You'll be on the ground out there, directing the operation."

Abdi attracted attention by raising a finger, "You're going back five years. Aren't these people going to be hard to trace?"

"Good question: to which the answer is no. They're the types who become bolder as time passes, thinking they're untouchable; and because of government lethargy, they're even more prominent than they were when they committed their first crimes. They're arrogant people, who've cheated the law, and grow fatter by the day as they vie to out-thieve each other. Money is a drug to them, and they can't get enough of it. Don't worry; I assure you you'll find them if they're not already in the graveyard. Now if by good luck, any are dead, contact me using one word, 'negative', and you'll get new instructions? Do I make myself clear?"

"Crystal."

"In fact, the example I demonstrated shows three targets led by Opugi, and we have selected them for your first operation. Again they're highlighted in a news item in June 2005, so I'll give you another code for 2005, but the first will serve our purpose. So let's have another dummy run to make sure we know what we're doing. He jotted down N28M60531 on a slip of paper. "Tell me Wainaina?"

"National dated 28 June 2005 page 3 column 1. Am I right?"

"Absolutely, and the three faces you'll see in column one are the same as those in the 2002 issue. It's a repeat article, because they're still at large and continue to enjoy the fruits of their ill-gotten gains. As usual, nothing has happened. Just seek them out and do what you have to do; and don't shoot any bystanders," he laughed. "Digby, you want to add anything?"

"Yes. I don't think it's necessary to send an e-mail about this mission; let Joseph and Abdi study the targets before they leave here, and we give them a copy of the paper. As far as I'm concerned it's all wrapped up. And for every ones further information, Rupert and I will be making some new selections from that pile on the floor over there." He pointed to the newspapers stacked and divided by slips of cardboard into each year. "I'll be fine-tooth-combing those over the next few weeks with Rupert's assistance."

"I agree with you Diggers, no e-mail." Rupert added his weight to the decision.

"Thank you for you support. Rupert. Now, logistics is the only thing holding us up, and that'll be handle by Jesse and I in the next few days. Any other comments?" no one spoke.

“Then that’s it.” Rupert interjected for the second time, in as many minutes-- he was thirsty. “Come on, Diggers! Where’s that nightcap you promised?”

“Delighted old boy… Mrs. Catchpole!” he rang a small hand-bell near at hand, relieved that the briefing was over.

12

Abdi had been searching for the ship on the horizon since early morning. His powerful binoculars were trained seaward from the shadows of the hotel room overlooking the boulevard of a bygone era. Nothing but dhows and small coastal tankers plying between Djibouti, Aden, and Kismaayo, summed up his watch as he handed the glasses to Wainaina.

"I see it!" an excited Wainaina exclaimed just five minutes later. "It's just a speck onthe horizon, but I can make out the prow, plowing this way."

Abdi took back the glasses, searched in the direction pointed out by Wainaina, and found what he was looking for. From the speed and direction, his experience told him the ship was two hours from docking, which left him adequate time to round up the teams and turn up at the port, in their look-a-like UN truck; painted in white with the blue 'UN' lettering on the doors. The weapons, hidden in maize sacks, were loaded in number-one hold, and forced the team to be first in the queue by the unloading sequence, to follow the tracer signals in the special sacks, that were activated when the ship docked. Leaving nothing to chance, Abdi's cousin had also arranged for the team to be waived through, before the cranes shifted the first pallets. It was a smooth operation, and within the hour, their bogus truck had melted into the convoy confusion to replace a vehicle hijacked by Abdi's friends as it left the port. The substitution of the genuine number plates from the hijacked vehicle, then sealed the deal, and a free load of grain came up for sale on local market.

After an overnight stop in Kismaayo, they turned inland and crossed the border into Kenya. Their column was one of the largest rescue operations ever mounted to feed the starving people of the region, and the timing was perfect to smuggle the group and their weapons into the country. The large air-conditioned Volvo with shock-absorber seats was a state-of-the-art creation, but the secret air-conditioned compartment behind the driver's cab for the field operatives was far from luxurious. It had a single light bulb that didn't allow for reading, and the white-steel wall only inches from their faces, was oppressive, as they listened to a squeaking Somali voice from a toneless radio. The minutes dragged into hours, and the monotonous pitching and rolling of the vehicle caused them to doze, dispelling the adrenalin-rush, which had been hanging around for days before their departure.

As commanders, Abdi and Wainaina, were up front in the cab driving the mission forward, with sufficient physical and mental energy to make up for the dispirited team in the back. But whatever the conditions, the majority onboard was eager to test their military training. Not that their lives had been wasted in the intervening years, but the tasks they had been pitched against had yet to stretch their highly honed skills. Internal Security in their home countries had needed quantity rather than quality, so their bosses trained specialist units at home to put down insurrection, as the people woke up to the happenings hyped in the media, about those in power, and their greed without any love for their people. Night raids in remote areas to track down and recover stolen cattle, had usually kept the elite forces busy, but barely taxed. They were trained for tougher things.

The second stop after dark allowed the team to walk around and stretch their legs without too much suspicion. Their position was approximately 100 kilometres inside Kenya and 800 south of Mogadishu, and their next halt was scheduled in Garissa at dusk on the second day. In the meantime, sleeping on top of the vehicle was inspirational, and the hate in the world was momentarily forgotten as they observed the myriad stars and a moon so bright that maps could be read without the aid of a flashlight. It was truly a heady experience, and a God-sent reward to recharge their 'batteries' drained by the truck confinement.

Abdi felt really comfortable, and at home for the first time in years in the Northern frontier province of Kenya, and Joe Wainaina, was looking forward to catching a glimpse of Mount Kenya the following day. The planned breakdown of the vehicle in the congestion of Garissa town was on schedule, and from there they would strike out on their own in the direction of Malindi. Again, one of Abdi's many cousins was in Garissa to execute this manoeuvre, and the final stage to abandon the truck in Malindi Township was also discussed. He advised, dumping it in an alley behind the DC's office, as a surest way for it to disappear. The manna from heaven would almost certainly be claimed, and the hiring out of it, to famine relief, would surely enrich the finder.

In the meantime, sacks of maize were handed out to the locals between Garissa and Malindi, and the weapons were removed from their cases to be stowed in the backpacks, specially designed to accommodate their various shapes. The sparse landscape was also used to zero their equipment.

It was five days since the ship had docked in Mogadishu and the group had now taken up residence in an isolated farmhouse in Karen, a suburb of Nairobi. The owner, a little old white lady, was thrilled she'd been paid in cash and had no intention of declaring her windfall to anyone. The Karen Langata area of Nairobi had been specially selected, because the people kept to themselves, as long as the neighbours didn't make noise. The cars parked in the yard had made the 500 kilometres journey from Mombasa to Nairobi in record time, after they were purchased for cash in Mombasa, within an hour of the Malindi bus, hitting town. Intentionally, they were a mundane assortment, selected to avoid attention. One 1999 Corolla, a battered Golf of 98 vintage and a rebuilt Land-Rover 110 from the 80's; all reliable and nondescript with their insipid grey, fawn and green colors—yuck! Abdi and Wainaina had treated themselves to a grey 190 saloon in good condition, previously owned by a *Mzungu* or White.

For personal documentation, the Kenyan Embassy in London had pulled out all the stops and issued updated passports to the six individuals over a couple of days, without adopting the high-handed attitude of a five-day rest period sometimes required. The service had been exemplary, and no money had changed hands besides the official fees. Eventually, the only thing false about their passports was the entry stamp, which had been added to show they had passed through Jomo Kenyatta International airport, Nairobi. The different dates in each passport were good forgeries, but wouldn't stand up to scrutiny, if matched to landing cards that didn't exist. National IDs were original as were the fingerprints, but the districts and vernaculars were all borderline areas without clearly defined tribes, selected to give the holder the initiative if questioned by the police. But if for some reason their explanation failed to satisfy, they could always resort to bribery, using the heavy gold wrist-chains supplied for the purpose, with the detachable links, each valued at $300 US, based on the present price of gold.

The fifth day was spent resting. Abdi and Wainaina were the only members of the team, who left the house to shop for provisions at Nakumatt Mega. They also checked for a coded email from Jesse, just in case, but nothing was really expected until they'd completed their first mission.

13

"Okay, sit down and pay attention." Joseph Wainaina was addressing the class of six, with Abdi Suleman beside him. Five guys and a doll occupied the huge plank table in the kitchen with benches running down the full-length. Jesse had purposely chosen Wangu, the doll, to instill competition and flavor into the venture. In her time, she had taken gold in the Olympics in the days when you ran for pennies. She had been accepted because she showed a need for money, and confessed to being ruthless enough to kill for it. She was dressed like the men, and had battened her tits down to fit the rough image she wanted to display. Other than her height of 5ft 8" she was a 'Grace Jones' look-alike all over again. That's how Jesse had described her to the Lords, who had welcomed the idea of a woman on the team. Wangu was mean, from the time the bastard had failed to turn up at the altar. And it was that meanness in Jesse's estimation that would serve to drive her on, making her partner the luckiest of the five.

"Targets: three people that society can do without. I've been through the morals of vigilante action with all of you before, and nothing has changed. So let's do it!" He paused for thought. "Any of you want to pull out?" No one moved. "I take your silence as affirmation. Suleman will give the shooter of each team an area map with a layout of some of the most likely places the target frequents. A number will identify each team, which will be the last digit on their car license plates. Ben and Wangu are number 9 their plate being 099. The Js, Justus and John, will be team 6 with their plate number 356, and the third team will be 4 for a similar reason. You'll be operating in areas familiar to you, although some of the recent building has changed the landscape since you were last here, but your local knowledge is still a plus. You'll be able to get around in the dark, even kill in the dark; you have night scopes, and whether you use them or not, is up to you. On the downside, is recognition by local residents, who could hang you in the end if you're caught? You set your time, and you pick your spot; the only proviso I make is..." he gestured to Suleman, who took over.

"You have two days to survey, and then you'll make the hit on the third, but do it sooner, if the opportunity occurs. Then make your way back here covering your tracks. Dump the car if you must, and if you do, make sure it's hard to retrieve from a river, over a cliff top, or set it on fire. I don't have to spell it out. Your team will retain the same number from the car registration whatever happens. The easiest part is gonna be the deposit of 50,000 U.S. into your accounts, when your mission's successful." Six pairs of happy eyes, danced at the thought.

"If any of you come unstuck and abort, key in the code on your mobiles issued for that purpose, and return here in a roundabout way, watching your backs for followers. Drive within the law at all times, unless you're being chased."

"Team 9, your target is one Philpot Zechariahs Liki; you have his picture. He lives in Taita-Taveta off the Voi, Loitokitok road, and on a clear day his mansion stands out like a sore thumb. He's known as the 'Rubyman' locally, because he owns vast mining rights. Team 6, you're nearer home, but that doesn't mean you'll complete your task any earlier than the others. I suggest you live rough and survey your target from a distance...he's a coffee farmer by the name of Opugi, and he's very fat, you have his land reference and picture; go get him. Team 4, you target Chege, he's called the 'King of Molo', and his palace stares down from the Molo escarpment as you cross the railway line. I'm told it used to be the "Farmers Hotel" before it was taken over by the GSU (para-military police) and later reallocated to him for services to the State. You have his picture, so earn your money, and don't get caught. I wish all of you, luck." He hesitated for a split second as if he'd missed something and then decided he hadn't. Wainaina stepped forward. "All of you have memorised my HQ number, the Sim-card is new and mustn't be used for any purpose, other than to contact Abdi or myself; and that's only if you've got to. Got it?"

"Got it!" they echoed.

"Questions?" A hand went up.

"Yes Wangu?"

"As you know, we familiarised ourselves with the weapons on the journey between Garissa and Malindi, and zeroed our sights. We've put a lot of time and effort into this job, so I would like to know if this is a one-off?"

"Wangu, I am surprised you're asking that, but I agree it's good to know one's future. To which my answer has to be wait and see, because until things begin to happen we can't know what the reactions will be. Okay?"

"Any more questions?" no one moved. "Then that's it, check your kit. You move out at 5 AM. I will be cooking your send-off breakfast and Abdi will do the serving." A muted cheer went up from the group, ever vigilant of their surrounds and nosey neighbours. "And whilst I'm talking food," Wainaina's memory had been jogged. "Your hard-rations will be rather grim over the next couple of days and I don't want any cheating; avoid public places in your area of operation if you can, and live rough. The only calling card you're going to leave is a .0388mm hard-nose... understood? And the Police will be left with a mystery of a lifetime. Now get some sleep; tomorrow's an early start. Goodnight all."

"Good night to you too," Wangu said, hauling her feet awkwardly through the limited space between the tabletop and the bench where they were sitting.

Wainaina was a good cook, no doubt about it, and the cars left at ten minute intervals with preference being given to team 9, who had the farthest to go. And as expected, teams 4 and 6 were the first to return to the fold on the evening of the second day. It had all been rather easy for them, and they were brimming with confidence with the mission behind them, and money in the bank to boot. But for Wainaina and Suleman the assignment was in the early stages; newspaper headlines highlighting their shootings is what they wanted to read. In particular, they wanted to know how the police were treating the deaths. A bullet in the head had to be murder by anyone's reckoning, but were the crimes being grouped together, and what importance was being given to their international connections, in diplomatic circles and gemstone trading. A leaked item to the press was only a matter of time, and would fall to Wainaina to instigate, if the press didn't reach an exciting deduction, without assistance.

"Where are the two from Taita?" Wainaina asked.

"They'll be here shortly," Suleman assured, "but even if they come in tomorrow they'll still be within the time schedule. I don't see what all the panic's about?"

"No panic. I guess I'm just a bit edgy; who'll join me for a beer?" He opened the fridge door and examined the contents, most of which was beer.

Team 9 took four days to do the job instead of the allocated three, and by the time they eventually returned, nerves had begun to fray in Karen, since telephone silence was absolute, and Suleman was the only one to adopt an optimistic view. When they did eventually arrive, Wangu explained their lateness was due to the sisal plants offering minimal cover, because they grew in such perfect rows. So in the end, they were forced to make a night attack, which entailed a lay-up for a couple of days until Philpot Liki relaxed at sundown, on his veranda. Finally, the drama had all seemed rather worthwhile in a macabre sort of way, as she had watched her partner fire the fatal shot, seconds after Philpot had drained his last whiskey, and placed the glass on the table beside him. No doubt, the police would check the glass for fingerprints, and traces of poison, in spite of the hole in his head; because that's what they always did. "But, what a way to go..." Wangu had said, in a deep voice with a sigh, and no remorse. "No nerves at all, he didn't even know what hit him; and the whiskey must have been coursing its way down his gullet at the time."

Wainaina smiled, "Wangu, is that it?"

"Yes."

14

Another morning dawned; the sun was breaking through the clouds in patches and Kariuki's car washing was behind him for the day, but for some unforgivable reason he was late for his tea break, when all hell broke loose in the direction of the big house. Within seconds, (he was never one to be left behind) he had joined the frenzy of his friends from the canteen, who wanted to know what the commotion was all about. It was even rumoured the workers had downed tools, because something as dramatic as Independence had just reoccurred; but what in truth could it be…? Everyone wanted to know.

At a rough guess, Kariuki estimated the crowds to be in the hundreds. His group stood in the driveway near the black Mercedes he had cleaned that morning, and the domestic staff were gathered under the portico at the house entrance. All without exception, were staring in the direction of the huge body that lay in full view, with its head resting on the edge of the steps. It was the big man himself, clearly recognized by all those present. Had he collapsed? Was he dead? What had happened, they wanted to know? But it was Kariuki's special interest as he stared more closely than the rest, that yielded the answer; fresh blood was oozing down the steps, drop by drop...

The call reporting the incident to CID HQ had been used by Nane Njoroge to instruct the servants not to move anything, there being no point if the Professor was dead. He had also taken the opportunity to inform the in-charge he was on his way, which gave him space to finish what he was doing – having his morning tea.

Eventually the jostling crowd of spectators, most of whom were household staff, had been pushed back beyond the taped-off-area as the butler took charge with an air of authority. Detective Assistant Superintendent of Police, Simon Nane Njoroge, to give him his full title, then used his cell-phone to summon a photographer and a crime scene expert, and at the same time he cursed his luck as the first policeman on the spot. His day for some reason had got off to a bad start after finishing his tea, when he found there was petrol in the vehicle to visit the area of contention. Why the tank couldn't have been empty as usual, he didn't even try to guess. True, he blamed himself for answering the phone during the course of his tea, but as much as he now regretted this act, he had at least tested its ringing to its limits, before he accepted it wasn't going to die by itself.

The battered Peugeot with broken blue and red lights on the roof eventually pulled up, and Kariuki the farmhand, who was only a hundred metres away felt the urge to press forward to make doubly sure the bastard was really dead. It was only the 'pressing forward experience' fresh in his mind from the bank that held him back. Strangely enough, Kariuki felt a weight had been lifted from his shoulders, in spite of the realisation that any hope of retrieving his cash had died with Opugi. But 'the goat' that Opugi was in his estimation, had been killed by 'the dogs' whoever they were. So now he was free to re-arrange his life with his obsession behind him, and become a full member of the coffee planting fraternity. He didn't like it, and Kamau wasn't going to like it either, but he would find a way to tell him gently over a beer, at the Kazi Kubwa Club, as they discussed the size of his new wife's belly, that had begun to swell for the second time...

Nane saw at a glance, he was crossing into 'new territory'. It was a first for him to set eyes on such a luxurious house, and he clearly recognised the body of its owner from TV newscasts. He was constantly in the company of the President. So with such eminence in mind, he stepped gingerly forward onto the marble floor and gazed down in awe at the body of Isaiah Opugi. And strangely enough, as he studied the detail and the size of the dead man's suit compared to his own, he gauged a person like him could fit into it three times over and there would still be room for a small one. Following this deduction, he reasoned the famine in the North of the country, where people resembled sticks, hadn't affected the farmers 200 miles to the south, living off the fat of the land; not counting the one lying dead on the floor in front of him.

The hole between the eyes could have been mistaken for a large Hindu good luck spot. It was almost an inch in diameter, and from the minimal blood letting at the front of the face it looked like a careless lipstick splodge to the untrained eye. Clearly, whatever had entered from the front had passed through the skull and left a large gash at the back, from which a magenta stream had begun to flow down the steps in the direction of the black limousine, before it was stopped in its tracks by the hot morning sun. Messy, Nane pursed his lips, picked his nose, and shook his head in disbelief; understanding full well the victim was just one more of the big people who weren't going to swallow all the money they'd amassed.

Once the crime experts had completed their task, the body was wrapped in black plastic and bundled into the ambulance. It was routine for the attendants and they showed little respect for the dead, as they roared off at speed, their hip-hop music shaking the trees with their woofer. It was now the turn of the pictures and measurements to tell the story from here on in, and the autopsy would determine, what dastardly method had taken the big man's life.

15

Ambassador Professor Isaiah Opugi, as he entitled himself, had been a pillar of respectability in the Riara set and was highly regarded in international circles. He had stamped his name on the portals of higher education by endowing a university in the highlands, and had built a church within his country estate to be at one with the Lord on a Sunday.

His magnificent mansion, ironically showed admiration for a colonial past, and was designed like a miniature Buckingham Palace. It would now be left to his children, all of whom held British passports from a long stay in the colonial heartland seeking a first class education. Patriotism, however, was only as deep as their selfish interests. British passports were better than those of their birthright for overseas travel; but to cross borders nearer home their local documents were used. They had learned well from their father, to exploit their historical exploiters for all they were worth, and to shout 'Foul, Unfair, and Persecution of the minority' if caught cheating. They were the new elite, and like him, they didn't care a damn for the starving masses.

Satirically, his lifeless body on the cold stone floor had just enjoyed the taste of a full English breakfast, and his early departure thereafter, had saved him the trouble of farting. Uji, the local porridge, had long since been abandoned from the time he'd vacationed on the estate of Lord Banks-- his mentor into the English system.

Opugi's brother Justus, the Honourable Member for Zita constituency, was a different kettle of fish, and owed a debt of gratitude to his brother Isaiah, who had hitherto led their tightly knit clan. His successful re-election was entirely due to his brother's clout and the power of his money to influence the electorate. Mind you, a backup plan was in place should votes fall short of expectations, but it hadn't been used in the end since a hundred shillings a vote had won him a slim majority. Of course, even at a hundred bob a time, the electorate hadn't been entirely trusted to do the voting themselves; so their cards were collected by agents in exchange for the fee, and the ballot papers were marked before they were fed into the counting confusion, at the right time.

In the same constituency, Festus Fila the freedom fighter was in opposition. Poor but honest, he had foolishly refused money from Tamaa to pull out of the race, and had eventually lost all-round. He had duly cursed his indiscretion, as he thought of the jobless years ahead, but if there was a next time, he swore to be more considerate of himself, like everyone else.

After the electoral dust had settled, quite naturally, the Honourable Justus Tamaa's elevation to power had activated his desire to stuff his stomach, in direct proportion to the importance of his government position. He already possessed an awesome reputation from his last term in office, as a gifted manipulator, to invoke escalation clauses and punitive penalties in road contracts, never to be challenged by the Attorney General.

Besides which, unlimited horizons greeted all elected MP's with bountiful gifts of 4x4s from a grateful government, plus pensions for life at forty, and emoluments to make the First World drool. Winning a seat was like winning the lottery, but that wasn't enough for the Honourable Justus Tamaa, as he viewed additional projects from his 'honourable status' to boost his income. Ill at ease, he had no option, when his friends were getting richer than he was, if he wasn't to fall behind in the race for riches.

There was no doubt in his mind; he had to break into the fashionable fraud that was minting millions for those working the ploy. Yes, that had to be the answer to his problem; he nodded his head in agreement to his flashing thoughts and decided to form an N.G.O. with the help of his wife; the target was, to 'milk' the donors. And according to his friends in the business, it was almost as exciting as getting elected, because it was difficult to judge the size of the windfall from the tear-jerking adverts they placed in the foreign press, before the money began to roll in. The rich and gullible, guilty nations to the North, were always worth a bob or two, provided pictures of emaciated kids with pleading eyes were there to jerk their guilty tears, at mealtimes, on their TVs in Europe. He had to get weaving before the idea was exposed...

In retrospect, before his demise, Honourable Tama's big brother Isaiah who had launched his political career for him, had been a shining example of an embezzler trying to disguise his assets stashed in European banks. But quite recently, he had been beset by a growing attitude he found difficult to comprehend. Hitherto, greedy government officials were now refusing bribes; and to add insult to injury, they actually wanted to recover his stolen funds, for the benefit of the nation. In his opinion, the whole corrupt system was 'rotten' and coming apart at the seams, and the thought of returning anything to anyone, was as outrageous to him as it was disgusting; so the rich thieves to disguise their wealth had turned their talents to building huge office blocks and living complexes, that dotted the sky-line in the capital city. Finance for such heady projects was usually arranged by back-to-back loans, to hide the true source of their illicit money hidden in Europe. And it was not without good cause that European banks colluded to hold on to their greedy profits; minted by accepting vast sums of money from law firms, which knowingly shielded their criminal clients.

To the innocent bystander, who had patiently read the local press over the years, and was not outraged by the rubbish therein-- a light was shining at the end of the tunnel. It had been reported that there was little left to steal, and crunchtime for the dishonest was manifesting doom. How long the National Treasury could withstand the onslaught, and pay the bloated 'Ali Baba' cabinet, was a matter of conjecture. Mind you, this was 2008, and it had been an uphill struggle to achieve a state of national insolvency, because the economy was booming, and the sell off of the national assets, had yet to be exhausted

But finally, a sharp-eyed office cleaner, had found that last bundle of dollar bills overlooked by the Governor of the Central Bank. His shout of alleluia praising his luck had reached the ears of the askari sleeping on top of the Kenyatta Conference Centre, or was it the one sleeping on top of the Hilton? Kariuki wasn't quite sure which building it was, because his wife who had got the story from a cousin of the cleaner, had told him about it several weeks earlier during the course of his visit to Nairobi. And by the time he had got around to telling Kamau, in the 'Kazi Kubwa Day and Night Club', his memory was hazy, and the beer was confusing his hitherto straightforward story.

"What size was the bundle he found on the top of the Hilton?" Kamau asked, as they made their way down the last stretch of a muddy gully formed by the rain, which conveniently led to their gates.

"He didn't find anything on top of the Hilton. I told you the askari was on top on that Conference place, and the bundle was found in the Central Bank." By now, even Kariuki was a bit confused about the exact location of the askari who had heard the cry, which really had nothing to do with the size of the bundle or where it was found. But, it was his story, and he would decide in which building the askari was sleeping, without any directions from Kamau.

"You told me the Hilton."

"I didn't! I was telling you the story, and I know what I said. It was on the top of the Conference Centre!" Kariuki was adamant, because by this time he had isolated the Conference Centre in his mind, though he wasn't quite sure if it had been the money, or the askari, on the top of the structure. He was also a bit confused, because he was claiming to be the authority on the subject, and he had yet to workout a large enough sum of money to be found by the cleaner, if he were to inspire Kamau, with his superior knowledge of the economy.

"Okay, I agree with you, it was on the top of the Hilton—how much was it?"

"Now, I'm not going to tell you!" Kariuki, fumbled to open his gate, and Kamau staggered on through the darkness—he knew, he was right.

Now the only thing left to sell was the wildlife, if whoever was in-charge could make a fast buck. Rumour had it; the scam was already set up, to sell this heritage through the back door to the newly rich nations of Asia.

But, under development wasn't yet dead, and thanks to the resilience of the crooks it was fighting back, after a hiccup from the newly elected government, which had merely, spelt delay. A second wind was in the air, with a helping hand from the judiciary using commas, full stops, and technicalities, to screw the system. It was business as usual, all over again, and the judiciaries were wringing their hands in scrooge-like devotion, reviewing their busy schedules. Crunch time, had been a false alarm... Spring, was again in the air.

Strange though it may seem, the cleaner, who had yet to disclose the amount of his luck to any one, had dropped out of sight. And in the finale to the fiasco the Minister of Finance had addressed the nation on the state of the economy, and had countered the malicious rumors that the cleaner was about to receive a government pension, and get a gold medal; by saying he was a criminal and reportedly armed, and a reward was offered for his capture. The whole saga had fired the imagination of the country, and had made the cleaner a national hero. His image had suddenly become the cheer of the masses, as they retold his tale over and over again laughing at the comedy, and increasing the size of the bundle found for the benefit of the wildest dreamers, who were listening and imagining what they would do if they too stumbled on such good fortune; and pressure to track down the 'bank robber' was just another joke.

16

The House of Lords felt snug. Lord Digby drowsily gazed up at the windows high above the thick panelled woodwork and watched the falling snow as it gathered at the edges of the lead-held panes and continued its build-up; the weather outside looked beastly and he didn't want to go home. Lord Rupert was on the Opposition benches at the back of the House that afternoon, for reasons better known to him. Poor fellow, thought Digby, he'd obviously lost his way after lunch and the Lord Speaker hadn't the heart to disturb him, as he joined the snoozing minority. Anyway, that was Digby's reasoning for their separation, after they'd left the dining room together. No matter, they'd meet up at teatime. He sent a note to him by the Sergeant-at-Arms, that urgent business needed discussion—Rupert would know what he meant.

"Thought you'd never wake up in time," were Digby's first words, as they settled themselves into their corner table for a cozy chat, and a cup of Earl Grey lemon tea.

"I saw you gazing up at the ceiling." Rupert responded, not wanting to admit that the debate that afternoon had bored him to death and was only good for forty winks, which had turned in to an hour, before the division bell had rudely jarred his nerves.

"I must confess, I was looking at the snow slowly building up on the panes and shivering at the thought of going home tonight. Are you inviting me, to share your roof across the square?"

"Why not. You do the meal, and I'll supply the digs. Suit you?"

Digby was used to supplying food to Rupert, so regarded the offer of digs as a free and a fair exchange; besides which, their 'Rescue Africa' programme needed discussion. Two elderly gentlemen crossed the square that evening, with the collars of their black mohair overcoats drawn up around their ears. Unbent by age, they walked at the pace of fifty year olds; their homburg hats were uniform and they held their umbrellas high, to ward off the falling snow, that was quickly churned to slush by the passing traffic. The ambulant ancients were observed by the likeness of Winston Churchill in bronze, who failed to attract their attention from his lofty perch, as he too collected snow, like everything else in the area.

"Bloody depressing weather at this time of the year, what?" Rupert uttered, as he mounted the single flight of steps to his entrance.

"Come in Diggers, don't hang about out there, you'll catch your death. Whiskey is what we need; I'll take that coat." Whatever Rupert was with free meals, he was an excellent host under his own roof, "it's over there in that cabinet." He pointed in the general direction before he dived down the hall with the coats and returned to see Digby holding a bottle of Grouse, and two crystal glasses.

"Over here Diggers, bring the bottle; I've got the ice and water." He held up an ice tray, and a jug of Thames water taken straight from the kitchen tap; in his estimation, bottled water belonged to namby-pamby ninnies.

"Three fingers for you Diggers, and I'll have the same; miserable weather," he repeated, as Digby did the dispensing. It was now Digby's turn to add to the one-sided conversation that had prevailed since they had left the House.

"Do we get down to business, or do you want to talk after we've been to Quaglino's?" Digby was paying for the meal and had picked the restaurant to his own liking, with the diligence of a seasoned politician.

"It's better to get it over with, then we don't have to cope with indigestion in the middle of the night." He didn't comment on Quaglino's, so Digby assumed it wasn't a bone of contention.

"What's the news, Diggers?"

"It's the best news you could possibly want to hear. Three down so far, and they're waiting for new instructions.

"You recall who they were…refresh my memory?" he asked, somewhat overwhelmed that their plan had actually worked.

"The three thieving bankers we identified in the National Daily on the 28th June 2005. You remember, we gave our people their details before they left. Well, now I have confirmation." He produced a tightly folded piece of paper from his pocket and began to straighten it out on the table. It was a copy of the National Daily; that he had somehow retrieved from the Internet. "Examine this, Rupert."

"Fantastic! Fantastic!" Rupert echoed, as he devoured the newsprint, and inhaled the breath of adventure he so desperately wanted to knead.

"I knew you'd approve, and what's more to the point, they're still in situ and await our further instructions. So if we go for a second round it's going to cost us a little less-- being on the ground out there and all that. What do you think Crooky? Is this present plan working-- can we be absolutely sure it's having an effect on the public, and are the authorities treating our actions as a hit-mission against corruption—or is each murder being investigated separately?"

"Quite honestly Diggers, I think we'll have to wait for a few more editions of the news to help it along, before we can form an opinion on that, but there is no reason why Jesse shouldn't arrange for a letter to be sent to the editor from 'a reader', on a who wants to know basis?"

"It's time to consider the second assault," Digby declared. "The fact that we haven't yet received feed back from the first, shouldn't deter us from going ahead." He enjoyed the words 'second assault' that suggested a military operation, which he supposed, it could well be.

"I agree, we have to pile on the pressure before he does that, writes to the media I mean. So let's get down to selecting three more targets, caught with their hands in the till. Contracts, rather appeal to me," Rupert announced his preference. "Roads, airports, ferry boats, and military secrecy quoted to cover up theft. You take your pick Diggers, and I'll take mine, and then let's see what we have between us." Rupert was so enthused by what he'd read; the lead was taken out of Digby's hands by his suggestions.

"Good for you Crooky, you're really sparking today; takes one to find one, eh?" He referred to Crooky to catch a crook, and laughed.

"Absolutely, and I'm starting my research first thing tomorrow. So be prepared to hand over a bundle of newsprint."

17

After a brief respite, the case for debt cancellation was again on the London agenda; deep waters drowning development were about to be plumbed for signs of remission.

The powerful delegation arrived on the inaugural flight of the A380 recently acquired by the "Pride of Africa", and to add pomp to the occasion, the last few yards of the official red carpet was unrolled as the Jet came to a standstill. It was the Minister of State for Foreign Affairs and his cohorts, who wanted the firm foundation under their feet to shake hands with the hoi polloi, and to pat the occasional back of a closer associate, with whom they'd wasted time and money on previous occasions.

Almost immediately, the eyes of the Head of Protocol began to widen, as he noted their endless numbers cascading down the stairs, with a well-worn pose of self-importance. The 100 mark passed and the end of the fifty-man delegation was nowhere in sight. By now his eyes were not only widening, but also blinking in disbelief; in fact, distinct signs of agitation had taken charge of his physical calm. He began to clench, and release his fists; he had lost count of the disgorging passengers at around two hundred. It wasn't his first time to meet such delegations from Africa, but on other occasions the planes with guests and freeloaders were much smaller. His sharp eyes took in the scene, and calculated the consequences; if the gush from the 380 demonstrated the number still left on board a problem was about to explode in his face. The lack of accommodation would make him look foolish... where were they all going to sleep? Wives and girlfriends posing as secretaries, had been expected to swell the numbers to the 100 levels, but so far only brief-cased officials had descended the stairs. He resumed his counting and questioned his schooling; he had always been poor at arithmetic, but these numbers were clearly out of hand. An urgent word was needed with one of his deputies.

In fact, just recently, his whole world had been filled with deputies, since the title of Personal Assistant no longer applied. Deputy, was deemed by the government psychologist to have more enhancing qualities, and increased self-esteem for the holder; but as far as he was concerned the outside of the sack had merely changed, and it still contained the same old potatoes. But whatever the score by designation, he prudently reasoned, someone else was going to take the blame for his lack of foresight, and what better choice could he make, than one of his deputies bearing the new self-esteem.

"Jason," he addressed a deputy, "how many of these Martians are there?" By now his mind had likened the visitors to invaders from outer space.

"I'm sorry Sir, I wasn't in on this from the beginning. I really don't know, but shouldn't they be red, if they come from Mars?" He chuckled at the cleverness of his wit, and thought he'd raise a laugh from the boss, but unfortunately the pressure of the situation had dispensed with humour.

"Make sure we have accommodation for 500," he instructed. "Within a radius of twenty miles of the city centre. And lay on coaches."

"Do you think that's going to be enough, Sir?"

"What do you mean?"

"Well, that plane can carry up to 800."

"Surely there can't be more than five. Can there?" He rethought his question out loud.

"I don't know Sir, but I think we should be prepared."

"Okay, okay, fix it. Add another hundred, but do it now! This crisis is about to happen, and I can do without these guys from the Third World laughing at our incompetence-- even if it's their own fault." He sought to reduce his responsibility by blaming others, "but we don't want to look…" he pursed his lips, "you know what I mean…" and left his statement unfinished. "Coaches first," he continued, "let them cruise around while we sort out their rooms; it'll give us breathing space."

He returned to the line-up, his face reflecting confidence, that the calamity had been nipped in the bud. Counting resumed, and he tried to assess the numbers that had invaded the terminal in his absence...since the end was nowhere in sight.

His Excellency, the German Ambassador, who was watching the arrival scene from the comfort of his London embassy, recognized the trauma as it unfolded and the numbers swelled. A knowing smile crossed his face; he sipped his beer, and recalled a similar incident when his country too, had also been caught with their pants down. But in those days, the planes had been much smaller for the usual shopping sprees, in Bonn, by Third World members. He had thought at that time, 'stolen money' coming back to roost was helping the local shopkeepers, and also his party's political image. Not everything was bad in the aid-camp in those days, but recently he had to admit standards were on the decline, and the local shopkeepers no longer benefited, because the size of the looting had forced a change from goodies to good properties, which didn't yield nearly so much goodwill to his political party. And he had to admit; the neighbors from Africa living next door were possessed of strange customs, about which the Germans knew little.

18

The black Jaguar, collecting a gentleman on a very different mission, departed for central London before the plane had disgorged its last passenger. Seated in the sumptuous silence that reeked of hide upholstery, was a dedicated man, who had trained at Hendon forensic laboratories. Naturally gifted, he had a reputation for solving the unsolvable, by extracting threads of criminal activities from dusty files in dusty drawers, after the clerks were bribed to lose them.

The epidemic that now occupied him was sweeping his country, and had to be stopped. He had never witnessed such a phenomenon before, and that was the reason Detective Nane Njoroge, pronounced narn-nay, had hitched a lift on the inaugural flight as one of the few worthy passengers. He was in England to seek advice from his old instructor, Chief Superintendent CID London area, Conrad Black, and shopping was furthest from his mind. It was a great pity the criminal activities recently challenging him had all but taken control of his life, and as he crept through the traffic engrossed in his thoughts, the familiar landmarks in the city he loved, failed to spark any interest. His sprightly steps as he got out of the car on arrival, were an attempt to shake off his gloom, and they quickly propelled him through the main revolving door.

"Chief Black is expecting you Mr. Nane. Kindly sign here and pin this visitor's label onto your person-- he's on the third. Turn right as you get out of the lift and it's the second door on the left. You'll see his name and designation on a door before you enter." Simon thought she must have given the same instructions a thousand times over, with her typically British, deadpan expression.

"Thank you, I'll find my way," he answered. The directions couldn't have been more precise and three minutes later he was knocking on the door marked Chief Superintendent... Stepping inside, he was struck by the bareness of the room, compared to the luxury displayed by high-ranking officers in Africa. It was positively austere; a doctor's waiting room without the magazines was how he would have described it. The woman behind the desk seemed to know all about him and offered a cool British smile in welcome—at least she had smiled; an improvement on the one downstairs.

"He's expecting you, please go straight in."

"Thank you," Simon acknowledged, and turned toward the inner door. Chief Conrad Black stood up as he entered, and seemed genuinely pleased to see his old protégé from Africa, if the size of his smile was anything to go by.

"How long has it been, Simon Nane?" He was the first person in the building to pronounce his name properly, and they continued to clasp hands. "Two, perhaps three years," he answered his own question. "I can still recall the unusual murder I helped you with… one of your top leaders, wasn't it?"

"You're right, and nothing came of our investigation."

"Yeah… it was that bod they burnt."

"That's the one... too hot to handle," Simon laughed, and immediately regretted his disrespect for the dead. The big fish in the government had slipped through the forensic net on that occasion, but this wasn't always going to be the case; he had faith in the new regime and genuinely believed transparency was beginning to bite.

"So tell me Simon, what can I do for you?"

"Conrad – am I allowed to call you Conrad these days? You're practically running the Yard and the country, and I'm still an underpaid overworked policeman from the Southern Hemisphere."

"Call me what you like. My mother thought Conrad was good enough for me when he landed on the moon, so let's stick to that. Now, what's the problem? Incidentally, I fully understood the obscurity of your phone calls in which you couldn't express your true difficulties... I hope you'll acknowledge me that?"

19

The catches snapped back on the pilot-type briefcase that was balanced on his knees. Simon extracted a black leather folder, and closed the case before returning it to the floor.

"This is what I have managed to collect so far," he was in no hurry to reveal his find, and noticed Conrad had moistened his lips in expectation. Simon, an ever-observant policeman, measured the Chief 's reaction and enjoyed his apprehension, but would now he have to release the tension before his helper lost interest...

"I'm sure they'll tell a story in the hands of the knowledgeable," he said, as he slowly took three small plastic bags from the folder and pushed them one at a time in the direction of Conrad, who picked them up one at a time, and examined them closely with a lighted magnifying glass switched on for the purpose.

"Mmm..." Conrad had quickly arrived at his own conclusion. He knew what he was holding, and could reasonably guess the type of weapon that would have been used to fire it; however, he had experts who saw such things everyday, and their opinion would be far more valuable than his experienced guess. "Simon, give me a day, and I'll tell you the colour of the killer's underwear when they pulled the trigger, eh?" He laughed at his own ingenuity.

"Of course, I need to keep these?" He held up the three packets.

"Be my guest," Simon replied. "I also have something else I'd like you to see, which might help."

He reached down into the side pocket of his case, and pulled out a sheaf of photographs showing the three crime scenes connected to the bullets. Turning them the right way around he pushed the collection across the desk. The photographs were explicit and would have shocked most viewers, but not so the Super, who was hardened by a lifetime of depravity that seemed to be getting worse by the day. The bodies and ragged bullet holes he saw were all part of his job, but after office hours his mind had been trained to forget the gruesome, in favour of his family environment.

"So what do I do for the next few days?" Simon asked, as he pushed back in his chair.

"Relax, what else?"

"Relax. How can I relax?"

"I'll arrange for you to visit the lab tomorrow if you like, but quite honestly there's nothing you can do, so why don't you go shopping. But tonight, you're having dinner with me, and we'll go over old times if you'll indulge an old copper... what do you say?"

"You're on, and thanks for the invite."

"See you at Brown's, eight sharp. It's just next door to where you're staying. You need a map or can you find it without?" he smiled.

"I'll manage. I'm not as dumb as I look." Simon was enjoying his friend of the past, and had easily slipped back into the old familiar conversation they always had at the pub after lectures.

20

"Simon! You enjoyed last night?" It was Conrad's jovial voice on the line. A bit early in the morning thought Simon, as he examined the dark grey sky from the warmth of his bed, and tried to figure out where he was. It had to be some ungodly hour, "what time is it?" he croaked, from a dried up throat.

"Have lunch with me at Brown's—one o'clock. I've got the report." Click, silence.

The digital figures on the TV time display eventually jerked him to life; it was ten o'clock and he was rotting in bed in spite of the jet-lag bonus from Africa. It was now or never; he threw back the covers and sprang to his feet to prepare for a jog in Green Park. He was about to fulfill a fantasy that had plagued him since his last visit to London. After a hasty breakfast in his room and a glance at 'The Times' he used the backstairs to street level for a preliminary warm-up, before he crossed into the park and began his jog down the right-hand side of the Ritz Hotel. The park was virtually empty apart from a couple of dog-walkers, and a few isolated newsreaders on the occasional bench, who were doubtlessly digesting the no news scenario, he had read in his room, as he gobbled his bacon and eggs.

The second 'reader' seated on a bench he passed was roughly of his own hue, and his instincts warned him of an unfriendly presence. He could be wrong, but he sensed hostility. He continued with his exercise, but decided to return to the hotel by a different route. Had he been in Africa, he would have known exactly what to do, but in London he felt so isolated and vulnerable. He was sweating as the doorman acknowledged him with a salute, and he jogged up the stairs in one final 'lap' to his room. The card slipped easily into the slot, the light changed from red to green with a buzz and he was in the vestibule… but he was not alone. He felt the closeness of another person, even before he set eyes on him.

"Good to see you, Nane." Simon was taken aback on hearing the voice from within. Why would, whoever this fellow was, think it was good to see him, and who the hell was he anyway?

"Although we didn't meet at the time, I glimpsed you on the Inaugural Flight. The steward told me you were responsible for security… what a load of crap! You see, I know exactly who you are, and that's why I'm here. I'm James Uko..." He didn't offer his hand in greeting and remained seated in the only armchair in the room as though he had every right to be there.

"So, surprise me again, you were one of the readers on the park bench I passed?" Simon by now had recovered from his initial shock, and began to fight back.

"How very observant you are. A policeman through and through; sniffing in all the smelly corners for something suspicious," he sniggered.

"Who let you in here? I'm calling security." Simon stepped toward the bedside phone; Uko was on his feet in a flash.

"I wouldn't do that if I were you." Tensions simmered, their faces were only inches apart and Simon backed down, catching a whiff of decaying meat.

"What the hell do you want from me?" He sat on the bed as he asked the question, and Uko, returned to 'his' comfortable chair.

"It's nothing much really." Uko, casually uttered the phrase.

"If it's nothing much really, you seem to have gone to the extreme to pass on the message… first you stalk me in the park, and then you break into my room and threaten me, when I want you thrown out. I take it you're the messenger-boy?" said Simon, with disdain.

"Call me what you like, it's not going to change the message, whether it's from me or anyone else," he produced a contemptuous smile, to match the messenger-boy taunt.

"So, deliver it, and get out!"

"Well it's like this...you've come over here to solve a crime, that we don't want solved. So the best thing you can do, is to pack your bags and go back home; and lose the evidence. We like what's happening."

"You have the advantage on me," he feigned ignorance. "I don't know what you're talking about, you tell me, which crime you don't want solved?"

"Look here!" He held out his hand to emphasize his point. "As a messenger boy, I have delivered the message. I am not here to tell you what you already know, but my advice to you from the messenger boy is to let it go, before you're stopped in your tracks. Now if you'll forgive me, I'm late; I have to deliver another message to someone else." He smirked, and walked over to the door, which he arrogantly left open behind him to cause more annoyance.

Simon, momentarily lay back on the bed, gazed up at the art deco light of mirrors and chrome on the ceiling, and slowly inhaled to calm his nerves. He then went over to the door and closed it. It had all happened so quickly his mind was in turmoil, and it was frighteningly clear to him, if he did his job and solved the crime, he put himself at risk. Who were these people, who balked at the apprehension of a criminal, and why? He stepped into the shower and built up the steam in a deliberate attempt to clear his mind, using the physical pain on his back induced by the over-hot water, followed by a shock when he switched to cold. He emerged from the cabinet physically glowing with a conversation in mind, he was about to have with Conrad, over lunch.

The Super stood up as Simon approached the carefully selected table, which was a decent distance from the serving hatch and the cutlery counter. Conrad Black, was a stickler when it came to choosing a table in a restaurant, he possessed a phobia of serving hatches, and would never enter an establishment if the tables were positioned in two's; in railway-carriage-fashion as he termed them, in his own special jargon. Brown's of Piccadilly, left space for choice, and was always his favourite facility when he could justify the expense, with a visitor from overseas.

Once seated, Simon came straight to the point with a question, even before they'd lifted their glasses to take a sip of the local ale.

"News, Conrad," each knew what he was referring to, but to make it absolutely clear he added, "from the lab, for me?" The smelly breath episode from the hotel took a back seat for the moment, but he fully intended to raise it later.

"Yes, as a matter of fact I have some news for you; interesting... very interesting..." The chief was enjoying his gentle unravelling of the information, creating suspense to match Simon's, of the previous day, at the time of exchanging evidence; and he even managed to hold back his humorous smile to add mileage to the situation. But Simon, knew his quirks from the past, and wasn't going to rise to the bait by showing his ire. He became equally matter-of-fact, and controlled any impatience he may have felt. "Do you want to share it with me?" he asked.

"Well of course I do," Conrad smiled. The game was up. "Excuse the intrigue, but I just couldn't resist it." The intervening years since college were rapidly fading with the subtle acts of daring and mischief between them.

"You'll get a full written report tomorrow, but for now, just let me quickly run over a few of the specifics to give you a sleepless night." He joked, took a mouthful of beer, and offered one or two theories from the specifics, to occupy Simon's mind for the next twelve hours.

"Shall we order?" enquired Simon. "I've no intention of having both, a sleepless night and indigestion into the bargain." Conrad liked this fellow from Africa beyond the call of duty.

They touched glasses, which he wouldn't have normally done with anyone else, and downed the last drops before the waiter was summoned. As the coffee arrived and the smacking of lips subsided, Simon decided it was time to relate the strange encounter in his room that morning, if only to solicit a second opinion.

"An extraordinary thing happened to me earlier today," Simon opened. "I'm not sure I should even be mentioning it to you," he declared, going back on his earlier conviction. "Perhaps after all, it's better left for my superiors in Africa," he thought out loud.

"Simon, if you feel uncomfortable with disclosures to me...my advice to you is don't." Conrad, had heard such hesitant remarks before, and in the end it usually resulted in a full confession whether he liked it or not, and in his opinion, an outside mind focused on a difficult subject, was worth more than ten held close to the chest.

"No, it's not like that at all. I want to tell you about it, but it's... just that my people are always so secretive and sensitive, and like to cover up anything that might be misconstrued in a bad light. But during the course of this meal I made up my mind to ask your advice, and I don't believe I have a choice, if I'm to get some proper answers; that's meant as a compliment."

"And I take it as such," Conrad smiled. "So what's the story?"

"Well it goes something like this...When I returned to the hotel this morning after a run in the park, one of my countrymen had actually accessed my room, and was sitting in my easy chair, facing the door as I closed it behind me."

"Aggressive?" Conrad asked.

"No, not then; but let me tell you the whole story."

"Sorry I interrupted, please go on." Conrad settled down to listen intently, showing a concentration, which had seen him through many, a meeting, in his meteoric career.

"This man made no secret of his presence, no apology, no explanation, nothing. Apparently he had come to deliver a message. Earlier, you asked about aggression; well, when I wanted to throw him out of my room he forcefully barred my access to the phone. 'I shouldn't do that if I were you,' he threatened. He was a big bastard from our lake region, if I'm a judge of places; so I chose to hear him out... well wouldn't you?" He smiled and felt comfortable with his story so far; he was using his African gift to weave a web of intrigue inherited from his grandfather's story telling days. "How am I doing so far?"

"Go on, I'm listening." Conrad didn't want a break.

"It's okay to continue then?" Simon fished for compliments..

"Yes, yes, carry on." Conrad showed his agitation, whilst Simon enjoyed his choice of carefully measured words, using the occasional adjective in precisely the right place, to spice his delivery.

"That fellow from Nyanza Province admitted to being on the A380, and told me the people he is working for don't want any of these murders solved, which means, he knows why I'm here. It's just possible, he's actually observing us now, and has rightly guessed the topic we're discussing. And this is one of the reasons why, I feel bound to tell you this story." He poured himself another coffee and offered to fill up his listener's cup, but Conrad didn't welcome the interruption, and refused with a wave of his hand.

"As you know, I'm only an Assistant Superintendent and I'm staying at the Holiday Inn, which is well beyond my allowances. The bare facts are-- I wouldn't be staying there without sponsors; and there's no doubt you'll want to know who they are, if you're going to give me advice. But first, let's examine that man I found in my room, and ask why his sponsors, which I assume he has, wouldn't want these murders solved. Whose side is he on? And finally, what do the victims have in common?"

"If you don't mind Simon, I'd like to interrupt at this point."

"Please do..."

"As I see it, the answer to this puzzle lies in the common denominator you've just mentioned, between the three dead men; assuming there are no more on the assassins' list. You're performing your job by hunting down the murderer and his accomplices; and experience tells me the hit man or the murderer, call him what you like, has to have accomplices," he stated the facts as he saw them.

"This can't be a one-man show, and someone out there doesn't want you as a law enforcer to catch the criminals, but you think otherwise and you're pressing on, and that has to be the right decision. Excuse my bluntness, but we aren't little boys anymore, and we know the score in Africa; your life could well be at risk. Now, I don't want to lose a friend, so if in view of what I've said you decide to bail out, and pass the business over to one of your colleagues, you'll have my full understanding."

"Thanks for your concern and advice Conrad, but there's no way I'm going to drop this investigation now, and if the Commissioner tries to take me off the case, when I'm getting so close to solving it, I'll resign from the force and go it alone."

"Message received and understood," Conrad, was proud of his protégé. "So let's get on with it; have you been approached by anyone seeking to bribe you to drop the case—even remotely; by insinuation?"

"No. At least not yet, but now let me tell you about my hotel booking in this country. My Commissioner was against it in the first place, which meant I wouldn't have a hope in hell of solving these crimes, unless of course, I had a lucky break. It was as though he didn't want the culprits caught—why I don't know. And now I can't help but wonder, if he's behind the occurrence in my hotel room,"

"Tell me more about the hotel booking."

"The hotel and my daily expenses are being paid by the family of the deceased Ambassador Professor Opugi, because they badly want the killers caught. But to get these expenses approved in the first place, they had to go to State House and seek permission, against the wishes of the Commissioner, who had refused their offer and blocked police funds as though he didn't want the case solved. Well, that's how it looked to me."

"What was the reaction of the Police Commissioner after that?"

"I really can't say, because I wasn't consulted. But what could he do about it, when the Opugi family went over his head to State House. He had to agree, whether he liked it or not. Now, the big question is, how is he going to react when I return? I imagine he'll be hostile-- what would you do in his place?"

"How generous were the Opugi family to you?"

"To tell you the truth, I've never had so much money in my life; mind you they're very rich and I suspect they teamed up with the other two families whose big men 'bit the bullet'." Simon enjoyed his 'biting' expression.

"And their wealth? Where did it come from?"

"No one can answer that for sure, but you must understand that most of the rich people in my country make it overnight. Ministers of

State and public servants rip-off government contracts, start financial institutions, grab land or government property, anything that's not nailed down to be precise. They are quite capable of embarking on virtually any scheme to defraud; they really are, the cream of the crap. They call it ambition and I call it theft. Don't get me wrong, there are many good and selfless people among us, but unfortunately, they're usually trampled under foot by the greedy hordes."

"Simon, you still haven't answered my question. Where did their primary wealth come from? Land grabbing, grand corruption, theft, larceny, legitimate business or what? Forgive me for pursuing this line, but from my experience, I believe all these families had something in common. Not only were they extremely rich, but also perhaps they were directors or proprietors, at sometime or other, of a single company. Were they ex-government servants, politicians, did they attend the same high school or live next door? That's the line you should be taking, and that, in my opinion, is where the answer lies."

"I haven't gone that far into the investigation, and anything I come up with may show the Opugis in a bad light, which means I'll not get their co-operation, to examine skeletons in cupboards – if you see my point. While there's no doubt they want the killers caught, and they're paying handsomely to this end, research into their family's history will not be their idea of the right direction-- even though, it's the only logical step forward. But you have given me an idea; I'll check with the Registrar of companies and research their family names, and see what I can turn up on my return. You know Conrad, I am sure I'll have reason to be grateful to you for this discussion, and I thank you right now in advance for the direction you've given."

Passing into the sunlight mid-afternoon from the subtle lighting of the secluded dining room at Brown's, lifted the weighty thoughts from their shoulders; the two friends shook hands and turned in opposite directions, an appointment fixed for the following morning.

Simon was due to attend an embassy party that evening to celebrate many years of independence; and interestingly enough, he had been invited by one of his sponsor's family, who was to be the guest of honor. Not often did Assistant Superintendent Simon Nane Njoroge, get the opportunity, to dust off his best suit and step out with members of the diplomatic corps. He knew many of the guests would be from the plane in which he'd travelled, pleased enough to gulp the booze provided by his government, but for him, it was a first time learning experience to be treated with caution. And as a crime scene specialist, he would find it interesting to guess the financial arrangement, he imagined to be in place, to make money from the outside catering.

21

The High Commissioner, a commanding personality, stood six feet tall and wore a gold threaded tunic of his own design-- so he confided to one of his guests. Black drainpipe trousers with a fine gold stripe down the leg served to show off his lean figure, and the black Gucci shoes of soft kid leather added the finishing touch. His Lady, who was also a fashion icon, was dressed to kill in a gold brocade bodice with Ugandan style sleeves and plunging neckline. The tight fitting ensemble hugged her figure as far as her hips, and gave way to a slim black skirt that emphasised her thighs and accentuated her buttocks. The slit at the back was long enough to allure, and practical enough to allow an unfettered walk. This gorgeous lady of medium height wore strapless high-heels in gold, and her 'kilemba', also in gold, swirled in an upward direction and gave her the extra inches to match her elegant man. In Simon's mind she was clearly the star of the show, and the quality of the diamond droplets that cascaded from her lobes to match the pendant in her cleavage could not be disputed. Graciously, the couple greeted Simon as any other dignitary, when the flunky from the embassy finally announced his name, 'Mr. Simon Nane Njoroge from...' before he shook hands at the entrance. He had discarded his police rank and was introduced as a visitor temporarily staying in London, which served to meet formalities and suited his purpose. At first glance his practiced eye estimated the guests in the chandeliered-ballroom to be about 700. Multi-cultural, multi-coloured, he'd never witnessed such a spectacle before. African and Indian fabrics produced a magical richness of colour. The Nigerian men stood out from the crowd with their colourful floppy hats that complemented their robes in pinks, greens and golds that were equally matched by their women, who were closely challenged by the Ugandans from nearer home. The milling textures and exotic perfumes had begun to affect his senses.

As he continued to absorb the atmosphere, his second host and sponsor from the Opugi clan found him in the mêlée, introduced him to Fatima from Tanzania, and charged him to escort her for the rest of the evening. He hadn't realised until then, how many well-wishers his country had, and in the back of his mind he knew one of them had to be, that fellow from the Lake. The one he'd sized-up as his national, at the time he occupied the only comfortable chair in his room. But after speaking to the Super, he was more than confident he could to deal with the menace, the next time they met. He would bide his time and research the background of this ugly fellow; though in truth, he conceded, he wasn't that ugly at all. As the evening wore on, most of the European embassies melted away, and the Africans got down to the business of enjoying themselves. Protocol was swept aside, and the tempo of the band was upped as the lights were dimmed, and Lingala music produced a sensual effect.

Simon moved to the rhythm, and his partner clung to his body as they exchanged the physical, and began to explore their common interests with probing questions, until they felt attuned. Fatima, a receptionist at the Tanzanian Embassy was free for the night, and hinted, with a sparkle in her eyes, that perhaps she could even be free until the following morning. Such a sparkle did not entirely escape Simon's attention; he felt lonely in the vast metropolis and Conrad was expected to contact him late next morning, so the timings were brilliantly coincidental all round.

22

At thirty-five Simon was single and prepared to mingle; tall, light brown and good-looking. The type of son-in-law a mother would give her back teeth for. But, unfortunately for the doting mothers, they would have to wait for the next few years as he played the field, and used his attractions, to catch and let go the most beautiful girls he could find. Such elusiveness had recently resulted in a sequence of loaded questions, from an anxious mother, during one of his visits home. She had opened the serious conversation over tea on the back veranda, which was her favourite place for family inquisitions, because of the scent from the garden that came in with the breeze in the mornings, and usually remained in the stillness of the afternoon. It was also her favourite place when she was on her own, since its tranquility was only disturbed by the hum of bees drawing nectar from the flowers as she concentrated on her library books, and a single glass of red wine would last for hours. On this particular occasion, she had specially baked his favourite chocolate cake to put him in a receptive mood; the thick icing spread with a knife gave the impression of a chocolate sea, and two slices later, she suspected, he was conditioned for what she had on her mind.

"Simon dear… your father and I are concerned about your future… is everything all right?" So, his mother was concerned whether 'everything was all right', from which he gathered the family had been discussing his sexual preferences in a roundabout way; he knew exactly what she meant-- and if everything weren't all right they would have to work out a scheme to cover up the family shame.

His father had only been mentioned to reinforce her concern, and those of her busy body sisters, both of whom had recently become grandmothers; thereby making his mother's position on the family tree, almost untenable. At first, he would usually smile in answer to her question. It wasn't the first time he'd been asked 'is everything all right'; and it wasn't the first time he'd answered by asking a question of his own to add to her frustration. 'Mum, I'm fine, how are you and Dad?' By now, he was far too wily, and knew how to play her along. She would then pretend she hadn't noticed his devious reply, and bring up the subject of the girl next door-- it was always the girl next door; of whom she approved as a possible match.

"Muthoni, called in yesterday; she particularly asked after you and I told her you were fine. I said you had asked me to pass on your love, and had insisted I call her over for a meal next time you're here; such a nice girl, don't you think?"

"Mum, how could you?" He usually never commented on her schemes, but recently he'd come home and found a bevy of pretty young girls with stars in their eyes from something she'd said. He knew she had his best interests at heart, but quite frankly, he found Muthoni a bore. He felt secretly guilty about tasting her honey in a weaker moment, but it had only served to prove his point—she was a nice enough girl, but the heat of the fire was missing. He just didn't want to be tied down when he considered the flood of new prospects, and he shuddered at the thought of marriage that was going through mothers' mind.

23

Tonight, Fatima was going to show him the sights of London, and what better launch could they possibly have, than an out of this world reception? She had lived in the city for the last four years and was due to return home to Arusha the following month; but it was the present that Simon's encircling arms told her he wanted, and from the first time they locked eyes they were bound to live out the night together-- wherever they found themselves in the morning. A tap on his shoulder interrupted his dancing. Simon looked around, and up, when he saw the size of the annoyance that said, "let go." It was a repeat of the warning earlier that day in his room and he still couldn't figure it out. But the threat had served to concentrate his efforts to solve the crime, if only to 'smack' the big guy in the face. He was a bastard with political clout, and the new government demanded transparency, which made Simon think.

"Who was that?" Fatima asked, "and what did he mean, 'let go'?"

"Nothing… he's an acquaintance from back home; a real pain in the arse."

"He didn't seem too friendly, and looked like he was threatening you."

"I know, but what can I do? I only met him for the first time earlier today and I don't particularly like him; mind you, if we're both working for the same government I'll most probably have to take his advice, but for the moment I can't figure out what's behind his remarks."

"If he's in the same government," she echoed his words of uncertainty, "it makes good sense to me, for you to take his advice if he's your boss, anyway, he's left.... Are you enjoying this evening Simon?"

"Now that I've met you...an unequivocal yes!" He flashed his brilliant white teeth and she noticed the perfection in his smile, which was something she had always wanted and admired in a man. She looked down at her large breasts and prayed that such a magnificent development was one of his hang-ups; she nuzzled closer and he held her more tightly, his fingers exerting the slightest of pressures as they ran up and down her spine. Chandeliers were dimmed to accentuate the sultry, and as time raced by they became the only couple left on the floor. And as they took their eyes off each other, the frosty looks from the other guests told them it was time to leave,.

"I think we've worn out our welcome," Fatima was an old hand at attending receptions, and had sensed the looks that made them break their clinch. "Simon, we have to go; time's up, and there's no one here to thank because the Biggies are already in bed. Excuse me a minute; I'll see you in reception and I won't be long, so don't get lost!" Strange though it may seem, they never did get to see the London lights.

The taxi ride to the Holiday Inn in Mayfair was only a matter of fifteen minutes, but during that time Simon's active hands explored the full extent of Fatima's legs to the very last inch with a will of their own. He too was squeezed in all the right places on a reciprocal basis. The fare on the meter was inconsequential, and the reception clerk didn't blink an eye when they collected his single room key. The power of money had spoken, and he became more indebted to the Opugi family, whatever James Uko was thinking.

Fatima enjoyed Simon's attention in the lift all the way up to the fourth, and she seized her knickers from around her ankles, as the doors hinted they were about to open. Did they have to run from the lift to his room? Neither had the answer to that, until they were safely inside and tearing at each other's clothes to reveal their innermost secrets, before they dived on the bed in a tangle as naked as the day they were born. It was Fatima, who cried out first in ecstasy, before all movement ceased, and Simon had echoed her passion with a sensual groan to couple his feelings to hers and those of her nails, that had scratched his back in their moment of passion. Their first experience was magical-- they lay side-by-side holding hands, exhausted, and oblivious to the world.

By a generous stretch of imagination, the tune from the bathroom could have been interpreted as Fatima's wake up call, as Simon lay in a coma and studied the overcast sky that pained his eyes from the drawn-back curtains. 'Who the hell had opened that bloody window?' He ducked his head under the covers to keep out the icy draft and shouted to Fatima in a muffled voice. 'Shut the window!' but she was far too busy in the bathroom shouting the joys of her newfound lover. He, therefore, followed the age-old adage drummed into him by his father, who always said, 'Son, if you want something done properly, do it yourself'. Stark naked, he sprinted to the window, shut out the draft, and dived back into bed to recover from the temporary exposure. Barely had he done this feat, than Fatima stood over him.

"Wake up, darling!" she shouted, stripping the blankets from his lukewarm body, as though it was the first time out of bed for him that morning.

"I have to go to work," she declared to his nakedness. "I'll let myself out-- see you at the end of the month." She leaned over, kissed him full on the lips, and was gone.

From that time on his mother was in for a shock with her enquiries, 'is everything all right?' For all he knew, as he lay there dreaming, she was already moving toward grandmother status.

24

Chief Superintendent Black had some interesting news he wanted to get off his chest, and ASP Simon Nane was to be the recipient. The expert assessment from the lab was open on his desk, and Simon was seated in the same chair he'd occupied only 48 hours earlier.

Black examined the page of tightly printed script in front of him, and endeavored to pick out the interesting points, to avoid the tedium of reading the full report.

"Simon, the gist of the matter is this…" he offered a thoughtful expression and continued, "whoever pulled the trigger in all these 'hits', was in possession of the 'Rolls-Royce' of sniping equipment, which tells us there's money behind this operation, and the perpetrators are prepared to pay for perfection."

"So what you're saying is, these murders haven't been committed by some thug recruited off the street."

"Precisely, they're specialists… could even be woman, but you're not going to know this until you nail them."

"Now you tell me Conrad, what's the colour of their underwear—pink?" they laughed, recalling the Super's boast.

"On that one, Simon, I feel we'll have to wait; I must confess, I was a little hasty when I made that statement." He fixed his eyes on the figures in the report, and his finger flowed in line with the detail, line by line. It was difficult for Simon to follow his reading with the wording upside down, so he waited for Conrad to speak, rather than trying to out-guess him from the other side of the desk. "My boffins say that all the bullets were of the same calibre, .338 mm, and each weighed 250 grains. They were fired from .338 Lapua specialised rimless centre-fire cartridges, manufactured in Finland especially for sniper rifles; the shape of the bullets picked out of the concrete from behind the target in all three cases, indicated a muzzle velocity as high as 3000 ft/s. Now here's the twist... my experts estimate that the range was less than a thousand metres in each case; in fact, they give a figure of nearer 500, because of the accuracy of the shot between the eyes in every incident, which they observed from your close-up pictures, and of course the shape of the impacted bullets. They are also convinced the latest sight technology was used."

"And the weapons?" Simon asked.

"Again, that's a difficult one. I don't know how they arrived at this theory, but you should start looking for the makers of such weapons among the Pathan manufacturers on the Afghan border. The same arms manufacturing base that was in full swing at the time of the Russian occupation. Furthermore, they believe the delivery tube, what we simpletons refer to as the barrel of a gun," he made a cautious attempt at a smile, "was at least 24 inches long with a single-shot bolt-action. There are some silhouette pictures on this page," he turned it over, "of what they think you're up against, and what you should be looking for… That seems to be about it."

"Well…" he sighed at the size of his problem. "I suppose it gives me some idea of where to start." Somewhat overwhelmed, he struggled to hide his emotions as a lonely man up against a system, which offered little assistance, if his experience so far was anything to go by—the odds were stacked against him.

"I wish I could be more helpful," Conrad offered. "But you know how it is…to get me out there to lend a hand has to be a government to government request, and as I see it, the government could be your biggest obstacle."

"You're right, of course," Simon agreed. "But after I was threatened by that countryman of mine, to desist, I've drawn a second wind to succeed. Off the record Conrad, I need you to be my consultant. What do you say?" the room fell silent with expectation.

"Simon, I want to help you, and I will, but it has to be low profile; very low profile for the time being. But if you come up with something really convincing, tell me, and our people who used to prop up your government with aid money, will try to bring some pressure to bear."

"What can I say," Simon answered, "besides to thank you a million." He smiled, and immediately felt less alone to tackle his awesome future. It wasn't the first time for Conrad, to see the effect of his support for an ex-student reflected in a smile of gratitude, and he knew it wouldn't be the last.

25

Simon had only been away for five days, but by now his mother was worried sick that he might have chosen to settle overseas like so many of his classmates, frustrated by the octogenarians running the country, like robber-barons from fourteenth century Europe. She was naturally possessive, and in her eyes her son would never grow up. No matter how old he became, he would always remain her little boy. So, to put her mind at rest, he rang her by landline from the airport police station and readied himself to answer the first question he knew she'd ask... "Yes," he said, even if it wasn't true; he'd taken his vitamin pills at regular intervals and would call at the house that evening to tell her all about his trip. Well, almost all, leaving out his encounter with Fatima. That particular subject, would have to be eased into the conversation at some future date, if she was to accept her as a means to an end, to gain grandma status. Clearly, it was going to be a balancing act between Fatima's religion and her foreign status, and the necessity of his mother to rival her sisters in the granny stakes. Fatima, after all, was a foreigner of the worst type; not of a different Kenyan tribe, but outside the country completely, and a Moslem into the bargain. But all things said and done his mother would have to adjust, and welcome her into the family, if he decided on marriage. His sporadic hallucinations had recently begun to develop a continuity he failed to understand, as he dwelled on the brief hours of bliss between them. The very image of her smiling face had even begun to haunt his waking hours, and from the tingle in his fingertips, he recollected sweet memories in the London taxi that verged on the super-natural.

He was in a mental mess, and beginning to question his sanity. Such feelings were new to him, and the more she was in his mind the bigger the ache in his chest became. The distance separating them was slowly killing him-- she was out of reach, and out of sight in the Tanzanian bush, bearing gifts traditionally demanded of her to compensate for her absence. Did she feel the same way about him, and did she also have sleepless nights with the agonies of love disturbing her? He wanted to know. But first, he would solve the case that was weighing him down, and then devote his energies to love.

Since the departure of Assistant Superintendent Simon Nane, all work in his office had abruptly come to a halt. He was the motivating power, and without him his specialist section flapped aimlessly in the wind, ticking over with mundane form-filling duties, and endless paperwork designed to frustrate the police in favour of the criminals. Simon, a hands-on-man, had no time for the forms that plagued his office, and of particular anathema to him was the supplying of answers, to parliamentary questions.

Suggestions posed by the Super in London were clearly uppermost in his mind when plain-clothes Inspector Michael Kamba, ex-military special branch, entered his office in response to his summons. Kamba, not acknowledging his boss's rank, immediately sat down on the standard government wooden chair in front of the standard government desk, surveyed by a standard picture of the President. The only other wall adornment was an animal calendar sponsored by Sadolin Paints. Kamba had been head-boy at their school when Simon was only a prefect, and now their authority was reversed. Mike was not insensitive to his position, but accepted it, because Simon was responsible for his last promotion, and a personal friend into the bargain.

Formality had been abandoned before it had even been offered, and Simon opened the conversation in a similar vein. He knew Kamba meant no disrespect for his rank; it was just one of his shortcomings that was more than compensated for by his brilliance. He liked the man, and placed more trust in him than anyone else on his team.

"Mike, before you ask, I had a good trip; and now we have to discuss other things with too many imponderables." He enjoyed his use of imponderables, and wondered if Mike knew exactly what he was getting at as he nodded his head in agreement to his own rhetoric.

"As the hunters say, we must get moving before the scent gets cold, but in this case it's more of a stink," he lowered his voice. "That's only my personal opinion, so keep it to yourself," they laughed. Mike appreciated the humour, as the happy-go-lucky character he was, who had endeared his friendship to his boss on a number of occasions. He was the only person in the unit who could call the boss by his first name when they were socializing.

"Mike, I need you and a couple of constables under your direction to examine these records, and don't discuss them with anyone else. If someone should come asking, no matter who they are, refer them to me; especially if it's the press. That also applies to the President himself, and the Commissioner; use tact, but tell them nothing."

"Why would the President be interested in such trivia?"

"Who knows, but when you begin to examine the connections it's possible that relatives of relatives and illegitimate sons with different names will be recorded as property owners to disguise their hidden assets; you get me? It is sensitive information and even the man at the top could be involved. Of course, that's highly unlikely, but nothing should be passed around, requested or not."

He pushed the new file compiled by him across the desk and Kamba focused his eyes on the plain brown cover. He was the first person to touch it after Simon had checked and rechecked his work for accuracy. The cover wasn't marked with the usual 'Top Secret' in red, which would have drawn attention to the program and increased curiosity, and the ruse was quickly recognised by Mike, who had worked under similar circumstances in his military career.

"Mike, excuse me tonight. I think you know what it's like; my mother wants to check on her little boy and I can't refuse." he shrugged his shoulders and sighed in despair.

"What about tomorrow?"

"Tomorrow I'm free; we'll have a beer and catch up on my trip. Tell you what, meet at seven, at the Simba Hill Restaurant—the evenings on me. And by then, I'll be expecting some feed back from you, to compensate for the goat you'll be chewing at my expense." He reached across his desk, and Mike recognised a familiar seriousness in the closeness of his face as he tapped the file significantly, "see what you can do with this?"

26

Flowers for his mother. She was thrilled, even though her garden was overflowing and the gesture raised suspicions, as to why he had bothered at all. Nevertheless, she preferred to give him the benefit of the doubt, and dismissed her thoughts of a previous occasion when he'd forgotten to tell her he was traveling outside the country. They embraced, before she held him at arms length to assess his well being and admired his good-looks, which in many ways reflected her own. His big eyes, fine nose, and full mouth with even teeth, were all gifts from a gracious God using her as his medium, and surprisingly enough, no trace of his father's genes could be seen.

His father welcomed his son with his usual warm handshake as though he hadn't been anywhere at all, but when Muthoni from next-door appeared from the shadows, and grabbed him like a much-cherished doll, he almost fainted. And as his breathing returned to normal a thought had occurred to him; that the delicate matter of telling his parents about Fatima, could now be postponed because of Muthoni's presence, if they ask why it hadn't been mentioned before.

Twenty-four hours back in the country and the persistent ringing of his phone was driving him mad; he shouted out loud, "Stop! Stop!" to relieve his tension. Important people, as the Commissioner termed them, wanted to know the score, and he was expected to enlighten them. Peace – he needed peace – he had to think. "Block all calls," he instructed his secretary; he was 'out' to whoever it was, and that included his mother.

Seven in the evening arrived soon enough, and with the prospect of the Simba restaurant on the horizon, he closed his office, leaving one of the most hectic days in his life behind him. A few guests only occupied the room as he slipped into the corner bench to await Mike, whom he hoped had the missing jigsaw pieces, to match the questions he'd underlined in ink. If the worse came to worst, the disturbing pattern of the family connections imagined by him, would be confirmed-- but what was Mike's prognosis?

"Wow!" The first cold beer of the day hardly touched the sides of his throat as it whistled down to the pit of his stomach, but it was the second that really counted, as it leisurely massaged his taste buds and produced the vibes beer lovers adore. His affinity with beer had been acquired as a curious kid at his parents' home. The cook, a dear lady, had scolded him on occasions when he'd been caught with a half-empty bottle, but finally she had taken their secret into retirement with a wistful smile and a memory.

"Mike…what news?"

"News …it's a conspiracy!" Mike declared. "But for the different names, dates, and various facts I've stripped bare, you'd think at a glance they're all different families.

My biggest obstacle was traditional naming, because I had to find out who was related to whom; sons taking grandfather's names, and daughters taking the first names on the female side. In most cases the main family name is not recorded in European style. Sure, customs are slowly changing to the European way if your father is famous, and you want to brag about his power and wealth. But if you want a second passport to hide your identity, the traditional system is still used to juggle the names, and that's what we're up against. Methodology used to obscure identities." He added 'ology' to 'methods' when simple old-fashioned methods would have sufficed. Everyone was doing it these days to show their knowledge of nothing, when addressing their colleagues, and he didn't want to be the odd man out. "In most cases, the name trails I've examined are littered with pot-holes to disguise their family structures."

"Not entirely unexpected, or was it?" Simon asked.

"No. I was just giving you the background; I'm not complaining."

"Sorry I interrupted." Simon said, defensively. "Please go on..."

"Well, I have some details you'll find interesting. I'm only griping because of the hard time I had, until I found a couple of old family retainers sacked after forty years of loyal service. You know how it is… one of the family members marries outside the clan and wants to replace them with their own tribe. So, I exploited this fact, and offered incentives for information. I hope you don't mind, but I promised a couple of places in the force to their grandchildren in return for deciphering a few of the name conundrums I needed, to construct the family trees. Mind you, I've yet to examine all the information in depth; but from what I've seen to date we've hit the jackpot." He waited, expecting a backlash from his confession to blatant bribery, but Simon's facial expression remained intact, without so much as a twitch to distract his attention. He motioned Mike on, using a come-hither wave of his hand that reflected impatience. Mike accepted the signal, and mirrored his boss's unblinking attitude as he picked up his hesitant thread and continued…

"So, I constructed several family trees from the information provided by these two grandmothers, who filled in the finer details showing a pent up hate; such as I've never witnessed before in all my experience of vendettas."

"Did they really understand why you wanted the family tree?"

"Perhaps not, but besides the family links, the extra information they offered will be useful if we can put it into context. It was vindictive but clear, and was most certainly topped off with a full portion of venom to settle old scores. Much of it was irrelevant, but I didn't choose to enlighten them. Anyway, it's all on tape if you want to hear it?"

"I'll take your word for it."

"I think this is what you've really been waiting for," Mike smiled confidently and reached into his inner pocket while moving around to the other side of the table, which was reasonably free from the clutter of their second round of bottles and glasses. He eased on the leather-type bench-seat in the corner next to Simon, and without uttering a word handed over four manila sheets for examination. He was on hand to explain, but was also aware that his boss usually liked to arrive at his own conclusions in true detective form; so as the seconds passed and became minutes, and Simon sipped his beer hardly lifting his head from the papers, Mike waited in expectation.

At last, Simon looked up, "Mmm… I just don't believe it… are you sure of these facts?"

"Sure, I'm sure," his repetition swept aside any doubt.

"But these family trees you've constructed look more like family bushes. There're hundreds of names, which are bound to obscure our starting point by the sheer numbers involved."

"I've also given thought to that."

"What do you suggest?" Simon had first thought to question farm workers on the estates himself, but that had been set aside in favour of a new idea to link businesses to common family interests, and look for a single motive; it had been suggested by Conrad that there was a distinct possibility of a single organisation being responsible for all the killings. Now Simon had a hunch that a single business connection could be linked to the deaths, and this would be found in the family trees. It was early days to cull the answers however, but he would block his office phone tomorrow and think without distractions. How he hated gossip.

"I just don't know," Mike replied, shaking his head in exasperation.

"It's time to eat Mike. I was in the office up to now, and after looking at these documents from you I can do with some brain food." He pushed the four sheets, back into their original envelope and consigned them to the warmth and safety of his inside pocket. His briefcase was readily available, but these pieces of paper were special and he preferred them to be on his person. It wasn't the first time he'd forgotten his briefcase as the evening wore on, and besides, a jacket was comfortably part of his person. And he wasn't the only forgetful person on the force: he recalled the incident of the laptop taken from the Commissioner's car and the full-blown enquiry now under way. Naturally, it would come to nothing, like all the other enquiries, and the pressures of life within the criminal environment usually got the blame, even though by now, such excuses were wearing terribly thin.

"Can I interest you in a fish? Fish, brain food, get it?" Simon made his point.

"Yes please, but whatever happened to the goat you promised me yesterday." Simon, ordered fish and took no notice of the goat remark. He was anxious to discuss his affairs of the heart with Mike, whom he conceded to be the more experienced man on such a subject.

"Now, do you want to hear about my trip to the UK?" Simon was dying to confide in one of his age-mates, and it had to be grist to the marriage-mill if the size of Kamba's family was anything to go by.

"Okay, okay, spit it out," was Mike's response, and Simon smiled.

"Not so fast, good stories have to be unravelled with great care... I'm sure you appreciate what I'm saying?"

"Okay, okay, then spit it out slowly... is that better?" He laughed and Simon abandoned all pretence of a sermon. Mike also wisely decided against further interruption. The pressure on Simon was so obvious.

"She's called Fatima!" Simon, declared, as though it had been his intention to proudly shout her name for all to hear.

"A real angel is the only way I can describe her." He sighed, and took control of his emotions by interlocking his fingers in front of his chest and pulling them tight, after which he unclasped both hands. "She's mine," he announced, "and I'm in love for the first time in my life."

"Calm down Simon, I don't have to be convinced; if you say you're in love, you're in love."

"I can't sleep at nights and nothing else matters. Is that real love or a passing infatuation? Advise me, Mike. She's beautiful and she's from Tanzania, so where do I go from here?"

"It's love all right," Mike agreed. Simon's description, without doubt, confirmed the bug had bitten him. "And you're asking me what you should do?"

"Well, it's never happened to me before, and as you're a married man I'm asking your advice, and… I don't want to make a fool of myself. I realise Tanzania's another world, and her religion could also cause a problem with my parents."

"Follow your heart, dear friend, and call on me for support. That's the best advice I can offer. Love occasionally takes a smooth course," he assured Simon, announcing the doubtful fact, and not believing it for a minute. It certainly hadn't in his case, but he was optimistic for Simon, and noticed the relief on his face as he had unburdened his heart to him. Hadn't someone famous once remarked, Mike recalled, and wondered if he should now make a joke of it... 'marriage was the only time you got to sleep with the enemy.' But perhaps, it was not wise to mention such 'theoretical triumphs' at this time, and wreck his hitherto receptive ear; he settled for silence.

When at last the Tilapia fillets arrived, packed out with chips and embellished with two enormous slices of lemon, a bottle of tomato ketchup was also placed on the table, at the same time as the beers. The switch from the large Tusker bottle to the more delicate Tusker Malt, was a sign of elegance that Simon associated with fish, and the more delicate glasses bearing the Tusker crest also replaced the chunky jugs. They wished each other, '*maisha-marefu*,' long-life; glasses touched, they took a gulp of the brew, and then they pointed at each other and burst out laughing, as though they'd never left school—both wore frothy moustaches.

27

The suffocating stillness of the night promised the long rains were on their way, if recent renegade patterns didn't prevail. Simon punched his pillow, sidled up to Fatima, and fitted his form into hers as she lay there in her usual coma. It had been a restless night of tossing and turning even before the whining mosquito had settled on his ear. Why it hadn't chosen Fatima, who was by far the tastier morsel, he found hard to believe, until he saw she'd covered her head with the sheet. He rolled over and snapped on the light to check the temperature, time, and date from the bed side digital clock, and confirmed he could get to the club for an early swim, avoid wetting his costume if he went nude, feel free, and snuggle up to Fatima on his return. She would always complain he'd come out of the fridge, but never failed to warm him. Her internal warmth was also there if time permitted, but he was never one to rush sensations, they were there to be savoured.

"What are we going to do about our problem?" Fatima asked, as Simon was admiring the symmetry of the Spanish omelette on his plate.

"Problem?" He looked up.

"Simon, you know perfectly well what I'm talking about. What are we going to do about our problem?"

"Don't think I'm not concerned: I am, and I've given it a lot of thought...I think we should get married."

"Simon Daarliing... you mean it?"

"Well it's a bit early in the morning and I'm still half asleep," he joked, "but do I have a choice? I love you-- didn't I tell you that?" He played it cool as he pulled back her chair just slightly to hint she should rise, and as she did so, he took her in his arms and kissed her, caressing the nape of her neck with one hand, and clutching her buttocks with the other to demonstrate his love for the 'family furniture'.

"I'm so happy Simon… never let me go." He held her for a full five minutes before they came up for air.

"Darling, the Champagne's on ice."

"What! When did you put it there?"

"Well if you must know; a couple of days back when I decided to propose… to you know who?"

"You mean to say you've been trifling with my affections since then."

"Oh…I wouldn't say that. It's just that I have been pre-occupied with these murders. There were another three last week, and I'm no nearer to solving any of them.

"Simon; I know your job is important to you, but sometimes you must let go and put me first. That's one of the reasons why you've remained a bachelor for so long; but I'm not complaining. I'm glad you waited for me. But before we finally tie the knot, I suggest we sort out when we work, and when we play. Don't want Simon to be a dull boy, do we?" She pinched his cheek as his mother would have done, and laughed.

"Champagne! Champagne!" he hadn't heard a word she'd uttered. The cork popped and froth filled each glass, which magically turned to golden bubbly.

"To hell with family objections! To us!" he declared.

"To us!" she replied. They entwined their arms to form a chain between them, and drank to a lifetime together.

"What about our omelettes?" Simon asked as she steered him out of the kitchen.

"You're my omelette," she declared, and led him toward the bedroom. She pushed him back on the bed, and stood between his knees to unbuckle his belt and unzip his fly that restricted the bulge in his pants; and unlike her omelette, he was piping hot.

28

"Sorry I'm late, but something came up as I was about to leave the house," was Simon's opening remark. They could have laughed together about what had kept him, but for the moment he had no intention of sharing his private antics with Kamba.

"I can see you're in a good mood. What's going on?" Kamba responded.

"Mike, if only you knew." He wasn't yet ready to confide.

"Okay, hang on to your secret: but I'll find out, you'll see."

"To business," Simon announced, looking at the records from the Registrar of Companies that littered his desk, which clearly indicated the Opugis wholly owned many an enterprise, when he compared the names from the family trees re-constructed by Kamba. It was true, the different names were one and the same person, but if Simon were to accept Conrad's theory that a common denominator existed between the businesses, and the killings, a computer analysis was necessary. He still wasn't sure that the names were as convincingly connected as Conrad surmised, for him to shout Bingo!

In his eyes, Bingo belonged to crime fiction and real life was very different; but based on the theory that the assassinated people were prominent individuals, he asked the local press to provide another dimension by extracting a list of high profile personalities, with their stories to hit the headlines over a four-year period. How London was going to analyse the data he wasn't quite sure, and the excitement normally reserved for a case of this magnitude appeared to be lacking, as the details were dispatched to the Yard.

"Can you take a call from London?" Simon's secretary was on the line.

"Put it through." It had to be Conrad.

"Assistant Superintendent Simon Nane?" Conrad's enquiry was clear enough to suggest he was in the next room, but he wanted to recognise Simon's voice, before he continued.

"Nice to hear you Conrad-- good news, I hope?"

"Perhaps… I can't say for certain, but Opugi came to the fore over two years ago when one of his companies collapsed. Not only is his picture in the newspaper in June 2005, but so are those of his two co-directors, who rank as uncles on the family tree. And what's more, it all ties up with the registrar of companies."

"Are you sure; why didn't my man pick it up?"

"That's for you to worry about. I'm just telling you what we found, and it only took a day when my experts got down to it. Look Simon, its sensitive information, so pick it up from the High Commission tomorrow evening at 5pm your time. I'll put it in double covers and tell the HC you'll collect it."

Black's report was bulky. The covering letter summarised the contents and initially associated Opugi, Chege and Liki, the murdered victims, with a hardware firm that had collapsed two years previously. According to the newspaper report, the company pension account monies had failed to reach its correct destination. Other legal obligatory remittances such as VAT debts to the revenue authorities also remained unpaid. In fact, it was these authorities that had eventually acted to close down the business with a loss of jobs and millions of shillings to the private employees, and to the exchequer.

Three months after the collapse of the hardware business, exactly the same people, Opugi, Chege, and Liki, had launched their own bank. Meeting the depository requirements they declared themselves as Directors, and became the controlling equity holders without a thought for their bankrupt status—and no one had bothered to ask. The report reasoned, the lack of questions was due to the high civil service positions they held at that time, and even then, they still owed money to the Revenue Authority from the hardware store receipts. When they died, a tug of war was going on between them and the Government, and they were claiming protection from prosecution based on a violation of their constitutional rights. Even now to this day, the court injunction against the government is still in force. Hear this, the paid-up capital of the bank was a hundred million shillings, and the name of their new enterprise was called the 'Rocky Bank Limited.'

The trio conducted all these frauds while moonlighting from their government jobs, which gave them the big-man leverage, to pursue their criminal activities.

Good hunting—Signed, Conrad Black.

"Mike, come over, I want you to see this." He leaned around the door to make sure Simon was alone.

"Yes Boss?"

"We have something here!" Simon proffered the single page synopsis he held in his hand. "Sit down and read this; then tell me all about Rocky Bank."

Mike breezed through the letter, but then paused to gather his thoughts as he tried to recollect that particular news item, and separate it from dozens of similar events.

"It was certainly headline news at the time, and I recall a picture of a corner bank in downtown Nairobi. But I suspect you know more about this than I do. It was one of those cases where the promoters gave themselves unsecured loans and broke the bank. Something about offering above market rates to draw in gullible customers, and once they were on board they robbed them blind."

"Congrats Mike, you're spot on...here's the actual paper dated 28th June 2005. The names in the paper are the same as those in the reconstruction of the family tree to support your theory. All of them, in powerful positions of authority in Government, managed to channel millions into Rocky Bank against regulations to invest in Government Bonds or Treasury bills. I blame the government for this whole affair. They should have chosen their custodians with more care. It says in last week's paper, they were some of the richest men on the social circuit when they were murdered. I'm not surprised. Strange, very strange…" a pin would have made a loud noise had it dropped, as they mulled over the position…

"As much as I sympathise with the losers of their money, we still have a case to solve. Three cases in fact, although I now suspect we're looking for one organised operation."

"What makes you say that?"

"Well, for one thing, two crimes were committed on the same day, and the third was committed on the day after, 200 miles apart. So whoever or whatever it was, couldn't have travelled the distance and taken the time to organise the crime, if they were the same people. Why, you may ask? Well it's really rather simple when you think about it; these types of crime need stealth, and tracking over days, if they're to be perfect."

"And you think they're perfect?" Mike asked.

"No. I don't think they're perfect. In my experience a perfect crime has never been committed. It's the investigators who miss the clues who are responsible for creating that illusion." He held up his hand and pointed across the desk. "We'll nail these people; I feel it in my bones. The only thing I don't know—is when?"

"Then let's do it," Mike enthused.

"First, get me the bank case file. I want to see for myself what exactly happened. I also want a court order to examine the bank records, if they still exist. And it's now time to employ a forensic accountant to find out who could have had a grudge; someone who lost big when the bank collapsed-- besides the government."

29

Roger Fitzpatrick was one of the best. Engaged by foreign governments on numerous occasions, he was known and respected by Conrad Black, who had cause to be grateful to him when ingenious thieves had stretched accounting fraud to the limits. On Sunday evening he landed at JK International Airport and proceeded directly to the Intercontinental Hotel, where the UK Overseas Development Aid had booked the boardroom suite for his use-- all paid by them, at Conrad's request.

Before his arrival, Kamba dusted off the incomplete files on the Rocky Bank case. They were actually hidden in the depths of the AG's Chambers, and blatantly required expert attention. Furthermore, Kamba was the only confidante to Simon's request for such an expert, since the Commissioner's support for the investigation had become sporadic after his return from London.

The secretive deputation to see Fitzpatrick on the Monday was comprised of Simon and Mike transporting two large cases of documents, and some hard drives recovered from the basement records of the Public Prosecutor's office, without the authority of the AG. Had he known, he would no doubt have refused permission to protect his career. Nane's investigation was now completely under wraps, and to avoid influential interference he no longer updated the Commissioner.

It was a fact that no one disputed – the owners of the Rocky Bank had resorted to devious tactics to cover their tracks, and it now fell to Fitzpatrick to trace them by using information extracted from their customer base. It was not an uncommon task for him-- he knew how to reconstruct data from ICUs crudely damaged by thugs, before the police in this particular case, were coerced to intervene. It was going to be a tedious job, involving a certain amount of travel in the company of plain clothes detectives, followed by delicate persuasion in private, with affected bank customers to reveal their balances. And to add to his difficulties, some victims actually believed that the relatives of the deceased bank owners, would reward them if they refused to co-operate.

A.S.P. Simon Nane and C.I. Michael Kamba were amazed by the speed at which Roger Fitzpatrick completed his task, which sought to pinpoint customers with a motive so strong that murder was the only explanation. It clearly divided the 'haves' and the 'have nots', and the temperament of the customers was another factor that would determine the direction of their investigation. The biggest loser, the government, with billions of shillings misdirected by highly placed civil servants, was not in dispute, but the government wasn't likely to resort to assassination. It was the other losers, the small individuals who had lodged their life savings, who needed assessment.

It was still early days to point a finger in any direction, but the most surprising disclosure was a customer base of less than 500, that clearly implied 'window dressing', and hid the fact that the bank was a 'shell', to siphon off government money.

From the Jomo Kenyatta International Airport to the office in the Industrial area was only a matter of ten minutes, after a grateful pair of policemen had seen Roger off on his return flight to London.

"Let's make this clear," Simon was speaking to Mike as they pulled out their respective chairs in his office and looked at the first pages of the report. "We both know it's a scam by some of the highest in the land, but we have to put that behind us. We're looking for murderers and not searching for morals…agreed?"

"But what happens if we unearth the stolen millions?"

"As I said, Mike, we're looking for murderers; but should we uncover anything else while we're looking, we'll put it aside and finish our primary objective first. I don't want any distractions from outside parties. Do I make myself clear?"

"Absolutely."

"Right; we see eye to eye...so what do you make of this report?"

"Well," Mike was looking at picture of the President above Simon's head to gather inspiration, "if I were asked, who do you think wanted to bump off these guys, I'd go for the little man who's lost his life savings. But it doesn't fit the sophisticated weaponry used. Another point...if it was the little man who committed these murders, he would have to know the clerical details, addresses etc, and that is extremely unlikely."

"But Mike, whoever it was would have seen newspaper details and have photographs to work on. So identification wouldn't have been too difficult. However, addresses are another thing; but one follows the other if you need it badly enough. And what if professional were hired?" Simon played the devil's advocate.

"Little men don't hire professionals. They either chop people up in the street, or wait for them to return home and hit them as they're waiting for their gates to open," Mike replied.

"Okay. Rule out the little man for the moment, which leaves us with a family feud...remember they were all on that family tree; or alternatively, someone who didn't get a loan; or a big depositor who lost out—such as the government."

"We have yet to examine this report in depth," Mike responded.

"I have the gist, but I agree with you Mike, it needs deeper examination if we're to come up with anything worthwhile. It's just not logical for someone to use sniper rifles, from God knows where – the experts suspect Afghanistan. When in our capital you can hire a hit man with an AK for 50,000/-. Ask yourself this: what would you do if you wanted to commission a killing for sheer satisfaction and immediate confirmation? Well, I if it were me, I'd buy an AK for 20,000/- in Eastleigh, and shoot the bugger myself, and risk the chance of a finger being pointed in my direction."

"Then you don't think we'll catch them?" Mike asked.

"I didn't say that, and I didn't imply it." Simon was annoyed.

"If you don't mind Sir," Mike introduced formality to massage Simon's testiness. "I suggest we adjourn for a drink."

"That's the best idea I've heard all day. Let's get the hell out of here! I'll lock these in my safe tonight," he collected Mike's copy from across the desk and added it to his own.

30

"What's happening?" Simon asked the *askari* at the barrier as he returned his salute for the first time that day.

"It's a robbery Sir."

"Was it cash?" After all, it was the end of the month.

"No Sir. I think it was your office safe, but I'm not sure?"

"What!" Simon shot toward his covered parking bay twenty yards up the tarmac. 'For what?' he muttered under his breath, and cast his mind back to the London encounter with the long black man from the lake. 'Surely not,' he muttered again, that had to be all behind him. He could see at a glance as he entered his office his safe was definitely missing, and from what he could judge, it must have been dragged through the door using his new red carpet for a skid. That was also missing. He called for a cup of tea and added an extra spoonful of sugar to soothe his nerves, and then pushed back in his chair to examine the room and confirm nothing else had gone astray. Finally, satisfied that everything seemed to be in place, including Fatima's picture on his desk, he picked up the phone and asked Mike to come over.

"I don't believe it," were Mike's first words, as he parked himself in one of the visitor's chairs.

"Look at that space!" Simon pointed to where they had both witnessed him locking the safe-door and rattling the handle the previous evening.

"Yeah, looks rather bare in here now; anything else in particular missing?"

"Are you blind…? My new bloody carpet's gone; they used it to drag the safe through my own bloody door! If things aren't safe in a police building where can they be safe? Answer me that?"

"So whoever it was, wanted to get hold of old Roger's report, and let's not lose sight of your new carpet," he grinned.

"Yes, my new carpet…why didn't I think of that?" Simon banged the desk with his fist and burst out laughing. At last, he'd have something to talk about in the bar at the Police Officer's mess. "Have some tea Mike, and let's see where we go from here."

The phone connection to London was surprisingly clear for a change; he didn't have to shout.

"Yes Simon, how can I be of assistance?" Chief Superintendent Black was on the end of the line

"And what makes you think I need assistance?"

"And what makes you think, I don't know you need assistance. You must need something, or you wouldn't be phoning me—am I right?"

"Conrad, you're not going to believe this…" he paused, and Conrad slipped into his usual phrase when talking to Simon.

"Try me?" he invited.

Simon swallowed. "Well…it's all a bit embarrassing."

"Hit me again, Simon." By now he was enjoying Simon's apparent discomfort, and in turn, Simon, was assessing how he could tone down his ridiculous state of affairs.

"First, let me say thanks for sending Roger over here; he's produced an explicit report on which we're working right now. I suppose you've read it?"

"Not yet, but I'm glad to hear it's to your liking. Is there anything else?"

"As a matter of fact, there is. It seems someone else also appreciated the quality of Roger's efforts and stole his report from my office last night—can you send me more copies?"

"No problem, I'll get hold of Roger and they'll be in the High Commission mailbag first thing tomorrow. And next time young man, put them under lock and key." There was absolutely no admonishment in his voice when he said, 'under lock and key', and Simon couldn't help but wondered, which was the worse scenario – losing the safe, or failing to lock up the documents. He felt honour bound to say he had locked them up and office security had let him down, but on second thoughts he would let the matter rest where it was. He couldn't bear to hear Conrad's familiar laugh, if he told him what had actually happened.

"Will do, and thanks."

As the call ended, Mike questioningly raised his eyebrows. "And when can we expect the replacements?"

"Tomorrow, I hope."

"What about the stolen safe?"

"I'll let the usual crime squad deal with that and we'll move next door in the meantime."

"Am I missing something here?" Mike was looking for the usual confidence that flowed between them. "You don't seem too concerned with the theft of the safe and the contents. I'd be raising hell and thumping the heads— in your position."

"Mike, I might not show it, but I'm more disturbed than you think. There're other circumstances I should have mentioned to you before today, and now this has happened, I think you should know what else occurred in London that could have a bearing on this theft. You see, on my first day when I returned to my hotel room after a jog in the park, this thug was sitting there."

"In your room?"

"Yes, in my room; that's what I said. He had evidently picked the lock, or had done whatever it takes to bypass these new card entry systems, because he was in my only easy chair waiting for me to return. He's a big bastard, I might add; and he introduced himself as James Uko, and that was a lie, because I've tried to trace him since my return, and he's not on any staff list-- secret or public. Anyway, certainly not under the name he gave me. It's the point he made at that time that worries me. If I can remember it rightly, he said, 'let go before you're stopped in your tracks', and he was referring to this investigation that he seemed to know all about. He also added, 'we like what's happening,' which led me to believe the 'we' was the government, and he's on the government payroll even if I can't trace him. And now we have the theft of my safe, that couldn't have happened without official connivance. So I have to conclude, the theft could be part of the 'stopping us in our tracks.' You don't think he's the one responsible for these murders do you?" the thought suddenly struck Simon.

"That's an interesting thought indeed, but where is he now?" Mike asked.

"How should I know? I can't find his name in the government lists, and his person, as big as he is, is nowhere to be seen. Do we start looking? I don't think so. But I should have mentioned this incident before, and put you on your guard, for which I now apologise. What was in my safe, you may ask? Well, besides my passport and bank cheque book there were a few shillings, and let us not forget the original family trees and of course our most recent addition, the report." His vacant expression summed up his feelings, and he wrung his hands in despair.

"So our opponents are now in possession of my passport, which can be replaced, a small amount of money and some blank cheques, and the report from Roger we hardly had the opportunity to see ourselves; not to mention the family trees we constructed as part of our enquiries, and that's about it. And they know we have some powerful helpers. It's a pity we didn't have some false information in there to lead them astray. You didn't mark your copy, did you?

"Hardly had time-- it was only in my possession for a matter of minutes. Did you mark yours?"

"No: so they don't know our thinking, and let's keep it that way. But be forewarned, they're on our tail, which brings me to a more serious note. Mike, you're a family man, I've known you from school, and I think this investigation could put your life in danger; do you want out?"

"No way! I have no problem with you watching my back; but thanks for asking." Simon reached across the desk, took hold of his partner's open hand, and there and then a pact was sealed.

Conrad Black was as good as his word, and Simon collected a copy of the report from the High Commission twenty minutes after receiving their call. This time they would remain on his person and Mike would retain a second copy in the same manner. The tedious analysis of depositor lists looking for motives to match the crimes was about to begin. He called Mike in.

"Mike-- now let's begin afresh. This fellow Fitzpatrick spent some time out here on our behalf, so the least we can do is to hang onto his report, examine it, and to come up with a theory; but quite frankly, when I saw his conclusion, I don't think he's nailed anyone or anything."

"What's your theory, Mike?" Simon wanted Mike to go first. It seemed rather childish, but that's how he felt in this particular case, and not without good reason. Clearly the bank had gone bust, but he sought the reassurance and confirmation of Mike to underline the obvious.

"Why are you asking me when you know the answer?" Mike questioned.

"Confirmation, I want confirmation; that's all." Simon insisted.

"Okay, I confirm it went bust. What more can I say; you've read the report as I have, and there's nothing more to add."

"Nothing more, I agree; and we seem to be no nearer to a solution. Fitzpatrick's summary said it all. This bank was set up as a shell to facilitate loans to the owners, who milked it, before the customer-base could grow to support their greed; they just couldn't wait. Sure, they hung on for six months after inception, but the high interest rates only attracted a few of the more naïve, who enjoyed collecting their interest each month from a solitary building—the full extent of the bank. And in the end, receivership was impossible, because when the building caught fire, the partly destroyed records recovered by the Central Bank became a recipe, for them to dance the fraudsters tune."

"Quite frankly Simon, I suggest we bin this report and look for a different angle, and we don't tell Black because he's your friend with our interests at heart. But what a waste of time, and effort."

"In fact, the only scenario that I can imagine to justify these deaths, as a result of his report, has to be some do-gooder or vigilante organization, with high morals to drive them on." Simon guessed, not knowing how close he came to the truth.

"At least we're in agreement on that; and you could be right about the vigilante angle" Mike accepted.

31

"Jesse, thanks for the information; I've discussed our next move with Crooky, and we've decided to keep up the pressure. Meaning, your teams will receive another target as soon as we've made the choice. Can you come over this weekend, we've things to discuss?"

"What time?" Jesse didn't waste words.

"Fifteen hundred hours, tomorrow Okay?"

"Yes." Disconnection was instant.

Rupert picked up the phone, knowing it had to be Digby on the other end. "Diggers?" he enquired. "Tell me, your 'ancient pile's' on fire!"

"Huh! No such luck; the insurance companies are still hanging on," he laughed. "Come over early tomorrow and we'll go through the papers together."

"Expect me, for brunch around eleven."

Rupert was on time; Rupert was always on time when he smelt the prospect of bacon and eggs. Even at home, the smell reduced him to a quivering jelly.

"Come in. Come in dear boy. We have work to do before three o'clock, this afternoon."

"And brunch?"

"Ah, thought you'd ask about that; it's already on the stove. We eat now, and discuss what we're going to do when we finish." Digby knew the proclivities of his dear friend so well. "Mrs. Catchpole!" he called out, and then reverted to the subject in hand. "Jesse, has to be given a second target today."

"What's the hurry, when I left here last, it was going to take several days, and now I find we've only got a few hours? You're pushing it too fast, and then we'll make mistakes. Note my words Diggers… I'll say no more."

"Rupert, I've heard you, now let's get on with it. And I don't want you to say 'I told you so', if things don't go quite according to plan. You take this bundle, and I'll take this one. Now start looking, all told I want six items from you." He handed out old copies of the National Daily from Kenya, which stretched over a period several years; and two hours later Digby called "enough!" By then they were reduced to gauging the serious of the crimes, having selected far more than the six required, and Rupert's choices lay on the floor.

"What have we here?" Digby stooped to pick up Rupert's bundle, and uttered a groan as the unused muscles in his back complained. He then walked over to the banqueting table and spread out Rupert's selections next to his own. "What do you think, Crooky?" Digby switched to Rupert's nickname, to gain his absolute attention.

"In my six." He'd counted out six of his selection, and then six of Rupert's to match his own, rather than have any overlap. "I've two cases of embezzlement, straight cash. Two cases of contract fraud. And finally, two cases where contractors have sued the AG's office, which cost the government millions in penalties, because no defense was offered. Now let's see what you've turned up."

"I'll tell you, don't even bother to read mine," Rupert volunteered. "To begin with, I've picked out two open and shut cases of fraud by the Social Security Investment Committee that bought grossly overpriced land from their cronies. There are also a couple of cases of government land sold back to the government – sounds like science fiction but it isn't. And a case of Airport tender manipulation. But to round up my selection, I offer what I think has to have the most merit: the misallocation of settlement scheme land for the landless, to the big bosses – hundreds of acres. I've read my articles thoroughly, and searched for reprimand or arraignment of the culprits in each case. I came up with nothing, absolutely nothing, and now I suspect they're living off the 'fat of the land', no pun intended. So you tell me Diggers, which of our choices is going to teach an important lesson to the greedy, and which is the easiest to execute?"

"By gad Crooky, I think you're right; land, the perennial issue! It has to be the best example, no doubt about it. A settlement project for the landless will cover the broadest spectrum of corruption. Another point in favour of land issue is, that we have written details, lists, records of payments, and secondary sales. Whatever else falls apart in African society, they're ever so particular about registering their title deeds; no matter how the land is acquired, they want their names on that little bit of paper – their own names, because they don't trust a soul – it's a type of religion."

"I must admit, before you mentioned that land issue-- I honestly thought the Airport scam was the best selection; where the tender was awarded to the highest bidder when the lowest pre-qualified. After which, an advertisement was placed in the National Daily to justify eight million pounds overpayment. The details couldn't be more explicit than that, and the reporter I see," he was reading the article, "says, the work was shoddy. That would have been my original choice." Digby waited for a response, re-reading the article to see, if he could perhaps add something more in favour of the airport scam.

"Diggers let Jesse decide." Rupert suggested

"What about a glass of wine?"

"Capital, capital."

"Stay over Crooky?"

"Thanks. Don't mind if I do."

"Sorry I'm late, the train broke down," were Jesse's opening remarks the following afternoon, as he showed up in an officer's greatcoat with substituted leather buttons-- a hat of any description, was not his style. "The bloody country's going to the dogs," he further declared.

"What do you expect with a Labour Government? They introduce taxes to make us all equal and vote themselves increases in salary; so much for equality." Digby scoffed, and headed for the library, where Rupert was dozing in front of the fire.

"Crooky... Good to see you." Jesse off-loaded his coat as he spoke and placed it on the writing-desk chair.

"You too," Crooky replied. In all, it took about an hour to arrive at the final decision, and by a unanimous vote they settled on the land-grabbing saga. It would give good publicity to the scourge of land grabbing, as they picked off a few of the guilty culprits from a list of the non-genuine participants. The project also contained a tinge of internationalism, because the 10,000-hectare Kiboko settlement scheme was launched by the Minister, accompanied by a foreign Ambassador, who gave away out-of-date tractors to advertise his country's products. Jointly, they had addressed a happy crowd that was so overwhelmed; it had failed to question the credentials of government officials about to become their neighbours.

It was to be the 'Kiboko Project' and the code for the exercise read N29M40411. Launched three years ago, plots for the landless had been unfairly allocated to influential people, who believed by now they had slipped through the anti-corruption net by selling their holdings on.

Wainaina collected N29M40411 from his email at the Nyayo Nakumatt three days after Wangu, and Ben her partner, had returned from their Taita Hills 'expedition', claiming a success of three out of three for the group.

The list was published in the National Daily of the 29th April 2004 and had hit the headlines on page one at the time. "The Landless Shame..." was followed by a list of allottees that were glaringly not landless. The decision was now Wainaina's, to select three targets from those who were not entitled to the land they'd grabbed. Conveniently for him, the front page carried the names of the greediest; before it continued on the inside pages, naming the lesser culprits. Names, occupations, etc., were all there... But Wainaina, who was a considerate person, sought out the architect behind the story to make sure the facts were true.

32

On either side of the timber-plank table faces were bright with expectation; something was in the air and they knew it. The preliminary scene that preceded their first mission was being replayed all over again, after a gap of only a week. They were as one as the seconds passed before the announcement, drawn together by the closeness of the house that had created a family bonding.

Wainaina opened the session. "You will no doubt recall Wangu's question last week concerning future activities; to which I can now reply...."

"Yes: we have another project, so be prepared...well prepared." He pursed lips and then nodded his head a couple of times, in a 'see what I've done for you' attitude, before he announced the bottom line of fifty grand a piece, which drew spontaneous clapping.

"Suleman will give you the details."

"Have a look at this," Abdi Suleman offered a couple of copies of the National Daily of the 29th April 2004 he had printed from the Internet.

"I haven't marked any of the copies in the interests of security, but Wainaina checked out the genuineness of the three people at the top of the list with the reporter who had researched the story. Interestingly enough, his editor subsequently fired him to save his own skin, in spite of having okayed the article before it went to press. The reason he gave, was possible incitement to violence between tribal factions. It seems, most of the names of the land-grabbers belonged to one tribe from outside the district."

"Why don't you take over from here?" Suleman invited Wainaina.

"As planned?" Wainaina enquired.

"Well it's up to you, but I think we should follow the route we discussed, rather than strike out with any new ideas at this stage."

"Okay. This is the plan. It may seem strange to you because none of the biggies are on site; they're what are commonly known as 'armchair' farmers. So you'll be looking for them all over the country…big job you may think, but not really, since they'll come to you... Yes, they'll come to you," he repeated. "In the shape of magnificent houses, flashy cars, and a lifestyle you'd kill for! Pun not intended" was easily said, and they laughed at the irony.

"In actual fact they aren't 'armchair' farmers at all, they have become landlords, and they rent out their land to their next door neighbours who do the toil and sweat. You'll get their business locations from their cards and trace them to where they live. Remember, we need the wide open country for our sniping style, if we're not to be confused with common thugs."

"Abdi and I recently collected these." He placed three white cards on the table face down. "They should make things easier for you. We actually looked your targets straight in the eyes as they handed them out like confetti, boasting about the companies they own. Observe the flamboyant crests that indicate the size of their egos. The cards are face down because one of them is marked with a red spot to indicate the high level of security that surrounds that particular person; so whichever team draws that card, keep it to yourselves and don't make a fuss. But be warned, that spot means beware, and I urge you take it seriously. The other two targets are more routine."

"The time allowed for the exercise will be the same as before; two days from tomorrow morning to stake out the area, and one day to make it pay, before you're back here. I can't emphasise strongly enough... lookout for the bodyguards, they're real mean bastards!" He finished and waited for questions. There were none. "Abdi. Anything to add?"

"Yes, as a matter of fact I have," he touched eyes with every person there. "Tomorrow morning," he paused.

"You'll cook your own bloody breakfasts!" Laughter followed, and the meeting ended on a high.

Wainaina collected a newspaper from the boy at the junction of Langata Road, and was gratified to see that their presence was at last being felt. Tall headlines posed the question... "WHERE IS THE LAW AND ORDER? Three harmless society greats have lost their lives to villains in the past week, and the country is much poorer for their demise. Senseless acts, for no rhyme or reason," the paper further declared. "The government must clamp down on illegal weapons that are threatening the innocent ...etc etc..."

The Lords would guffaw, when they read such rubbish as they were bound to do, and they would down an extra whiskey to celebrate success. Neither was Wainaina, so sure about the 'innocent' part of the news announcement, and certainly, one Johnson Blackstone Kariuki, who had been on the scene of one of the killings, was not very pleased at all. He felt cheated by the one small bullet through the front of the head, that he had actually seen with his own eyes. In truth, it had saved him the trouble of killing the man himself, but where was his satisfaction?

33

The cars pulled out of the Langata compound at broken intervals, carrying the teams toward 'ivory towers' where their targets were closeted in relative safety. The men in business suits blended with the early morning crowds, and Wangu looked particularly chic in her long provocative skirt, with a slit up the back to distract the security guards. She had examined her position as they went toward town, and queried the misfortune of the red spot warning; was it that serious, and can it be handled? Alighting near Barclay's Plaza, clutching the customary brown envelope when in search of a job, she left Ben to look for a room for that night in the Jivanjee area, with the two single beds she demanded.

Her aim was to take a closer look at land-grabber Kiprotich, as a likely employer, and the charm was with her as she approached reception on the fifteenth floor. Good fortune, plain luck, or perhaps autosuggestion played its part as the big man himself appeared, flanked by a couple of bodyguards. "I'm going home for the rest of the day," he declared to his receptionist, "so whoever calls, just tell them I'm in a meeting." He, like everyone else, used the standard brush off: 'I'm in a meeting'.

"Yes Mr. Kiprotich," the girl replied, as he turned on his heels and walked toward the lift ignoring Wangu's presence.

In those fleeting seconds, she had got to know what he really looked like, and could relate to Ben the number of hairs on his head, and the size of the rings of fat that made up the back of his neck. He didn't seem to be the bad person newspapers had made him out to be, and she liked to think he had given her a kindly glance as he had waited for the lift doors to close in front of him. But whatever her emotions she had her orders, and had made a positive ID. She flashed Ben to locate his position and started walking in the direction of Jivanjee Gardens, only to find him parked on the corner of Monrovia Street.

"What are you all worked up about?" he asked as she bounced into the passenger seat.

"Over there, over there! Kiprotich!" she thumbed in the direction of the petrol station on the other side of the street. "He's in that black S500 behind the curtains, complete with his goons. He's going home."

"Okay. We follow, but how do you know he's going home?"

"I overheard him telling reception."

"Oh my, Wangu. What big ears you have."

"Just drive with the big eyes you've got and shut up," Wangu gave as good as she got. They chugged up Museum Hill and slid through New Muthaiga, before passing into Muthaiga proper and turning toward Limuru; a tailgating matatu was allowed to pass to increase the distance between them and the Benz.

"Tea country, here we come," Ben sang. "Hilly and plenty of bushes is just what we need. Hope the house is on a hill?"

"You're so stupid. I'm in this for the money or I wouldn't be with you."

"What the hell's eating you?"

"Who ever builds a house in a valley? Perhaps a foolish European, but never an African!"

"He's turning right onto that track; we follow at a distance, and when the dust stops billowing we stop and wait for him to enter his gates."

"Who says he's got gates?"

"I do. Plus a sentry box with a direct line connected to the house. It's standard equipment for these big peasants." She laughed at his comments, and they were back on track with their smooth operation as they came to a fork in the road. "Now what?" Ben questioned himself out loud, and quickly followed it up with a "thank God," when he observed fresh tyre marks in the mud yet to refill with seeping water from an isolated shower. It confirmed a left turn, and the marks of cultivation further along foreshadowed a barrier ahead. He sensed danger, stopped, and automatically reversed into a field track to turn the car around. "You take over Wangu, I want to observe as we proceed. Head for the high ground and we'll look at this place from a distance." Ben by now was in his element, his training to the fore. "We'll use those hills over there that are not too distant, but far enough to hit and run."

Wangu said nothing; her training had only been elementary, and she had never pulled a trigger on the lines of a human face cross-marked in a powerful scope. Like all the other seconds in the hit teams, she was back up, but confident she could do the job if an accident occurred to her partner. Attractive, she had actually been recruited by Jesse as the only female in the team, to act in the part of a courting couple, should the necessity arise.

They pulled up under a tree specially planted to shade the tea, and observed the house on the opposite ridge, only slightly below their own elevation. Ben got out of the car, retrieved the scope from under the floor of the boot, removed the lens covers, and examined the surface for specks that might interfere with his viewing. He had trained with the best, and steadied the scope for a preliminary assessment against the trunk of a nearby tree. He fixed his right eye to the light excluder for a full five minutes before he rested, rubbing his eye to relieve the strain from its high-powered magnification.

"This position is almost ideal; 600 yards to the entrance of the house, and I'm betting this fellow will turn around to face his goons, and tell them something before he leaves the premises."

"Why would he do that?" Wangu asked.

"That's what they always do...I just know it...it always happens like that; and that's when I drop him. We could do it today and go home if we waited for him to come out to the car again, but then we'd have to drop down this hairpin bend in the road one more notch to reduce the target by 100 yards. Let's go home; we've done enough for today."

"Ben?"

"Yes?"

"Why can't we finish it today?"

"I told you; we've done enough for today."

"Okay, but don't think you're going to get into my knickers tonight, because we've got to watch TV in the room together."

"Quite honestly, Wangu, I didn't know you were even wearing any. I'm told they have pockets these days to hide your cash," he laughed. "Did you have anything else on your mind… besides your knickers in a twist?" he laughed again.

"No."

"Now let me continue if you please! Tomorrow we stake out this place from 6 AM and wait for him to emerge. I'm betting he'll stand still long enough, to present the perfect target. By the way Wangu, you'll be driving."

The night was warm and the mosquitoes affectionately kissed the occupants of room eighteen at the 'Get in Hotel,' Jivanjee Gardens. Tossing, turning, and smothered by sheets to keep out the flying insects was a certain recipe for a restless night; not to mention the suspect knickers with the suspect pocket, he suspected Wangu wore. It was only brought to an end by a wake-up call at 5 AM. Getting out of bed was painful-- but once motivation got under way the room was stripped clean of evidence and their bags zipped closed. By then they had donned black tracksuits bought from Gikomba market with the 'Nairobi Club' marking mysteriously blacked-out. Personal documents other than licences and IDs had been left in Langata.

It was still dark as they pulled out of Jivanjee Gardens, posing as early morning joggers looking for a patch to use. A roundabout route was selected in the general direction of the previous day, avoiding places where police roadblocks could cause a problem. But in spite of their care, it wasn't long before a uniformed policeman waved them down with a torch and pulled them over in front of some uneven spikes, seemingly tested on many occasions. His light picked over the details on the screen and showed the insurance to be in order, before his voice at the window demanded that the boot be opened. Ben got out of the car to help with the operation, quite prepared for aggressive action should the policeman become too nosey. But it was the muddy sack and tools spread over the floor that did the dissuasive trick. And the policemen actually closed the boot himself after lifting the hessian with the muzzle of his gun—showing disdain for the mud he waved them on. For no obvious reason, the hold-alls in the foot-wells behind the back seats containing their clothes remained undisturbed, not that they held any secrets.

Wangu slipped into the driving seat at the point where they turned off the tarmac and the road changed to murram soil. She was immediately cautioned by Ben to slow down. "I don't want to raise dust and tell them we're coming; we have plenty of time."

"Sorry." There were no quips; life had suddenly become very serious. She slowed down to thirty and the dust hardly lifted as she pushed forward, accepting 'the journey' was going to take half an hour to cover a distance normally timed in minutes. Patience. She glanced at Ben, who looked cool. She had seen him in action once before, and couldn't help but wonder the number of 'notches' he had on the 'handle of his gun'.

"Turn left here," Ben commanded, as the sun began to push through the morning mist and the birds were all of a-chatter.

"Stop!" He surveyed the scene; the house was still partly shrouded in mist.

"Now, go down one hairpin bend." Wangu slowly manoeuvred the car round the bend without comment.

"Stop!" Ben got out of the car and surveyed the house for the second time. The mist was rapidly clearing and the dawn bleeding into the sky had begun to fade with the brightness of the rising sun.

"Damn! Damn!" he realised his error and openly cursed his predicament. Wangu, alarmed by his outburst, slipped out of the car and closed the distance between them.

"What's wrong?" she asked.

"The sun will be in my face as I take the shot. I should have seen that yesterday, even if it was past midday. Anyway, it's too late now to change our plans, and this still has to be the ideal spot, whatever the time of day."

"So, what shall we do?" Wangu asked.

"We go ahead, I'll overcome my incompetence, but I'm really pissed off. How could this happen?" He would have punched something or someone to vent his frustration, if he hadn't needed the energy, and tranquility, for the job on hand,

"Right, let's get on with it. Both of us get back in the car and I'll assemble my weapon before he surprises us. I want to be waiting for him when his vehicle comes round to the front of the house."

Ben drew on the fine black leather gloves he liked to use for such occasions, and then began to extract the pieces from his rucksack with the sensitivity of a sniper in love with his weapon. Wangu, watched from the driving seat in fascination, ready to take off if danger threatened. The clicking of metal parts as they matched their mates failed to disturb the stillness of the scene, and when the scope was finally mounted, Ben raised the weapon with a single hand and took a cursory look through the lens, before he seriously grabbed the stock and aimed toward the opposite ridge. Cautiously, he'd placed three extra .338 mm lupus bullets of the hollow-nosed variety on the back seat beside him for backup. They were different and more damaging, compared to the pointed bullet that presently nestled in the breech with the name of Kiprotich on the tip.

"Wangu, I'll stay in the back; can you just move the car forward a couple of yards?" The car crept forward yard by yard.

"Stop! Now all we have to do is wait." Ben stated the obvious. "I don't like this sun in front of me, but as I can't move the house, 'Mohamed must go to the mountain'," he quipped.

"Something's happening." He rested the barrel he held in his left hand; on the black cushion purchased from the bazaar, and steadied his aim using the edge of the open car window to assist elevation.

"Wangu, don't even cough-- absolutely still. The car from yesterday's coming round to the front of the house with a driver and a couple of Goons. Ah…now they've stopped…they have to be waiting for the big-man."

Kiprotich, kissed his wife of thirty years goodbye in the hall, and the servant held open the door. "Tonight we have to go to State House; meet me in town at six in the Range Rover, and we'll go there together. I'll shower and dress in the office suite." The top floor of his building had been entirely occupied by him, after some serious soul searching about the rent he would lose by such an extravagance. But eventually he'd given way to his vanity, and the envy he saw in the eyes of his competitors more than balanced the loss of rent. They never actually commented on how fantastic his office was, but as their mouths dropped open in awe, he lived their feelings and smiled within as they coughed and cleared their throats, to master the boldness they didn't feel. He enjoyed their discomfort, but never said anything, and neither did they-- he knew them so well.

The bodyguards smartened up and adjusted their ties as their boss stepped into the fresh morning light. He stood for a moment to take in the air, and glanced at his diamond Rolex. It showed ten minutes past seven, so he had time to spare before his first meeting that morning. Life had indeed had been good to him, and he was full of the joys of spring, without any shame for the poverty around him.

Understandably, he wanted more land if he was to challenge those who owned areas the size of Provinces, but give him the time, he philosophised, and he would grab the whole country, well… almost all. He had the financial clout already to further his aims, and the political arena was now in his sights. He rather fancied an 'honourable' title. What State House held in store for him that evening, he could only guess-- exciting times lay ahead.

34

There was no trigger guard on the beauty he cradled and his finger was bared through a hole in the glove, designed by him for sensitivity. He employed a feather light touch to tension the mechanism as recommended by Umar Khan to Brian Stewart. Glued to the scope, his eye was searching for the head of the man about to die. He zoomed in; took a deep breath and held it – the pin struck home. A chill swept down his spine, and the victim's face dropped out of sight, leaving his greedy aura behind him. Ben, a perfectionist, knew his trade, and never followed them down.

"Move off slowly Wangu, we don't want to attract attention." Ben remained in the back seat and slipped one of the hollow-nosed cartridges into the breech for defensive action – he was on full alert.

The Goons were not the fools most people believed them to be. Their Boss had hit the ground at an angle that indicated the direction from which the bullet was fired, and as the shot rang out they had also scanned the compound in the general direction of its report, before they looked up and further a field, to notice a glint on the opposite ridge, from the window of a moving vehicle. Ben's very worst nightmare was being played out; the sun shining on the car had given their position away.

"Stop the car," Ben commanded. He wanted to observe the activity. Two Range Rovers had joined the boss's S500 and were lined up in front of the house. Ben took aim, fired, and the group of people pointing toward him panicked and ran into the house. The front tyre of the lead Range Rover burst and Ben smiled, he was enjoying the people's reaction. The second Rover took the next shot and curtseyed just like the first – the tire collapsed. And his final message, a coup de grâce to the head of the S500 caused steam to hiss from its bonnet.

"Drive Wangu! Drive like the devil!" The car actually lifted slightly as they surged forward, but the engine was basically rotten and it took time to build-up to a charging sixty miles an hour. Early in the morning the roads should have been clear of traffic, and Wangu reasonably expected them to be so. Similarly, the driver of the milk truck collecting churns at road junctions didn't expect any traffic as he hurtled along at breakneck speed past the Kiprotich farm. The gradual bend in the road appeared through Wangu's screen at about the same time Shadrack Chemilil powered his way into the corner from the opposite direction with three friends squeezed into his front cab.

The power unleashed by the explosive impact killed six people that morning, before the momentum of the colliding metal came to a halt, and the rifle was found in Ben's arms.

The tragedy of the speeding vehicles that had met head-on while negotiating a dusty corner on a murram road in Limuru hit the headlines, and came to the attention of Wainaina, as he stepped from his shower to catch the tail-end of the 8'oclock news... 'Two vehicles, travelling at high speed in the Limuru area early today, lost control and crashed head-on. There were no survivors...stay tuned for an update on the half-hour.

"Abdi!" Wainaina shouted. "Did you hear the news on Classic?"

"No. What happened?"

"There was an accident in Limuru and the occupants of both vehicles died. I've got a bad feeling, it could be one of ours."

"Well, we can't do anything about it; we can't break silence because you have a bad feeling about something. You're right, it could be one of ours, but let's wait for the half-hour updates. Turn on the TV, and if we're lucky we might see the car involved."

"We interrupt this programme to bring you an update on the early morning road accident in Limuru, in which six people died, and another person, whose name is being withheld, was shot in the same area, at about the same time. The first people at the scene of the accident told our reporter that a weapon was recovered from the dead man in the car, which was being driven by a lady at the time. "Seven deaths in seven minutes," was how the local Police Commander described it. "A tragedy of great magnitude," were the words of the Honourable Member for the area. "Yes, the local residents, whom I questioned at the scene," the reporter came through, "couldn't recall a parallel within living memory; some of the more emotional residents have placed flowers on the road at the point of impact. A Police spokesman said, it was too early to comment on the causes...This is Tom Maina, on location in Limuru... returning you to the studio."

Wainaina and Suleman smelt disaster, but couldn't be sure their team was involved from the information received so far. They had their suspicions since a man had been shot in the area where the weapon was found, but was it their doing, or was it a disturbing coincidence? The Police Commander had covered that point when he put the number of people killed at seven, of which six were involved in the accident. It therefore followed; the waiting period was going to be difficult for all concerned, with another day to wait, before their suspicions could be confirmed-- one way or the other. Could they continue or would they have to close down, was the next question to be addressed. One of their exclusive weapons was in police hands.

The two remaining teams checked out of their operational lodgings early on the morning after the Limuru crash. They too, had heard the breaking news the previous day, and by the time they pulled into the Langata house the pictures from the National Daily were clearly on their minds. Like Wainaina and Suleman, they knew in their heart of hearts it had to be Ben and Wangu, and they lamented their fate as they pictured them rotting in the city morgue and winding up in an unmarked grave. Their money would be paid in full to their beneficiaries as requested when they were inducted into the group, but sadly there was no triumph for them. The fruits of their labour had truly become their legacy, as offered by the Lords in their original text on the Internet.

The urgent meeting called by Wainaina brought together six sad faces in somber mood, which had by then accepted the inevitable loss of their colleagues killed in the Limuru crash. The fact that they were all in the business of killing, had no bearing on the consequences of their loss. It was sad, and in a twisted way they regarded their work as noble, and compared it to fighting a war where it was legal to kill and medals were struck to honour such heroes. To them, they were waging their own private battle against corruption, about which they had only the slightest inkling, but it could be won.

"I'd like to congratulate all the teams, including our brothers who are presently missing, and for whom we can hold out little hope. You have completed a great mission. Six targets, six dead." His voice was calm, flat, and lacked emotion. "Sadly, Ben and Wangu will miss our reunion; be prepared for the worst on that one. So… pack up, clean up, and we get out of here tonight using consecutive flights to Europe; no fingerprints and no trace that we've ever been here. The three cars will be burnt with the house. We walk out of here and get a bus at the junction to wherever we decide to go. And finally, I'll set an incendiary device in the roof and trigger it by mobile before I fly out. It's quite possible the flames will be seen from the airport. Now for the weapons and ammunition; we dump them piece by piece in out of the way places, and one car will be used to do that as soon as this meeting is over. Abdi, what are the alternatives?"

"Joe has told us," Wainaina's Christian name was used by Abdi to match the brevity of his own, "how he intends to wind up the mission according to our London instructions. But there are also other options he's asked me to mention; instead of flying back to London you might choose to stay on in the African continent. Each one of you has a hundred grand U.S. in his account in Europe, and it's yours to start a new life wherever you want. But it goes without saying; it will go much further here, than in London, so perhaps you should consider starting a new life in Africa. Our continent is so huge it can easily hide you if you decide to take an inter-African flight tonight in place of the intercontinental; the choice is yours. And if you feel particularly brave, take your chances here in Kenya, but as far as Joe and I am concerned we have almost finished our leave of absence, and have to get back to our jobs in London. Think about what I've just said, and in the meantime let's get busy."

Joe issued the orders. "Team 4, take the weapons and ammunition and completely dismantle and disburse them. Suggestions for disposal are the middle of the Nairobi dam; the wet concrete mix for the extension to the new Mbagathi Way. Hell, there're only forty pieces at most; just get rid of them as best you can."

"Consider it done," replied leader 4.

"Team 3," Joe continued. "All rubbish to be stacked in the house and prints wiped clean from the furniture, glasses and all surfaces where possible. The fire will take care of the overall picture."

"Wilco," team leader 3 acknowledged.

"Joe, what chances for the survival of Ben and Wangu?"

"I truly cry for them as family and remember them as they were, since I doubt their chances. What should worry us the most is, have the authorities one of our weapons?"

"Can it be traced?" Suleman asked.

"If the money is right most things can be traced, even Bin Laden, at $100 million, but in this case the government hasn't got the money to spend, and quite frankly I doubt if they have the conviction." Joe stated the position as he saw it. He was ignorant of the powerful backing by the Opugi family and associates, who had become more determined than ever as the killings continued.

"How much do you think this house is worth?" was Suleman's next question.

"How should I know? What are you thinking?"

"Come on, give me a rough estimate?" Suleman pressed.

"Well, to start with, it needs rebuilding, and quite honestly the only thing worth having around here is land. But without a borehole, forget it!" Joe stated the facts.

"You've read the papers and property prices this last week. Give me an estimate?"

"In the U.S.?"

"Yeah, in U.S."

"I'd say a hundred grand is generous."

"That's settled then. I'll fix it with Jesse when I see him, and we'll arrange to pay the little old lady compensation for a her house burnt to the ground. Agreed?"

"I'm with you all the way."

"Now everyone disband, before you get burnt." He was sprinkling the contents of a jerry can throughout the house as he told them to get out and disappear. The exercise was over.... no lengthy good-byes and no sentiments exchanged.

35

"Kamba, I want your input." Simon always called Mike by his father's name when he needed his absolute attention, and today was one of those days. The question was how to deal with the sniper's rifle recovered from the crash.

"Yes?" Simon picked up the telephone energised by a weak electrical charge. The old instrument was the only one in the building and had followed him throughout his career; it had become a unique friend and was personal to him.

"It's the Commissioner," his secretary whispered with a tinge of reverence in her voice.

"Well, what are you waiting for? Put him through." She wasn't the only one surprised; he covered the mouthpiece and whispered to Mike. "It's the Commissioner; wonder what he wants?"

"Good morning, Sir."

"Is that you, Nane?"

"Yes Sir."

"I have a senior member of the Opugi family with me. He's called to congratulate us on catching the two assassins; I told him you were the one responsible." He winked in Opugi's direction.

"He wants to come over and see you, to offer his personal thanks... so don't go anywhere in the meantime."

"Yes Sir!" He recalled his London trip sponsored by the Opugi clan and the tussle with the Commissioner over paying his expenses, and how the President had ruled in his favour. But now with a solution in sight, that was all behind them and everyone wanted to get in on the act.

"You heard that, Kamba?"

"Only what you said."

"One of the Opugis wants to come visiting; to thank us no less. The downside is, I'm stuck in the office for the rest of the morning, but the upside could be the answer to our prayers."

"Go on..." Kamba urged.

"The Chief in London, said these weapons were made on the Pakistan Afghan border, so it follows... if we're to trace the manufacturer of the one we now possess we have to go to Pakistan. You hear me?"

"I'm all ears."

"That gun is the only lead we have, so one of us has to sniff out the source, and to do that-- we are going to need money."

"Will the Opugi clan pay again?"

"Who knows, but we should have the answer to that before the morning's out."

"You want me to sit in on the meeting?"

"No; I know these people. When they offer something they usually like a one-on-one in case there's a dispute, so they can deny the meeting ever took place if they don't want to pay up. My original trip to London speaks for itself. They financed it and they negotiated directly with me, rather than the Commissioner. The secret is, to get your hands on the money before they change their minds."

"Why would they change their minds, if it's in their interests?"

"I can't answer that, but it appears that the more you have the more tight-fisted you become, when it comes to helping anyone—relatives included. Anyway, that's my personal theory and that's how I see it."

"I'm learning," Kamba acknowledged.

"So Mike, go home, take the morning off and I'll see you this afternoon; and by then with luck, who knows...?" He leaned back in his chair, and laughed for the first time that morning.

"Janet." It was almost eleven o'clock in Nairobi and he judged that Conrad would have either arrived, or be about to arrive in his Scotland Yard office. "Get me Detective Chief Superintendent Black in London." he replaced the receiver and began composing the questions he had in mind to ask.

"Superintendent Black's on the line." Janet announced.

"Yes Simon, and what can I do for you?"

"Conrad, I've recovered one of the weapons used in the shootings."

"Good show Simon... I just knew it; something had to turn up sooner or later."

"Thank you, but this now raises the issue of travelling to the Afghan border to trace the source of manufacture, which could prove difficult for me to do on my own. Either, I need an expert from London to come with me, or a contact in Pakistan. What can you suggest?"

"Well if you ask me, your best bet has to be Pakistan Interpol. Hang on a minute, I've someone in mind." Simon waited, and waited, and finally shouted into the phone, "Conrad, say something!"

"Sorry about that Simon, but I've just been speaking to Chief Inspector Akbar Ali of the Interpol division where you'll be going, and he says you're to be his guest for as long as it takes. He also tells me there's a posh hotel up there you're bound to enjoy. Phone him as soon as you're ready to travel." He then read out a number, and Simon repeated it back as he wrote it down.

"Simon, I'm sure you've made the right decision to go there, but if you're expecting these people to betray their customers you'll need wads of cash, which brings me to my next question. Where the hell are you going to lay your hands on, that type of money? Anyway, good hunting." He chuckled, and rang off with the question still ringing in Simon's ears... 'hands on, that type of money.'

Was he ahead of himself and had he been foolish to discuss an expedition yet to be funded, when the possible answer was still an hour away, and hinged on Opugi's family's desire for him to succeed, backed by their copious pockets. He looked at his watch: it was a quarter to noon, and fifteen minutes remained of the morning, for him to find out if Opugi kept time.

At precisely noon, Janet, his secretary, announced that a Mr. Amos Opugi was in the outside office and was anxious, which translated into the local vernacular meant… "Can he come in?"

"But of course, show Mr. Amos in." Simon stood, and after shaking hands waved him to one of two basic chairs in front of his desk, that was hard enough to be uncomfortable, and guaranteed to keep his visitors on the move.

"It was kind of you to take the time to call on me. I know how busy you must be with all your enterprises." Simon massaged Opugi's ego from the word go—he was after his money.

"You're really very important to me Chief Inspector." Simon was demoted a rank by being addressed as C.I., but didn't think it worthwhile to mention. "It is I, who don't want to take the time from you, that you're devoting to my family's investigation. I'm really only seeking a personal update."

"Jack," Opugi used the Commissioner's first name, "tells me you've made fantastic progress and killed a couple of the assassins." Jack had apparently failed to mention, it was a milk truck that had actually done the killing, but why should he correct an error that clearly made him a hero.

"I must admit, we did get a couple of them," he owned up with a casual modesty, wondering how he could massage his advantage to squeeze more money out of Opugi.

"Tell me about the details?" Opugi furrowed his brows in a quizzical manner, indicating he genuinely wanted to know.

"All in good time, if you'll forgive me for saying so Sir. The investigation is on-going and I have an emergency on my hands to track down the source of the weapon used to kill your uncle."

"That's interesting, very interesting. Perhaps you can fill me in on that particular aspect. You know I'm the type of person who always likes to see things through to a positive conclusion," he offered a self-assessment of his determination for Simon's information.

"Well, as I see it Mr. Amos, whoever commissioned this weapon we now possess, has to be behind these murders. May I ask you a question Sir?" Simon paused, and there was no going back.

"Fire away, that's another reason I'm here."

"Well Sir, if I'm going to crack this case, I have to visit Pakistan to track down the source of the recovered weapon. And like the London visit, I'll need funding if I'm to be effective. But quite frankly, to ask you again so soon after the London visit is causing me deep embarrassment; not to mention the size of the amount, I'll most probably need."

"Inspector," Simon was reduced in seniority by one more rank, and wondered how far this ignorant man would go, before he finished up as plain Constable. "Put the pros and cons to me, and I'll decide about the size of your embarrassment."

Here goes, thought Simon. "I need $20,000 to cover bribes for information and travel costs; most of which I'll not be able to account for."

Opugi took the declaration in his stride. "What's my guarantee if you get the money?"

"No guarantee-- I might even lose your money."

"And what are the odds of success?" Opugi, sought to gauge his risk.

"I really don't know, but if I was a betting man, I'd say you have an even chance: but it's up to you, Sir. The only alternative is for the case to die and join the millions of unsolved mysteries."

Simon was taken aback by Opugi's next announcement. "I'll see it through: I demand my pound of flesh!" He clearly wanted blood to run in the streets and was prepared to pay for that privilege.

"You'll get your money tomorrow... good day Mister Nane and good luck." Opugi had finally retired him from the force altogether, as he addressed him as plain Mister, but why should he worry-- he had the funding.

"Mike, where are you?" Simon squeezed his mobile tightly and pressed it more closely to his ear.

"I'm in the parking lot, on my way to town."

"Not now. Opugi's gone and we have to discuss my weekend departure."

Kamba shot through the door, "Yes Boss?"

"Right: here's the deal. I want you to book me on the first Pakistan Airlines flight out of here after you sort out my visa. Give Inspector Akbar Ali of Interpol as my reference; this is his phone number and address." He pushed the details across the desk together with his brand new passport issued after the robbery. "Negotiate for these things today and tomorrow you'll get the cash to pay for them... questions?"

"No. It'll be a piece of cake, compared to the nonsense at the British High Commission."

"Wait one...I also want that multiple British visa transferred to this new passport; who knows, what might transpire?"

"Leave it to me..." Kamba was on his way.

36

"What a pleasant surprise." ASP Simon Nane heard the words from the shadows of the plane as he stepped onto the tarmac in Rawalpindi. Inspector Akbar Ali casually saluted to declare his considerable presence; he was a big man with smiling eyes and a heavy moustache.

"Good to see you Sir, welcome to Pakistan; allow me," he relieved Simon of his pilot-type briefcase packed for the week. "The car's over here."

Simon was impressed, and wondered if Akbar Ali would have been handled so perfectly had he been on the welcoming end at Jomo Kenyatta Nairobi; he filed the thought for future reference. It was a standard black police car with two uniformed escorts, who smartly saluted and closed the passenger doors, before they entered the front of the vehicle and drove off.

Ali leaned toward Simon in the back of the car. "Call me Akbar. Everyone calls me Akbar."

"Thank you Akbar. I'm Simon."

"I take it you brought the weapon with you."

"Only the barrel, the problems of travelling with a complete weapon and the implications would have been too much to bear," he laughed.

"I can well imagine it," Akbar nodded." I can also imagine where we'll have to go to pick up the trail. We're booked on the night train to Peshawar," he informed Simon. "Why don't we fly, you may ask, but I thought the opportunity to talk on the train and view some of the spectacular scenery before sunset would be more beneficial to both of us."

"I'm entirely in your hands, Akbar; I'd even accept a donkey-ride, if you thought it beneficial for my health." Akbar laughed. "Didn't Conrad tell you what I was looking for?"

"He did; and if I can examine the weapon on the train, I might be able to narrow it down to an area, where I think we should start looking."

The car pulled into Rawalpindi station, and the driver who was on Simon's side opened the passenger door for him. Meanwhile, the escort who had grabbed the bags from the boot began to force his way through the bustling crowd, closely followed by Akbar. At the sight of the reserved sign on the compartment window, Ahmed, who carried the bags, elbowed his way on board, and switched to the power of his uniform to make the steward unlock the door. He placed the luggage on the overhead racks, and was about to leave, as Akbar, somewhat breathless, arrived on the scene with Simon in tow. A cursory 'thank you' followed, and the helpful Ahmed disappeared into the crowd. Akbar slid the door shut, and they jointly sighed as they plonked themselves down in the oppressive heat. Simon tugged at his collar to gain some relief, and waited for the AC to take effective.

"I agree," said Akbar. He too began to open the neck of his shirt, and sighed, as the popping of buttons released folds of flesh. Finally, he pressed his head back into the seat, and briefly closed his eyes.

"An hour to go," Akbar shook Simon's shoulder, and disturbed his heavenly dream of Fatima at a crucial time; he noticed a subconscious grin on his face as he shook him again. "Wake up, we're almost there."

"What's the time?" a detached voice asked.

"Time to get up, wake up, we're almost there," Akbar repeated.

"Okay, okay, slowly does it," Simon was adjusting to the time difference, the train journey, and the altitude all at once, whereas Akbar had been in local orbit for the past five years. His feet eventually touched the floor to coincide with the train pulling into the overhang of the station platform.

Akbar flicked his fingers, and the hungry taxi-man was there for business.

"Morning Sahibs," the driver observantly addressed them in English assessing the black man to be a foreigner.

"The Hotel, the one opposite to where Dean's used to be." Akbar gave a description because he had temporarily forgotten the name. The porter threw both bags into the waiting boot that had conveniently snapped open from the driver's seat.

"The Hotel?" the driver repeated for reassurance as he cranked the engine.

"Yes, the old colonial one opposite to where Dean's used to be." Akbar reconfirmed the destination. There was only one other hotel of any historic value after Dean's was pulled down, and that was where those in the know now stayed, to soak up the pre-independence atmosphere of the place.

"Simon, see you at eleven on the veranda," was Akbar's parting shot as their porters split in different directions.

"I see you've now adopted a rucksack to carry 'the piece'," was Akbar's opening remark. Simon sat down on a chair, pulled out by an attentive waiter.

"Join me in a juice?" Akbar asked. "It's orange," he volunteered.

"Don't mind if I do." Simon accepted, in spite of his longing for a beer.

"You found everything in order?"

"A beautiful room, thank you." Simon gazed up at the long line of fans on the ceiling that stretched the length of the veranda; he was enjoying their gentle wafting in the stillness of the air. "First class... first class, and these fans are really something; they fit the scene of the wicker chairs and the glass topped coffee tables. It's all so cool and relaxing."

"Enjoy while you can, because in another hour we'll be in the shanty part of town," Akbar, chuckled, and sipped his drink, making sure his 'Saddam Hussein' moustache didn't dip into the juice.

A short taxi ride dropped them at the beginning of the road that led to the East and Islamabad in the Dara-ada-khel area; they were in the industrial side of town. The same area, in which Jesse and Brian had dared to tread some three months earlier, with the biting wind from the mountains burning their faces. But now it was spring, and the double metal-doors on which they had knocked in the biting cold, had been passed by Akbar and Simon, as they walked down the street in search of bearded man, reputed to be-- the 'Guru of Manufacturing'.

"What he doesn't know about manufacturing isn't worth knowing," Akbar announced, and Simon being the new boy on the block, accepted his words as gospel; but he had yet to prove his worth by identifying the part he had in his rucksack.

"Come in, come in," Nazeem beckoned, urging them to step further into his parlour.

"Akbar, sahib, what brings you here?" he asked.

"Meet my friend from East Africa, Simon Nane. He comes to me with the highest credentials from Scotland Yard, England!"

"Scotland Yard, England!" Nazeem repeated. He was suitably impressed and got straight to the business without further comment, "So what can I do for you?"

"Simon sahib, needs to know who is capable of manufacturing a master piece such as this..." Simon took his cue and offered the gun barrel for Nazeem's inspection, which he immediately hefted to determine the density of the metal, and then squinted through the barrel directly into the naked light bulb to inspect the quality of the bore.

"Interesting," was the only word he offered to describe his finding, as he recalled similar rifling, recently seen. "Akbar sahib, who did you say wanted to know?"

"Simon sahib, here, wants to know, and would be very indebted to you if you could point us in the right direction."

"I'm an old man Akbar sahib, and I lost one of my legs to those Russian bastards during the war. Sadly, I didn't get any compensation, and now I have the responsibility of sending my grandchildren to school in Peshawar after the Americans killed their father. I'm living from hand to mouth, and sometimes, I don't know where my next meal is coming from…"

"Enough! Enough!" Akbar pleaded. "I'll give you $500 US in advance for the information, and a further five at the hotel tonight if you send one of your grandsons to me with a note…provided your information's correct. But if it's bogus, may Allah grant my prayers and infest your underpants with fleas from a thousand camels—have we a deal?"

"May Allah bless you," he was happy on two counts; he never ever wore underpants, and his lengthy list of grief had paid off. Only that morning the larder was empty, and now he could fill it to overflowing. "Allahu Akhbar! I'm rich," he cried. "Go back the way you came for 300 yards, and you'll see a large garage door on your right with a smaller door inset. It is the entrance to a bus garage, but at the back, there is a most modern engineering shop. It's owned by the Khan Brothers, and only they are capable of producing such quality, as we have here." He handed the barrel back to Simon. "Ask him what you want to know, but please be careful not to say anything about my directions."

"Nazeem, send your boy to the hotel tonight, I'm sure we'll find what we need; and peace be with you my friend."

How Umar Khan, wouldn't know that Nazeem had tipped them off, was beyond belief. Simon was a novelty in the area by his colour alone, and so far, they had walked at least a mile down the shanty street surrounded by urchins. Mind you, Nazeem could be a relative of Umar, or perhaps he had a long-standing agreement to pool any payments when strangers came asking questions. The large door was nearer than they expected, and like the approach of Brian and Jesse it opened as if by magic, and the watchman welcomed them in. "The shop at the back Sahibs?" He sensed their intentions and led the way; Umar Khan, stood as they entered.

"Welcome, welcome Sahibs, have a seat, how can I be helping you? Tea! You must have some tea," he insisted, clapping his hands for a servant to appear.

"Yes gentlemen, now tell me, you want something special?" he enquired, before Akbar had a chance to speak.

"Mr. Khan, we have a couple of questions we'd like to put to you in the strictest confidence." He gestured toward Simon to produce the barrel, and watched for Umar's reaction, as it came into view.

"Have you ever seen this before?" Umar's eyes flicked ever so slightly, when they first fell on the item, handed to him directly by Simon. Like Nazeem, he hefted the piece and looked through the bore into the naked light bulb, which was hanging shamelessly from the rafters. "I know it; I made it here in this workshop. Do you want something like this or perhaps a modification?"

"We want to know who it was supplied to…and we don't come to you empty handed…"

"Ah, so it's a case of how much you'll pay me to betray one of my customers, is it?" He sounded hurt for a fleeting second, at their very thought he would do such a thing.

"I suppose you could put it like that. I'm thinking it might be worth 5000 U.S. depending on the value of the information. That is of course, an opening bid for three questions, and every one after that is a thousand a time. Do you feel comfortable with that?"

"I might…it depends on the questions?"

"Well, you work it out. There are only so many questions I can ask – what do you say?" Simon placed a wad of US currency notes on the edge of the desk to nudge Umar in the right direction.

"Three questions for 5000 you said?"

"I did," replied Akbar.

"What are your questions?"

"Over to you Simon?" Akbar waved his hand in the direction of Simon who took up the prompt.

"Mr. Khan, had you ever seen these people to whom you supplied this weapon at any time before they placed the order with you, and can you describe them to me?"

"That's two questions, you agree?"

"If you answer them helpfully, I'll count them as two, okay?"

"One, the younger one, I had seen before because he was a collector of weapons. But not the older one with him, who was the boss and paid the bill; an impressive gentleman he was. Tall, with a red face, thick white hair, and he wore a moustache. I also remember his big blue eyes."

"Next question – any names mentioned between them during your conversation?"

"The small one was called Brian, but the other man, who gave me a cheque to hold until they come up with the cash, wasn't called any name by his friend. But I do remember that his cheque was from Coutts Bank, because he made a point of explaining the bank's reputation to me, and I returned this cheque to this Brian in exchange for cash when he came back in two weeks time."

"What was the name on the cheque?"

"Is that another question?"

"Yes, if you can answer it?"

"It was either Stop or Holt. I know it was something like that, because I laughed to myself at the time, but I can't remember any other details.

"One more question. How many did you supply?"

"Three."

"Is there anything else?"

"No. I think that about wraps it up," Simon counted out $7000. "Seven thousand okay, Mr. Khan?"

"It's a pleasure to do business with you Sahibs. If I can be of more assistance just contact me, and may Allah bless you 7000 times." He ceremoniously bowed them out into the yard, but didn't step into the sunlight himself, because the smile on his face he was obliged to show to his customers, was never there for his workers to see. To them he portrayed a sad picture of poverty to keep their wages in check, when he occasionally sought the warmth of the sunlight.

"That was a good interview," Simon remarked to Akbar, as he ordered a beer to celebrate his coup. By now it was apparent to

Simon, that Conrad's assistance was needed yet again to iron out the London connection. He placed a call, and gave his details to Conrad's secretary in his absence, and she confirmed he would be met the following day. The money left over from the bribe allocation and the multiple visas had miraculously come into play, and he secretly praised himself for having the foresight.

"Thank you so much Akbar," he turned and walked through the final barrier at departures.

37

April in England and the temperature was still in the single digits; but his new cashmere sweater came to the rescue as he dived into a taxi, and gave an address off Russell Square, central London. A modest hotel had been booked for him by Conrad, there were no plush travel agencies involved and he was travelling economy on his own initiative, from which he expected results, to more than justify his lonely decision. He checked in to a basic room, took a shower, and struck out for the Yard.

"Is the Chief in?" Simon asked Conrad's secretary.

"Mr. Nane, what a surprise; how nice to see you." He could see by the depth of her smile, she was genuinely pleased to see him, and he carried the warmth of her feelings into the boss's office.

"Simon, dear boy! Thought you'd never make it out of the Indian Sub-Continent." They both laughed, although Simon didn't think it particularly funny. "Take a seat and tell Uncle Conrad all about it. Coffee?"

"Wow! I see you're coming out of the middle-ages since I was last here," Simon remarked, "a new coffee making machine and all that."

"Well, to tell you the truth it's not all that good, you'll see; biscuits?"

"Don't mind if I do."

"Now tell me Simon... how'd you get on?"

"As you know already, when we got hold of one of the weapons, it was our first major break-through; thanks to a car accident as the assassins were exiting the crime scene. Both died on the spot. The driver was a woman, and the man who had to be the killer, was in the back of the car cradling the rifle. Your first identification of the bullets fired from a specialised weapon made on the Afghan border then began to make sense, and as you now know, made me seek out a lead in Pakistan to trace those behind it."

"Thank you for the intro to your friend Akbar Ali, who met me on landing in Rawalpindi, and from there we travelled to Peshawar. So, to get to the present, I'm on my knees again and need your assistance, to process the information I gathered from there," Conrad smiled and let him continue. "I have now reached a point where I'm looking for two people in London who possess firearms licences, or who are antique weapons collectors-- or something like that. I haven't a clue how you control such collectors in this country, but I do know one of these characters is called Brian, and the other goes by the name of either Holt or Stop as the Pakistani liked to call him. I also have a detailed description of Holt or Stop, and it goes something like this...he's tall, has bushy white hair, big blue eyes and a moustache, and I rather suspect he's the leader. I'm told he did all the talking and he issued a cheque, which I now believe, was his biggest mistake. The other one had black straight hair, and no other distinguishing features that my informant could recall. Now here's the break – the cheque from the bushy white haired fellow was drawn on Coutts Bank to cover production until he could replace it with cash."

"How's that for information?" Simon sat back and waited for the applause. There was no applause; Conrad was biting his lower lip, deep in thought. He picked up the phone and dialed a number. "Jack, we need to talk. Please come over."

"Simon, I like it. I've got the firearms chap coming over, and after we've finished with him, I think we should get a court order to see an account at Coutts. You're going to solve this crime young man," he smiled; "have another cup?"

"It's better than I thought, thank you." Simon accepted.

"Jack, come in; meet Simon Nane from Kenya."

"Welcome to England, Simon," Jack extended his hand.

"Now tell me, how I can help?"

"Let me do this Simon," the Chief held up his hand to forestall an objection.

"Jack, this is what we want. Assume there are two separate antique arms collectors; one is called Brian, and the other has bushy white hair, blue eyes, a moustache, and could be called Holt." The name 'Stop' seemed unrealistic, so he plumed for 'Holt'. "Can you find these guys?"

"Is that it?"

"That's all the info we have for the moment, but mug shots on the licenses will give us a more positive identification. I take it the requirement is similar to that for a firearms permit?"

"You're right there; and I'll tell you something else, there're not too many of these licenses in London, or in the whole of the country if it comes to that. Now I suppose, you want to know how long it'll take me to make a short list."

"You, tell me?"

"A couple of hours and it'll be on your desk."

"Thanks Jack. I'd really appreciate it before lunch, if possible."

"Can he do that?" Simon asked in amazement, the moment Jack left.

"If he says he can I'm sure he can, but in the meantime I want to get that court order as a matter of urgency." He lifted his phone receiver and dialed a number selected from his diary. "Can you put me through to John Manners, Crown Council?"

"John, this is Conrad Black, Scotland Yard; perhaps you recall my name from the Haig case?"

"What can I do for you Conrad?" He cut the chatter short.

"I urgently need to examine an account, of one Mr. Holt. He banks at Coutts, and I know virtually nothing about him, but some evidence run by me, suggests he's involved in arms trafficking."

"Tell you what Conrad; you swear an affidavit and I'll get you a warrant tout-de-suite."

"Give me a time frame?"

"Well, if I can get hold of a judge to sign it as a matter of urgency, you should be able to pick it up from the courts in the Strand first thing in the morning. But make sure I get your affidavit now. Good luck."

Conrad hung up and turned to Simon. "You know there's really nothing you can do here for the present, so why don't you come back tomorrow."

"Here, take this," he offered a mobile from his drawer. "I'll contact you if an emergency comes up. And by the way, don't get any fancy ideas; it only receives calls from me." He smiled and stood up to indicate the meeting was over.

"Tomorrow at nine, Simon. See you then, and have a good day if I don't contact you sooner." Simon, still in a state of shock by the speed at which Conrad had disseminated information, shook his head in disbelief, as he admired the revolving symbol of Scotland Yard outside the building. There was absolutely no other way to react; he recapped his thoughts and walked toward Westminster Bridge.

9AM. Simon was seated in the outer office and Conrad had yet to arrive.

"Don't worry Mr. Nane," the secretary said. He phoned to say he's at the Law Courts picking up a document that concerns you. Why don't you have a coffee while you wait?"

"No thank you." He picked up the newspaper and flicked to the sports at the back to look for Kenya's gold medal tally at the games. Disappointed, he consoled himself it was early days and the runners had yet to perform. When Conrad did eventually arrive, he swept through reception at break neck speed and called on Simon to follow him into his office. Such swift motions to move from one office to another he'd never witnessed in Africa. He sensed another fast day was about to unfold.

"Know this man?" Conrad dropped a portrait picture about the size of a passport photo on the desk in front of him.

"Never seen him before in my life, but he could just be the one to fit the description given to me in Pakistan."

"He's James Holt of Richmond Surrey; a collector of antique weapons. That picture was taken from his license application, and strangely enough your man in Peshawar has identified him. So now we won't need this warrant for Coutts." Conrad dropped the warrant on the desk in front of Simon.

"I agree," Simon could see it was now irrelevant, "but out of this comes one more bit of information I think we should note. He isn't the man found dead in the car crash. So I suspect Holt is still around and in London, and whether he's ever been to Kenya, I couldn't even begin to guess."

"Listen to his background, Simon. James Holt, was a senior member of the Special Air Services, and retired as a full Colonel – no less. The other man with whom he travelled to Pakistan was also a member of the SAS, but by the colour of his hair, I suggest he had to be his junior. Wasn't it described as straight and black?"

"Yes, I agree with that."

"Well now I can confirm they were both in Pakistan on 14th January this year, around the time your gunsmith admitted they placed their order."

"How so?"

"Because they applied for visas here in London, which were issued on 12th January to one James Holt, and one other, who turns out to be Brian Stewart. Incidentally, Brian Stewart, whom we couldn't trace originally by using Brian alone, is also a collector of firearms. His license turned up in a search based on his full name, conveniently written by him in neat block letters on his visa application form. So where do we go from here?" he pre-empted Simon's question.

"Precisely; where do I go from here?"

"Well, as I see it from my angle Simon, offences under British Law have definitely been committed, but this whole issue has international connotations involving extraditions and politicians. A similar case some years ago never saw the light of day, and as far as I can see nothing has changed in the meantime. There're wheels within wheels, if you see what I mean."

"I don't see what you mean at all; if an offence has been committed the perpetrators must be prosecuted—it's as simple as that."

"I wish it were Simon, but it isn't."

"What are you saying?"

"Well, there're so many consequences to be considered. For instance, Britain has good relations with Kenya. Grants, trade, military training facilities, universities, which can easily be soured if a couple of Brits are extradited in chains, to face murder charges in a country practising capital punishment. It just can't happen."

"But we haven't hanged anyone in the last ten years."

"It doesn't matter whether you've hanged anyone or not; the law exists and you're not going to change it for a couple of murderous Brits. What did your own Minister for Home Affairs say to his police last week? 'Shoot to kill, all those found with weapons.' Wouldn't mind a little of that over here, but the do-gooders would be up in arms, until one of their number was raped and robbed at gunpoint. I could go on all night with this, that, and the other, and make a stronger case as I quote instances of refusal to extradite, even to countries without capital punishment. If the people who commit murders are caught in Kenya, they will be tried under Kenyan law, whether they're British or not, but if they escape to Europe there's no way to extradite, because of the capital punishment issue. They'd be punished in Europe, not as you would want them to be, but that's the law in Europe. However, all is not lost." Conrad said in a doubtful voice.

"Really Conrad, you could have fooled me. You're on their side because they're British and they're whites!" He regretted his words, immediately they left his lips.

"Simon, that's not fair and you know it." Conrad understood his feelings as well as he did. "Think about what you just said, and justify it if you can? You're frustrated by the law and so am I, but remember we are little people who vote MPs into power on the strength of their manifestos, and after they win they tear up their promises and pursue their own selfish agenda. It's the same the whole world over. You and I think the law is an ass, and we're both most probably right, but to change it we haven't a chance. That's life, and I accept it, because that's how it is. Another thing, I don't want ulcers." He smiled to show there were no hard feelings.

"Sorry, sorry Conrad, I was very wrong and I pray I haven't ended our friendship."

"Don't talk such rubbish; if I ceased my friendship with someone every time they made remarks like you just did, I'd have very few friends indeed. We're having dinner tonight at our old haunt, Brown's Hotel in Piccadilly, if you're on?"

"Thanks, I'll be there early.

"Incidentally, strictly between us, there's a raid at sunrise by the anti-terrorism squad on both these blokes' houses, and some of those boys in the squad are black if it makes you feel any better. On the surface of it, I may not appear sympathetic, but deep down inside me Simon... I'm with you all the way. See you tonight." Conrad held out his hand, and shook Simon's, in a gesture, to re-affirm their friendship.

38

"What's your poison?" Conrad asked, as soon as Simon was seated.

"What's that you're drinking?" He pointed to Conrad's half empty glass.

"The usual draft I order, when I'm meeting a dignitary from overseas." His deadpan expression held for half a second, before it made way for a scandalous grin.

"You're up to something Conrad; I don't know what it is-- but I'll catch you out," he wagged a finger at shoulder height and offered a knowing smile. "Give me the same." Conrad signalled the waiter, pointed to his beer, and raised an index finger.

"Cheers!" They touched glasses and quaffed a good linear inch before they turned their attention to ordering food, which would be followed by a brandy and official discussions, if the previous meetings were anything to go by.

"You know Simon, I don't go on these raids myself," Conrad admitted. "Must be getting past it..." he mused. Simon held his peace and showed respect as he would for an African elder. "But I should have a full report before the morning's out, and for what it's worth, I don't think they're acting on their own. Over the years, I've always been led to expect the unexpected, but what the unexpected is in this case-- God only knows. And the longer I get in the tooth, the less surprised I am when something grotesque crawls out of the woodwork. So be warned-- I'm not getting up to something, as you suspect," he briefly smiled. "That 'dignitary' title was flannel for a good friend; but putting all that aside... this case could be your introduction to a really murky crime. This is not just a fight in a bar that sparks instant reaction, and someone drops dead. There's more to this than meets the eye; it's becoming a saga."

"And the extradition," Simon asked. "What can you do for me on that?"

"I told you – nothing."

"How can you dismiss it like that?"

"Because it's the law, and experience tells me the instigators aren't going to prison."

"Why?"

"Well, for one thing, you'll have to find a jury in this county to convict them on this delicate subject of corruption; even if you and I think they're evil people, it's the jury who'll decide, not us. So come and see me tomorrow, and we can talk things over, before you confirm your ticket home."

"My ticket home…that's the only thing I don't have a conflict with at the moment. But on extradition, I still don't want to let go, if there's a chance." Conrad, recognized the youth in Simon, trying to put the world to rights, and saw his own reflection twenty years ago. Simon, would mellow with age, as he had, and there was nothing anyone could do or say, to influence his present day thinking. Time and knocks, and hands-on experience, would be great teachers.

"Good night, Conrad," they shook hands. "Thanks for being my friend."

"I'll always be your friend Simon; you can't get rid of this old dog as easily as that. Good night, Simon."

39

"Good morning! Good morning to you Angela!" Conrad was on the crest of a wave as he greeted his secretary.

"Ooh… we are in a good mood to day," she cooed.

"Yup, I had a wake up call from the Home Office, to go over there and study some revealing documents, found on the premises of a Mr James Holt. It looks big-- really big-- could even bring down this lousy government; but I'm told, that's wishful thinking."

"I'm just passing through to collect my briefcase, and by the way… young Simon Nane will be here this afternoon. Treat him with care and pamper him a bit. He's still rather bruised from yesterday, when I dashed his hopes about extraditing these criminals if they're caught. He can't accept that the law would prevent it, and he's taking it personally. Tell him, I'll be back by mid-afternoon, if I can't escape lunch with Sir James-- you know what he's like."

"Sir James, good to see you, "Conrad, approached the Home Secretary's desk with an extended hand.

"Take a seat dear boy. How are the wife and family?" He didn't care a damn, but asked just the same. "Haven't seen you for ages; it seems our paths rarely cross these days… dare I say, we're a lot poorer for it."

"Absolutely," Conrad agreed.

Sir James pushed a button on his desk. 'Where is that girl?' he muttered. "Ah, there you are," he acknowledged her standing in the doorway.

"A spot of tea Mavis, and some of those rock-cakes for our guest. You'll take tea?" he presumed.

"Please."

"Examine these," Sir James, offered a fist-full of papers for Conrad's inspection, "take your time, no hurry."

Conrad read the first page that contained a list of names and shuffled through the rest before he looked up. "Whoever is responsible for this," he waved the pages to emphasise his point, "is in serious trouble."

"That's what I think. At least we concur on that."

"Who's behind it? "Conrad asked.

"Well, since you were the instigator of the raid you have a right to know. Incidentally, I've reclassified this enquiry—it's now top secret. We don't want the government to come to a sticky end, do we?"

"Go on…you're tempting me," Conrad laughed.

"Well, perhaps not a sticky end, but if ever it came out, we would of course deny everything. I think you'll agree-- there's no shame in politics."

"Do I?" Conrad's expression was flat, and without a hint of humour.

"Now, you stop that Conrad," Sir James wagged his finger.

"Well, it was worth a try, just to see the expression on your face." He laughed, and Sir James joined in good-humouredly.

"Now listen up – on the surface of it, there appear to be two bad boys in the House of Lords, who need a good caning." Sir James laughed. "This list says it all. The people at this email address have tried to recruit mercenaries for some vague cause, and now that I have the other end of the story I know what their intentions were, before they changed direction. In the end, they didn't use this list at all, or they would have come unstuck a lot sooner. So I have to conclude that someone with more brains, and experience, must have advised them."

"You know who they are James? Come on, spill the beans." Unable to contain his emotions, James grinned from ear to ear before he apologized…

"I'm sorry, but I can't believe it. It's so ridiculous, but it's happened, and to cap it all people have been murdered."

"Who owns that e-mail? That's what I want to know?"

"Okay Conrad, I can't hold out any longer. Lord Digby Banks is the person at the end of that e-mail, and his old colonial crony Lord Rupert Crook-Smith, is also up to his neck in the plot. That's according to statements made by James Holt and Brian Stewart, their 'expert advisers', who are currently detained at Paddington Green police station."

"And their Lordships…where are they?"

"Well, at a rough guess, because the House is sitting this afternoon, I imagine they'll be in their usual places. They're always there for a kip before they have tea and then go home, or overnight at their club in St James's, if they don't use the flat across Parliament Square. I intend to have a word with the Lord Speaker, and propose an interview during their afternoon tea session. They're old men, very old indeed; dare I say 85, or thereabouts, but with all their faculties about them," he conceded. "Quite honestly, Conrad, I need input from all sides on this one, but because of its sensitivity I can't consult too many people."

"Have you told the PM?"

"Not yet. I have to reconfirm the facts, and of course there's the African angle; where I know they'll want their pound of flesh. So I'm working on options to pacify the Africans, and cover up the whole beastly affair. Perhaps the Ministry of Overseas Development can offer a soft-loan or an outright grant, but whatever we do to sort out this 'indiscretion' is bound to be mind-blowing, and we've only just scratched the surface."

"As I've already informed you, James, I've a Police Officer friend from Kenya with me at the moment, who knows all the details up to the raid this morning. He was the one who actually found out about the two ex-SAS officers from his investigations in Pakistan. He's in on the project in Kenya, and if it becomes a Government-to-Government process, he's likely to be my opposite number out there.

He's young and inexperienced, but he and I go back to his training days, and he's upright and honest. Can I put him in the picture?"

"And your reasons, Conrad?"

"Well, I believe it's better for him to be on the inside now, rather than find out by himself from other lists floating around on the Internet. He could even come up with some useful suggestions."

"I'm not too happy about it, but you go ahead and swear him to secrecy, and make sure he's the only one in the know for the present. It might also be a good idea to feel him out for his government's reactions. We're treading on very thin ice and I'm nervous – how about you?"

"Now that you ask, I'm also shaking in all the right places, but what to do? It's happened." he raised his hands in despair.

"By the way," Sir James, added an afterthought, "you're having lunch with me in the Commons today... it's good to get used to the atmosphere of the place, if you're going to interview Peers of the Realm in the coming days."

"Thank you James; on the job training I suppose," he laughed.

"Shall we go?" Sir James paced toward his coat rack, and collected his overcoat and bowler from a bygone era. "My car's outside."

Simon was waiting in Conrad's outer office when he returned from the meal at the Commons. "Come on in Simon," he signalled him to follow.

"Since last night there have been certain developments. I'd call them embarrassing developments," he was groping for a way to describe them, and finally settled on a question to present the details.

"Simon, supposing one of your most senior government ministers committed murder for the good of the state, naturally, without the approval of the state, but as a result of which... conditions for the masses in your country improved. You're the policeman investigating the crime, and it is a crime-- I don't challenge that. What would be your position? Remember, this Minister has alleviated the suffering of thousands because of his actions, but nevertheless he has committed murder. But by committing, shall we say... limited murder, he's hit corruption so hard, there's a renewed awareness, and corrupt officials now go in fear of their lives. Would you say the law must take its course and prosecute him, knowing your efforts could be fruitless, because the very corruption he's fighting will be used to defeat your purpose? You see Simon; he's fighting for the most precious thing he owns, his life… so he has to embrace the very corruption he hates, since life is more important than principles, when it's his own. That's the circle he's living in. So whatever your efforts to prosecute, you will lose the case, and reap the agony that goes with it."

Simon paused for thought, before replying. "Conrad, you're trying to tell me something and I think it goes like this… Someone in England has been caught as a result of this raid last night, and he's a prominent figure. Am I right?"

"I wish you were on my force; you're perceptive, and absolutely right. So what's your answer to my scenario?"

"I don't like what I'm saying, because it's against all my training, and it's also morally wrong, but in this case, I would look at the overall picture. Not because I'm weak, and not because I respect authority, but because I feel for my people in the rural areas who have been suffering for years since independence, and before that under colonial rule. I know there has to be an end to all this, but without a beginning there can't be an end."

"So, as a policeman, you would let this murderer go-- is that what you're telling me?"

"If I did that, I'd be betraying my profession and words would stick in my throat; but that's exactly what I would do, and God help me."

"Well, I agree with you Simon, and I'd do the same." Their thoughts and moistened eyes gave them the strength to undermine their professions in the name of relief for the masses. Simon was the first to blow his nose, followed unashamedly by the Chief, who had resisted the act until Simon had led the way.

"What was the result of the raid?" Simon asked

"We believe two old men, very much like the minister figure I mentioned earlier, could be responsible for these murders. I emphasise, nothing yet is confirmed, but I'm interviewing them in the House of Lords with the Secretary of State for Home affairs tomorrow afternoon, when I hope to get to the bottom of it. From what you've just admitted to me I'll make sure you're kept in the picture, and I'll contact you by mobile if anything unusual comes up, but for the present I suggest you take some time off." The Chief blew his nose once more and returned his hanky to his pocket, "and thanks for the weep." It was now behind him.

"Me too." A red-eyed Simon showed himself out.

40

"Conrad," it was the Minister on the line." I suggest you come over here and we proceed to the House together. The Lord Speaker's got these 'naughty boys' by the ear, and he's guaranteed to drag them before us. If you're here by two thirty, we'll be there by three."

"Look forward to it Sir James. Do you want me to bring anything?"

"Just yourself."

Three o'clock that afternoon couldn't arrive too soon for Conrad, who had been on edge since the revelation of the previous day. He had never interviewed a Lord before on a criminal matter, and looked forward to the first time experience.

"Lord Banks, may I introduce Detective Chief Superintendent Conrad Black from Scotland Yard crime branch." Sir Humphrey Dodds, the Lord Speaker, was seated at the head of his conference table dispensing the introductions. "And this is Lord Crook-Smith, he gestured toward Rupert, who had already heard Black's name. Of course you know everyone here Sir James, so I won't labour any more introductions."

The Lord Speaker turned toward Conrad, "Chief Superintendent Black, will you please proceed."

"Sir Humphrey, I have to take one person at a time; may I ask if it's possible for Lord Crook-Smith to step outside until I have finished with Lord Banks."

"That seems reasonable," the Lord Speaker acknowledged. "Would you mind Lord Rupert?"

"Not at all Humphrey, I'll be in the canteen when I'm needed."

"Do you have any objection to my recording this interview Lord Banks?"

"No: why should I?"

"I asked you that Sir, because you could be facing very serious charges, and perhaps you want your lawyer present."

"Young man, I did what I did because nothing is being done about corruption in Africa, and in my opinion it has to be tackled. I'm eighty-five years old, and at my time in life I see the world as a disgusting place! Now tell me young man, what do you want to know about corruption… or anything else for that matter?"

"Sir, we have traced six murders in Africa to you. Can you explain these documents we found in the flat of one James Holt. Examine them, and tell me if you've seen them before?" He passed them to Digby for inspection.

"Well, of course I have; what type of an idiot do you think I am? It was my secretary who copied them off my computer at home, and if I remember correctly, I left them in Jesse's flat..."

"Who's flat?"

"Jesse's of course. Jesse or James, it's the same thing."

"I follow you Sir."

"Rupert and I took them over there when we first decided to hatch our plot." He didn't reveal that the list hadn't been used, but nevertheless, he had to admit the evidence was somewhat damning.

"Do you deny, that you conspired to commit murder in East Africa, and sent agents there to carry out your intentions?"

"Of course I don't deny it. Something had to be done for Africa: maybe you don't realise it, but the whole damn Continent's falling apart, and our help is needed to stop the rot. You as a policeman should know more about it than I. The law out there's an ass!" He thumped the table and surprised himself, as much as all those present.

"Sir, I feel it's my duty to caution you, and from what I've heard so far I suggest your lawyer accompanies you to the next meeting. For your information, I'm wiping this tape clean because of the complexity

I see in this case, which I shall have to refer to my superiors before we proceed."

"Sir Humphrey, I recommend this meeting be expunged from the records; it's a meeting that never was, as far as I'm concerned. Mr. Lord Speaker, Sir, please excuse me." Conrad slipped the recorder into his pocket and left the room.

"Lift, Conrad?" It was Sir James making the offer, as he caught up with him on the stairs.

"I'll take you up on that."

"Well, what do you think, Conrad?"

"It goes without saying, they're completely mad, but to the public they could become heroes overnight. They'll admit to everything, and what's more they're proud of it. They've set themselves up as the champions of the miserable masses affected by corruption; and they know it's too noble a cause for any jury in Merry England, Magna Carta or anything else, to find them guilty. And that's my reason for trashing the interview – a penny for your thoughts?"

"Huh! Only a penny; you'll have to pay more than that. I'm devastated, my mind's blank, and I keep asking over and over again what we're going to do about these two naughty boys! They're killers, but their cause is so noble, it would be popular with the World Bank, the I.M.F. and donor countries. Behind the scenes, I'm sure these institutions would approve of their nonsense as the only way forward, assuming they got wind of it."

"You're also going mad. Stop here and let me off. I want to walk the rest of the way."

"Wait Conrad. Wait!" he dismissed the driver.

"I'm walking with you."

"Don't talk to me James, I need to think."

"You think you're the only one, who needs to think? I'm sorry I even got out of bed this morning. Have a drink?" Sir James offered as they were passing 'The Rose and Crown'. And when they emerged two hours later, life had become more tolerable.

"We'll talk tomorrow; I'll contact you with my news in the morning. Okay, Conrad?"

"See you, James." Different platforms, different trains, they parted in the Underground.

Conrad waited in his office and shuffled his paper work around as he nursed a thumping headache, and waited for Sir James to call. At last, his secretary genteelly buzzed his desk, once only.

"It's the Home Secretary," she whispered, aware of the delicate condition her boss was in.

"James, what's new?" he asked.

"Only a thumping headache. But I did have a word with the PM this morning after the cabinet prelims. He said it was up to me to sort the matter out, he was off to the G8, and after that he had something else to attend. His parting words were, 'I have absolute confidence in you James, and I will back whatever you decide.' So it looks as though it's going to be difficult, to off-load this one onto some unsuspecting idiot. However, there is a ray of light I'm pursuing this afternoon, when I meet the AG. You can never know until you try, but perhaps he's willing to take it over, if I can disguise it sufficiently and downplay the cunning of the Lords. Wish me luck, Conrad."

41

The logs were crackling in the hearth, the sun had dipped in the sky, and Digby and Rupert were enjoying their first whiskey of the day. The sound of the ice chinking in Stuart crystal glasses, and the evening bird song on the balcony, oozed charm and melody into the occasion. It was an idyllic setting for the 'Lords of the Manor,' who were poised to discuss their victory of the previous day. For a change, they were not reminiscing about old times but were bang up-to-date with the inquisition, which in their opinion had been rather successfully repelled by Digby's outrageous conduct, under cold war cross- examination, as he liked to describe it.

"Actually Diggers, what did they want?"

"Well, it went something like this; that 'Peeler' fellow," he referred to Conrad the policeman, "produced a tape-recorder after you left the room and asked if I wouldn't mind him taping the interview. 'No problem' I said. He then asked if I wanted my lawyer present. 'No' I answered."

"He then asked me, to deny I had conspired to commit murder in East Africa. To which I replied straight to his face; 'I did it because corruption has to be tackled.' I then told him my age, but I think he knew that already. Then I told him the world was a disgusting place. Should have seen their faces! I had to pinch myself under the table to control my laughter. They all looked quite mad to me— absolutely crazy. He, the Peeler fellow, then asked me about those documents found in Jesse's flat. 'They're mine' I said, and again they looked rather shattered. Can you imagine they didn't even know James was called Jesse, but I soon put them right on that score. A couple of more questions and the Peeler threw in the towel. He just couldn't cope; so he scrubbed the tape and aborted the meeting, declaring 'I have to seek further instructions,' and that's about it. Round one to us Rupert, what do you say?"

"Capital, capital, I think you're right, and the battier we appear the more likely they are to give up. I bet by now they've consulted the PM, because they don't know what to do. Mustn't let our people down Diggers, and remember they think we're idiots because we're so old, and I say, let's keep it that way."

"Incidentally Rupert, I have another project in mind that targets a First World country, which we should be able to launch fairly soon if we can keep these fellows off our backs, and distracted by this contretemps over here. The 'New World', in the words of Christopher Columbus, has definite prospects for us, and I think you'll be pleasantly surprised with what I have up my sleeve."

"Diggers you're not thinking of the Americas…are you?"

"Where else?"

"Now you're as mad as they are."

"Those were the same words you used when we started our African campaign, if I recall them correctly."

"Maybe…" Rupert admitted reluctantly, "but the US is another ball game, and security over there is a bit tight.

"Tight security is the downside, but the upside is, we have weapons on the spot and a lot of people who could do our bidding for nothing. And if they don't, we'll just have to pay them like our African recruits, if we want to make a 'splash'. It's all down to our planning, and how we pick our participants, from the shareholder's in the companies that went bust from insider trading. Another plus point we have to consider, everyone over there has a machine gun or a rocket launcher in his or her house. It's something to do with their constitutional rights, I believe."

"Oh, do they? Well, if you put it that way it sounds like a piece of cake; but shouldn't we wind up the African campaign first?"

"Why? While they're busy with Africa over here, they'll have no time to think we're planning another, somewhere else."

"You really believe, we could pull something off over there?" Rupert asked.

"Definitely; and they won't suspect a thing."

"Don't you feel sorry for Jesse and Brian? You know they'll be going to prison."

"Of course I do, but they knew the risks and we paid them well. If they're unlucky they'll get three years, which means they'll be out in two, if not before, and with this new electronic bracelet they might not even be detained."

"And us?"

"We'll not be going anywhere. I predict the PM and the President of Kenya will confer about these two 'mad men', who sleep in the august House every afternoon, ex Governors, who set about trimming corruption in 'their colonies' so to speak. 'Mad as Hatters', is the phrase they'll use to describe us, and that's fine. It suits us well, and for sure we're not going to be extradited with the laws down there. And just supposing for the sake of argument, they put us in prison over here at our age. Well, that just isn't going to happen, because if the politicians did something as foolish as that, they wouldn't get back into power for fifty years. And who wants to be out of a job that long; so we remain free to fight another day. Good reasoning, Rupert. What do you say?"

"I just don't understand you anymore Diggers, but count me in whatever it is. I must confess I enjoyed taking part in this present operation, and I imagine there're greater challenges ahead if we take on the US. Look at this;" Rupert was holding the whiskey bottle upside-down to shake the last drop free; "it must have been half-empty when we started."

"Or half-full, depending on how you see it. Rupert, I'm tired; I think I'll turn in. Help yourself to another bottle from the bar. And don't forget: put the fireguard up before you switch off the lights. Good night, old boy."

"Sleep well Diggers… they're on the run."

42

"Yesterday Simon, I interviewed Lord Banks in parliament. Now I'm sure you'll agree there's a first time for everything, there always is, and this interview turned out to be a first time for me.

As a result of this meeting, I now know what Lord Banks was thinking when he recruited his crony Crook-Smith, to help him come up with an idea of summary justice, to lessen the suffering of the little people. According to him, it's the big time criminals stealing millions, who are responsible for their poverty. In fact, during the interview he readily admitted to his involvement and declared the law to be an ass. He further stated, that he and Crook-Smith had put their heads together to level the playing field, and to send a message of fear to future embezzlers – death was the reward they would reap, if they didn't stop stealing. At that stage, I terminated the interview, because I just didn't know how to cope when it became clear to me, that murders had been commissioned to kill some of the more notorious crooks. He clearly stated his intentions, that the bigger the crooks the harder they would fall, and the better the example they would be. His brashness, blew me away; and that's where it stands for now.

You know, Simon, I seriously think there could be a link between their actions, and the murders of the three owners of the Rocky Bank that collapsed. If I remember correctly, the bankers jerked the law around and were never prosecuted. Well, perhaps that's not entirely true – they were prosecuted, but when it came to hearing the case the evidence had disappeared. The usual nonsense."

"To be fair to the Lords," Simon reflected. "I don't know what my own reaction would have been, had I lost my life savings as some of those little customers did. The sums were quite small when I checked out the list, but to them, they were big enough to be looking for blood. And I don't think for one moment, they would have thought twice about killing these people themselves, if the vigilantes hadn't stepped in to help them out. What I can't understand is, how such people as the Lords can sleep at night after committing murder?"

"Let me assure you Simon, they sleep in a very prominent building in London every afternoon, so I'm perfectly sure they have no trouble sleeping at night. You and I might find it difficult to sleep if we were in the same position, but not these old men, who are acting out their warped philosophy."

"Conrad, I'm booked on the plane in the morning. Visit me this year; come to beautiful Kenya on holiday?"

"Soon, very soon, I promise you that..."

43

Mike was there in his official police transport to haul Simon through customs at four in the morning. But it was the happy laughter he detected in the back of the car that really lifted his spirits, and Fatima, was all over him as he slipped in beside her. An adoring puppy couldn't have shown more affection. "Where have you been my darling? You've made me so miserable with your absence. Say, come with me next time."

"Anything, Honey, just name it."

"When are we setting the date?'

"*Aiiee*! What did you say?"

"When are we setting the date?"

"I thought that's what you said."

"Well you did say anything. Didn't you?" she laughed.

"Okay...set the date. As I said before, anything Honey... just you name it." He thought it was good they both had the same thing in mind, but next time he must watch his tongue just in case their ideas weren't harmonious. After all, he had already proposed to her sometime back with Champers, and all she wanted was to hurry it along.

"I love you, daarling," she cooed.

"Straight home Mike. I'm taking the day off." Simon, had no qualms about taking the day off, he felt entitled; London had stressed him beyond belief.

"Mike, the case is virtually out of our hands." Simon announced, as Mike slipped into his usual chair opposite the boss.

"Brilliant; how did you wrap it up?"

"Well…actually… I didn't. It became a political 'hot-potato' and was taken out of our hands. I suspect it will now pass between Heads of States."

"You're pulling my leg—what actually happened in Pakistan, London or wherever?"

"Well you're not going to like this Mike, but it now falls under the State Secrets Act and I can't discuss it with you for the next thirty years, assuming we live that long. But if it's any consolation to you, I feel really mean, after all your efforts."

"So you should. Anyway, I quite understand. It's just one of those things in life that always comes along at the wrong time. So, what now?"

"Nothing… absolutely nothing; London is taking up the matter through diplomatic channels, and we await orders from the top. And I rather suspect they'll come directly from the President himself through our chain of command, but they'll be from him, you can bet on it."

"Okay, so I'm back to my usual routine."

"That's about it." Simon agreed.

The telephone rang. "Sir, there's a General James Uku waiting to see you. He says he's a personal friend."

Simon covered the receiver with his hand, "Mike, stay exactly where you are; I want you to meet this man. He has to be the one, who broke into my hotel room in London."

"Show him in." Simon was right, but this time Uku was dressed in the uniform of an army Major General, and suddenly Simon and Mike found themselves standing to attention. Uku threw them a courtesy salute and asked them to be at ease and seated. He then occupied the only other empty chair on the same side of the desk as Mike.

"Nane, I told you 'to let go.'" He beamed in Nane's direction, and took Mike into his peripheral vision.

"We are so grateful to you 'Mounties' for getting your 'man,' and it's turned out rather well as it so happens, for all the actors in the cast. But it could have gone terribly wrong, if our President wasn't so dedicated to the anti-corruption fight. Who am I, you may ask? I'm a specialist appointed from the military SIB (Special Investigation Branch) to reduce the enormous backlog of corruption cases. And you gentlemen, by not catching the Lords in England, before they took out the three land grabbers, helped us reduce the backlog by a final total of six. A miserable figure compared to what's out there, but had you 'blown the whistle' on the Lords much sooner and prevented that last crime of theirs, I would have been very angry." He wagged a finger, pointed at both of them in turn, and then roared with laughter.

"Thank you Nane, and thank you Kamba. I know I acted the bastard in London Nane, but who could foresee the outcome we ended up with. Mind you, it was the Lords' own fault their key men got caught, or they might have continued to help our statistics. I think you'll agree such accidents, if I can call detention of their commanders an accident, always happen at the most inconvenient times. What say you, Simon, am I forgiven?"

"General Uku, Sir, now that you have explained your position, I must confess I'm beginning to like you-- Sir!"

"Thank you, Simon, and that's just as well, since I've chosen you and Inspector Kamba to expand my team. It's a new formation, top secret, very select, and the brainchild of a few people in power to weed out corruption. These people are the backbone of the government, and demand zero tolerance whatever the cost. We'll have their absolute support and take over from where the Lords left off. While I've hand picked you, this has to be a volunteer force if you have the stomach for it. I emphasize, you're under no pressure to accept, but I would deem it an honour to have you with me. Think about it over the weekend, and give me your answer on Monday."

"Gentlemen…" he stood and they did the same. He then threw a 'smiling' salute in their direction, and was through the door in a flash.

"Phew! What do you think of that, Mike? If I understood him correctly, we're going to organise our own internal hit team. So in the next few days I suggest we drum up some hate for the thieves who are stealing medical supplies, exchequer money, famine relief…and possibly those who don't give value for the enormous salaries they squeeze from the taxpayers. That's also a form of theft."

"I'm all for it." Kamba declared. "Our lives won't be worth living if we have to revert to dull routine. I vote we join Uku; what do you think? Whatever happened to your safe?"

"I don't really know what to think, but I do know we should forget about that safe," Simon replied.

"What do I do about the snipers from London who are running free out there?" Mike asked.

"Nothing. They've served our country well and perhaps we should award them medals. We don't pursue them, but at the same time we don't let them know they are free to roam unmolested; let them feel apprehension. We don't know who they are, so why waste time trying to find out. It isn't worthwhile."

"I don't agree. They are killers and should be caught."

"Mike, let go. Up to last week I thought the same as you, but now I have changed my opinion, based on the reasoning put forward by my guru in London. My problem is how to explain my position to the Opugi clan, who put up the money to no avail. I feel I've betrayed them, and on reflection the Police Commissioner could have been in this whole thing with Uku, from the beginning, 'to let go or else'. He opposed my going to London in the first place to solve the crimes. So when the President overruled him in my favour, even he wasn't in on the plan. I think, when the Opugis enquire of me, I'll now refer them to their friend the Commissioner: that's got to be where the buck stops, as far as I'm concerned."

"I'm ordering you Mike, to let go. I'm letting go…I'm getting married this weekend, and I want you to be my best man; I've got to get on with my life, and you do the same."

"What! Get married again…never."

"You know what I mean…"

"I'm beginning to understand." Mike reached across the desk and shook Simon's hand. It's a deal. I'm the best man around here," he declared and laughed.

They were going to make a great team, in their next venture.

44

"Diggers, I'm distraught. Jesse's been sentenced to seven years, and Brian his chum to five. Both convicted under the new anti-terrorism laws. It seems the international flavour of their crime slotted them into this new legislation. I don't understand it. It's so unfair. I'm going down to see them this Sunday; do you want to come?"

"You bet! Is there anything we can do for them to organise an appeal?"

"I've already briefed my own lawyer to contact their fellow to confer. What else do you recommend?"

"Let's see what happens; maybe a reduction on appeal, who knows? Anyway that's what my man said. I feel so guilty that we as the instigators get off scot-free, and the people we used to carry out the exercise have to pay the price."

"Now you listen to me Diggers; they knew the score and so did we. Of course it's sad it turned out this way, but they took the risks and went down. How many people do you know out there who qualified for our offer, and would they have turned it down? I'll answer that—none! I also feel responsible, and I'll help all I can. Does that satisfy you?"

"There's no need to attack me. But I'll promise you this: the new venture is going to be different. We'll do the briefing ourselves, and if we get caught our arses will fry." He laughed and appeared to be back to his old-self, but felt far from confident that it wasn't to be his arse to fry, if their luck ran out on this second adventure.

"The PM is flying out to see the Kenyan President on our kerfuffle." Digby told Rupert, who was gingerly sipping his Earl Grey tea to test the temperature, and at the same time eyeing the cream-cakes over the brim of his cup to spot the most succulent, with that extra blob!

"Who told you that?"

"Carruthers, that's who. He's PA to the PR to the Home Secretary, and he's going with him. Wheels within wheels; quite honestly, it surprises me any of them knows what the other's doing."

"The PM won't go. It'll be the Home Secretary," Rupert re-assessed the importance of the mission, "you'll see."

"Whoever it is, I can't see what on earth they're going to discuss. It can't be us, can it?"

"That's precisely it. He's going out there on our account to see if the President wants to lock us up."

"What!"

"Well, that's what Carruthers says, and he's in the know. Also that meeting in the House last week left them in disarray. But by now they will have picked up the pieces and decided on a way forward. What Carruthers says makes good sense, but it's not all over yet, by a long chalk."

"So what's the President going to say?"

"Who knows? I suppose it depends on whether our action has had an impact on corruption. He has political advisers you know, and even though his cards are wearing thin he's bound to see the truth, and if we've made a difference we'll be home and dry; he's a magnanimous man."

"And if he doesn't?"

"Then we have the politics on this side of the fence. As I told you before… jailing eighty-five year olds for fighting corruption in Commonwealth countries, is just not on. But I'd prefer forgiveness from the President, if it weren't going to turn messy for him over there. Anyway, with a Labour majority of ten, the 'worms' over here will find a way out."

"Now, you mentioned another project. Am I allowed to know what it is?"

"All in good time...Rupert."

45

"Tell the Commissioner of Police I want to see him at ten this morning," the President instructed Wangari his secretary. "Excuse me Sir, you are addressing the *Maendeleo ya Wanawake,* 'Progress of Women,' at ten. You promised your wife."

"Yes, yes, I know," he was irritated. "Make sure the Commissioner is here at ten, and tell the *Maendeleo* I'll be there at twelve. I also want the Chairman of the Anti-Corruption Commission here with the Commissioner. Inform the *Maendeleo* directly of my change of plan, and don't mention it to my wife. If she telephones from over there at ten I'm in a meeting... I'm in a meeting and can't be disturbed. Not like the last time when you put her through."

"But Sir, I could lose my job."

"Mmm... so help me God," the President murmured under his breath.

"Commissioner, come in and sit down," the President, gestured to one of the vacant chairs. It was five to ten.

Wangari then showed in the Chairman of the Anti-Corruption Commission, who was spot on time. He sat on the right-hand side of the table with the Police Commissioner opposite. There were only three of them in the room and formality was minimal. The President wanted answers-- he scratched his head in thought and studied the notes in front of him; he then looked up, and announced the object of the meeting.

"The British Home Secretary is flying in today to discuss the case of the six murdered people. Apparently, and I'm as surprised as anyone-- they've caught two of the criminals in London, and want to discuss, what can be done about it. Commissioner-- what's happening in your department; caught anyone?"

The Commissioner cleared his throat. "Nothing concrete Sir, the only break-through we had led to London via Pakistan where I sent my man." He conveniently forgot about the Opugi family finance, without which nothing would have happened, not to mention the initiative of ASP Simon Nane Njoroge, who had challenged his judgment throughout.

"Nothing concrete, you say. Doesn't that make us look rather foolish?"

"No Sir," the Commissioner hid his offence. "Whoever is behind these crimes is a professional, so they're going to take time to solve, but I'm sure we'll get them in the end."

"Really?" The President was not convinced.

"And that brings me to you Mr. Chairman," the President looked the ACC Chairman straight in the eye, with all the qualifying preliminaries of challenge, mirrored in his face.

"Supposing, these deaths influenced future corruption; do you want the killers brought to justice or do you think we should let them run around free without prosecution, like the people they caught up with and killed in the end? Should the Commissioner, waste his time tracking them down, or do we devote our efforts to looking for other worthwhile criminals? What's your opinion, Chairman?"

"There's no denying, Mr. President, that the first three killed were hiding behind the law, and the land grabbing speaks for itself. The details are recorded in the Land Registry."

"Tell me this-- were these six on your most wanted list, and how have these killings affected your Commission's activities?"

"Mr. President, Sir, I can't deny we've only prosecuted a handful of the corrupt, since the Commission was established, and for trivial crimes at that. And if I may mention, I also suspect the only reason why we succeeded with them, was because they didn't have the legal clout of the 'fat-cats', who are still laughing and making an ass of the law."

The Chairman had a list of over a hundred big-fish on the end of his line, but thought it not wise to mention the dallying of the AG at this point, since he had survived many regimes, and no doubt was in his job for life to appease as many friends as possible. But as the Chairman fumed at his hapless situation, and accepted a negative press, the prominent crooks were about to feel his wrath. His moral beatings over the years had painted him into a corner, from which he sought release-- his own attack team was almost ready to act.

"So in your opinion, the six that died were criminals cheating the law?"

"I can't judge the legalities of their cases, that of course is up to the law," wherever… became a passing thought. "But personally, Mr. President, from the evidence I sifted through, they were guilty, but the legal process was being challenged every inch of the way, and the Judges were dragging their feet. But in the meantime, I have to seriously question; did their crimes justify murder?"

"So barring the severity of the retribution, it appears these killers in London have helped your statistics along?"

"If you put it that bluntly Mr. President, I have to agree."

"Under the circumstances Commissioner, I instruct you to redeploy your police forces to track down other criminals. Close these files Mr. Chairman. I expect you to recover the loans they gave to themselves that broke the bank, and I'll re-allocate the land myself." Timely politics he thought, as we come up for re-election. "I'll hand out the certificates after the Commissioner of Lands has identified some genuine cases—for a change."

"Gentlemen, that's all." He looked at his watch; he had fifteen minutes to spare before noon, and the *Wanawake* ordeal.

The Head of Protocol, and the Minister for Home Affairs, greeted their opposite numbers at JKIA, and the party took off at speed with escort vehicles to the front and rear of the column. The President, by this time had returned to State House under intensive care, and was recovering from his *Mandeleo ya Wanawake* experience, which had drained him more than a speech to the U.N. General Assembly. He was contemplating the conversation upstairs that night, when the door was opened…

"Sir James, welcome to Kenya. I trust you had a good flight?"

"Thank you Mr. President, it was comfortable."

"In that case, Sir James, may we get down to business?" The President waved him into the inner sanctum and surprisingly held up his hand to exclude his entourage. It was the first stage of a logical step to call off the hunt, due to the extenuating circumstances, which could have been misinterpreted by his staff as a weakness; so the fewer in on the meeting the better. Excluding his confidantes of today, who might become his enemies of tomorrow, was a calculated risk he was prepared to take.

Wangari appeared at the secondary door to his office, looked over to the high backed easy chairs and caught the eye of the President. He took the prompt and turned to Sir James. "Tea, coffee, juice?'

"Good coffee and Kenya are synonymous, there can be no other choice, Mr. President."

"While we're waiting Sir James… shall we begin?"

"Please."

"We in Kenya view the killing of our nationals within our country by external forces as extremely serious, and if this were to get out into the International forum, there is no telling where it will all end up. Under the circumstances, I shall appreciate your assurance that this conversation remains confined to this room."

"I respect your confidence Mr. President, and I agree with your thinking. My government extends an unconditional apology to you and the people of Kenya, for the actions of some of our more responsible, irresponsible citizens, if you see what I mean. Although your capital punishment laws prevent extradition, we could prosecute the culprits in Britain, if it weren't for the undesirable press it would attract internationally, and the problems we would reap for ourselves back home. The fact that the organizers of this dastardly crime are members of the British House of Lords is the first stumbling block, and the second has to be their age, which makes them foolish eighty-five year olds who should know better. Now, just supposing we put them on trial and found them guilty of murder. It would be like detaining criminals who are past their use-by date, or at the other end of the scale, like putting babies in prison. That's our predicament in England, and it's tantamount to political suicide if we proceed. As a prominent political figure yourself, Mr. President, can you offer a solution?" the Home Secretary was at a loss.

"Cheer up, Sir James, it's not all bad news," the President beamed re-assuringly.

"I've instructed my Police Commissioner to drop all pursuit of the killers in this country, and the same goes for Interpol. We are withdrawing on all fronts." The President leaned back in his chair and studied Sir James's face, noting the sweat on his brow had not reappeared after the last mopping exercise. A good omen-- he perceived.

"Why are you doing this for us? I don't understand."

"Let's say you have your reasons and I have mine. You have already told me yours so I suppose I owe you an explanation, and it's really quite simple. Earlier this morning I met with my Police Commissioner and the Chairman of my Anti Corruption Committee. It seems the activities of your octogenarians have in some small way altered our crime pattern," that's how he chose to describe it, "and these killings have apparently benefited our country in many ways. For instance, crime levels among the rich have fallen, and six wanted thieves have been removed from the scene, which means we can now recover some of their stolen assets without too much legal wrangling. Not to mention, smiles from the World Bankers, that have been lighting up State House with their presence just recently."

"What do I tell my PM when I return to London?"

"Tell him that over here it's 'all quiet on the home front', if I may use that idiom to explain my situation. And while I'm about it, I offer a word of advice from an ex-colony in the distant past," he smiled, and shook Sir James's hand. "If you want to stage something like this again consult us first, and we'll do a better job together."

"But... Mr. President."

"No buts about it Sir James. Advanced consultations and we'll achieve a lot more. Safe journey." He turned and left Sir James standing alone with his thoughts for a second before the High Commissioner appeared.

From London Heathrow, Sir James, telephoned Conrad, and asked him to meet him in his office within the hour.

"Yes Sir, I'm all ears," Conrad extended his head around the door.

"Come in, take a seat."

"Do I detect a sun-tan from your African travels?" Conrad enquired to break the ice. "I was in and out like a visit to a cheap brothel...you know what I mean?" "Perhaps..." Conrad nodded and winked to add to the conspiracy. "Would you care to explain?"

"The upshot is...the Lords are home and dry, Scott-free. The President, a most gracious man, told me the next time we want to kill a few thieves in his country we should consult him first, to up the numbers. Can you believe it?"

"Sir, I can believe almost anything these days. So tell me, why have I got this sinking feeling that you're now going to ask me to do something even more unusual than the unusual?"

"Call it premonition if you like, and of course you're absolutely right... and it is rather unusual into the bargain. I want you to drop all proceedings against the Lords and forget the case ever existed. This instruction comes from the horse's mouth – the PM himself – not that he has a long face," he joked.

"Is that unusual enough for you?"

"I'm not disappointed if that's what you think, but I know some people who will be?"

"Who?"

"Those publicity seekers in the Lords."

"Save me!"

+ + +

46

The New World

Digby stood back from the tourist crowd at Gatwick airport. His chauffeur who was there to take charge of the luggage and drive them back to the family seat accompanied him. Almost twenty years had elapsed since Lord Banks had touched flesh with Charles Edward Eisenbaum Junior, and then it had been on his Texas ranch, where he herded cattle and sold beef at premium prices.

At the age of seventy two, Charles Edward or Chuck as he was popularly called, stood six feet tall in his socks and nearer seven as a 'Marlborough Man' in boots and Stetson. His silver hair, presented an image of a glamorous rough, tough, Texan cowboy, and the only thing missing was a pearl handled gun he toted on special occasions.

In the span of time neither of them had changed dramatically. Their oneness persisted from their hunting days when Digby was Governor, and Chuck a young millionaire who liked to shoot elephants. Originally they were drawn together by Chuck's generosity, when he donated boreholes to drought stricken areas visited on his hunting safaris. Not to mention their mutual love of the African bush.

On one particular occasion they had left their retinue in Nanyuki, and hiked as pals in Ndorobo country; rifles slung over their shoulders, they carried backpacks and old-fashioned water bottles clipped to their belts in military style.

The night descends quickly in desert terrain, and until the moon rises, the company is drawn together by a darkness, that spells fear for lesser mortals than Digby and Chuck, who used such time to kindle twigs with a splash of whiskey, before cutting thorn trees to make a protective fence. An hour or two later, the whiskey bottle showed distinct signs of exhaustion as the logs blazed on, and the descant of the crickets matched by the growl of predators was the wilderness of the night. But step outside the heat of the fire and the mosquitoes demanded their blood; so they slung their nets from the trees to keep out the bugs and cushioned themselves with liquor. Such was life in the fifties, when they bonded as brothers, and exchanged their innermost secrets. Digby reliving his youth as a District Officer always overwhelmed Chuck, as he described his foot safaris twenty years in the past. And Chuck responded with stories of his escape from Nazi Germany with Eisenbaum senior in '38, relating atrocities witnessed, as they made their way through France to the Spanish Border. He also explained, how he had inherited the family business on the death of his father, and sold out to buy his Texas ranch.

Digby, from a different mould, was born with a silver spoon in his mouth and the vagaries of business building were foreign to him. He was merely a merchant banker fond of adventure, who had landed the position of Governor using family connections, coupled with his previous D.O. experience. From his mandate, to prepare the colony for independence, he perceived his present was about to become his glorious past, and his powers would ebb as independence dawned. So, in the meantime, he intended to live as 'King', and that was the era when civil servant and entrepreneur were bonded by the African bush.

"Diggers, what's the big secret you couldn't spell out over the phone?" Chuck asked, as he relaxed with a scotch on the rocks in front of the roaring log fire.

"We're having British roast beef for dinner tonight."

"Goddamn it, Diggers, you're avoiding the issue; and where's the British sportsman these days? There's bugger all to shoot around here!" He plucked the thought out of thin air, and his deep-throated laughter shook the baronial hall as he punched the arm of his chair in frustration.

"Says who?"

"Huh! Those sparrows we blew out of the sky in 86!" The hall took another pounding and so did the arm of his chair.

"They're called pheasants; and since you were last here they've stopped almost bloody everything...fox hunting, badger baiting and anything else worthwhile. So you may laugh. I'm now reduced to keeping chickens! Sign of the times I guess. Everything's gone to pot since the Gulf war. The country's falling apart...bloody economy... bloody government...just can't take the strain of this so-called modern living."

"Shit Diggers! Sounds to me like you're in it up to your neck. Come back to Dallas, and I'll stick my balls on the line. You won't even have to climb the fence from Mex...." He laughed.

"To us!" Digby proposed a toast, and threw back his head in tough Texan style draining his glass in one.

"Diggers... answer my question. Why am I here? You told me it was important and now you won't discuss it."

"Well of course it's important, but let's wait 'til after dinner when we're more relaxed."

"You mean more pissed.... well it's up to you."

47

The time had arrived for Digby to show his hand. "Chuck, I'm in trouble with the law," he declared as he swirled the brandy in his goblet observing its richness of colour.

"Diggers, we go back a long way, how can I help?"

"Well, when I say I'm in trouble with the law, I am and I'm not. It's difficult to explain unless you were in on this whole thing from the beginning."

"Diggers, if you need a shoulder to cry on, I'm a good listener, I'm your man, and we've the whole night before us, even if the log in the grate is not an African fire. Mind you, we always knew in the fifties, our nights under the African stars were too beautiful to go on forever. Why don't you bring that bottle of whiskey to hand, and let me listen to your story."

"You know something Chuck; I really don't know where to begin, and it's no good telling me to begin at the beginning, because the whole thing's so damned ill-defined. The position we now find ourselves in was a passing thought at first, and then all of a sudden, the idea got out of hand. Rupert and I, well… to tell you the truth it was my idea – decided to do something about the corruption plaguing Africa. It was an article in "The Times" that sparked off my interest, and which I blame, for our present predicament. It said, lawyers in Africa, made an ass of the law using technicalities, to keep the criminals out of jail. So, to cut a long story short, we organized hit teams to make examples of some of those criminals, theorizing that life, was even more precious to them than money.

In the end we bagged six, like ducks on a shoot. Shot them stone dead by way of examples. The Anti-Corruption Commission wanted every one of them; we just lent them a helping hand. Otherwise, it would have been years before they were jailed for their crimes, and in the meantime they would have continued to prosper. Finally, we were caught by our own stupidity, and as I speak, two of our team are rotting in a British jail, and as far as I know, four of our shooters are still at large in Kenya. Our two African team leaders have safely come back to this country, and returned to their jobs. Our bad luck was, two of our shooters died in a road accident, and their weapon was traced back to us. Now Rupert and I are on 'probation', so to speak, with a wink and a nod from the authorities over here, and Kenya is rather pleased with our activities, to serve as a warning to other transgressors. Can you imagine, some of the crooks are actually negotiating with the government for voluntary disgorgement; a term you use in the States to describe the return of ill-gotten gains. I might have overlooked a few details, but I'm sure you get the drift." He took a large mouthful of his drink, and sat back to observe, Chuck's response.

"Fantaaastic...! Absolutely fantaaastic...wherever we go from here, can only be down hill...Diggers you're absolutely fantaaastic! Goddamn it... why didn't you tell me before?"

"I'm glad you feel this way Chuck, since there could be a spot for you in our new mission."

"Count me in Diggers...Whatever it is, I'm your man—count me in."

"Why don't you check this out?" Digby handed over a copy of the Task Force one-year Anniversary Report, about combating corporate fraud in America. "Give me your opinion in the morning, and you tell me if they're putting the fear of God, into these fraudsters."

"Am I part of the team?"

"I'll try and fit you in, if only as a getaway driver." He chortled, and picked up his unfinished drink. "See you in the morning Chuck, around eight; sleep well."

48

"Hi there, Chuck, trust you slept well?" Digby stood at the foot of the Adam staircase, that hugged the outside wall of the house as it crossed from the minstrel gallery, and ended up with a flourish at the entrance hall. "Sure did; like a kitten, when once I finished this," he held the report in his hand.

"Shall we go in? Collect what you fancy from the sideboard and take a pew. Mrs. Catchpole is making the coffee and toast. Buckwheat, waffles, and peanut butter have been replaced by my traditional toast and marmalade. You Americans eat too much."

"Too early in the day for a dispute Diggers. I give in, if that's what you want. Anyway, I agree we're overweight, over sexed, and over here, as they used to say during the war. Remember that saying?"

"And over paid," Digby added. "Yeah…I forgot that one, why didn't I think of it?"

"Convenience, I reckon."

"Do you want to hear about this report, or not?" Chuck had burnt the midnight-oil and was ready to offer an opinion.

"Fire away."

"The number of cases investigated is in the hundreds, which indicates a great deal of work; but if you look at the overall picture, it's a drop in the ocean. The terminology stinks, and when crooks are caught, the law expresses a hallowed respect for them. Just listen, to this," he searched through some pages. "They've agreed-- that's the crooks-- to pay civil penalties and not to serve as officers or directors of a public company for 5 years…now, how the hell they did that, I really don't know. Again, they've 'agreed' to pay several millions in disgorgement, and have entered into settlements with the SEC for the payment of civil penalties. I ask you... how pathetic can you get? I added up the money involved and it's as though the crooks countenance the SEC to knock on their doors and beg for payment of penalties, fines and disgorgement, which in some cases are so minimal, it means nothing to the individuals—who remain millionaires. In fact, I doubt the cost of this exercise covers its implementation. Nowhere could I find a list of individuals sent to prison as a result of their transgressions. So where's the deterrent? The whole exercise is a sham and is based on who went to college with whom. In fact, I believe the SEC is using kid gloves, because they don't want to find anything nasty. The fines and disgorgement agreements are paltry, compared to the crimes. Sure, they're taking hundreds of millions in fines, but that's against a background of trillions, which amounts to little more than a tap on the wrist. And I'll tell you something else; the International Community is not so gullible as to believe such cheating is going to change because of these actions. Restoration of faith in American business; shit! Outsiders, who know the figures, read these reports and laugh. They know the SEC is talking pennies whereas trillions are involved, and in many cases the businesses have paid fines for the individual culprits. What happens to the individual? Zilch! They're left in the job to rob, on a promise to undertake reforms. I've never read such crap in my life. Left in a job on a promise; it has to be a joke!"

"Ask the little guy about Enron or World. Com, and corporate kleptocracy, and then ask them about the life savings they lost, and the lavish lifestyles of these manipulating CEOs. The language they'll use to describe these bastards will be new-- even to me."

"Stop right there, Chuck. Where's the justice, that's what I want to know."

"Justice? I assume you're referring to the size of the penalty to fit the crime?"

"Couldn't have put it better myself. That's precisely what I'm referring to. Of course, we don't know the ins and outs, so it's difficult to judge the issue. However, in some cases the guilty have actually got life if you count a ten-year sentence awarded to a seventy year old, but whatever the cost, the Directors have to be held responsible for their actions. I'm talking about those who vote themselves unjustifiable gluttonous salaries. They're the ones who have to be taken to task. Agreed?"

"Diggers, am I in or out?"

"I'll let you make that decision for yourself after I've explained what I had in mind. Rupert and I want to go to America with equalizer policies to sort out some of these crooks, who are jerking the law around; and to do this we could use similar tactics, to our African campaign. I emphasize could, because of the danger involved, which has to be much greater for you as an American national. Rupert has also, to agree to your participation."

"Goddamn it! I'm always being pushed around," he offered the injured person syndrome he loved to play; when he realized his wishes might not be granted. "What do you want me to do?"

"In the first place Chuck, we really do need to have Rupert in on this: the last thing I want is to upset him. I'm also thinking, since the Home Office is watching us, it won't hurt to keep them occupied using him as a decoy; and in that case, he shouldn't be anywhere near us. They'll never guess you came all the way from the States, to plan a criminal act with me."

"Have I?"

"I thought you wanted in."

"Well… yes, but how criminal is it?"

Digby sensed second thoughts, and reassured Chuck. "It's really nothing to worry about, because at our age they're not going to bang us up, even if we're caught. It's all a matter of politics, and no government worth its salt, can be seen as uncaring for its elderly people. So, if two eighty-five year old idiots like us, commit a capital offence, they're either going to commit us to the loony bin, secretly warn us off, or even congratulate us. It all depends…"

"On what?"

"On the circumstances, of course. If they're favorable, they'll warn us off, and if they're not, they'll bang us up in the loony bin. Do I make myself clear?" Chuck was a man of the world; why Digby had to explain in such detail, he really didn't understand.

"Now, if you want to pull out just say so, because if I tell you any more, you'll be an accessory to the plot. I don't know what you call it in America, but if you know the plot and don't report it, to whomever, you're as guilty as I am."

"I told you, I want in." Chuck saw his chances fading.

"That's settled then, well almost-- provided Rupert agrees." At that point, Digby realised that it might have been more expeditious, to have had Rupert there from the beginning-- in spite of his doubtful, 'decoy status'.

49

"It's no good knocking just one of these guilty guys on the head. We did things in threes in Africa, which means…?"

"We're looking for three?" Chuck queried.

"You're, looking for three," Digby corrected.

"Me?"

"Yes, you Chuck. You're over there, and you know the aggrieved, and what's more we're looking for shooters, who have lost it big – whole lives ruined, by CEOs. And we mustn't use the same shooter, to take out the actual culprit, who is responsible for his loss. We don't want a link between our equalizer man, and the one who caused his hate. We want to hit the cadre rather than a particular person, and that in turn will give satisfaction to the shooter, and distance him from the crime. And the money they earn, will provide some small restitution—what do you think?"

"Diggers, it's your show, so you get to pick the targets. You decide like God, who's going to live, and who's gonna die."

"Chuck, that's not fair, and you know it."

"Sorry; I withdraw that," he held up his hands to cool it.

"I suggest we pick our targets from this Corporate Fraud task-force list, using some of the companies therein, and the actual criminal insiders, who got off so lightly. Whatever we decide, we have to move fast and leave no tell-tale documents behind." He recalled his Internet boob, and the foolish idea he had devised with Rupert to recruit, which Jesse had immediately scrapped as foolhardy; and how it had eventually caught up with them, when the papers were found in Jesse's house.

"Goddamn it Diggers; wish I'd been in on that."

"You're going to be the main actor in this one, so what are you whining about? We'll go through the list tonight, and I'll call Rupert over in the morning; three heads are better than two." How the three instead of two slipped out, he couldn't conceive. Anyway, he knew Rupert wouldn't forgive him if he was found to be making plans behind his back; he must reel him in as soon as possible.

"Chuck, I'll do more planning with Rupert, and in the meantime, it might be a good idea for you to mentally run through a list of people, who might want to take revenge for their losses and help our plan along. Incidentally, I'm offering more remuneration than I paid for the African venture, and it's not out of the goodness of my heart; it's because the chances of being caught are much higher…sixty-grand for a man or woman down. Is that gruesome enough for you?"

"No way." Chuck hailed Digby's statement, and his mind flashed back to Vietnam where the bodies had lain thick on the ground, without a thought for morality. But that was war, not a sniper operation that required a gentlemanly approach, and a highly polished weapon lovingly wrapped in chamois.

Now, whom did he know, and was there a really deserving case? Indeed, he recalled one already. The guy, who sprang to mind, was his regular golfing partner, Henry Legg, who was always bitching about the money he'd lost in Enron. He'd bought a million shares the day before the collapse, on the recommendation of his financial advisor, who was off-loading millions before the bubble burst. That advisor had to be held severely responsible for his actions, and Henry had mentioned his name on a couple of occasions. Whether he was still doing community service for ruining dozens of lives, he wasn't too sure, but he could certainly get the details for Digby. And for someone else to be the shooter according to Digby's plan, was going to suit just fine, because Henry certainly wasn't a killer-- no matter what his pain. A freelance shooter, with an inclination to kill because of his own suffering, had now to be found for Henry's purpose, but in the end, the final decision belonged to Diggers. Nevertheless, he felt good he was able to put forward a name so quickly, and he knew Henry would be pleased to see the back of this man, who had received such a light sentence for stealing millions.

"Rupert, we're starting phase two, and I'm offering you a working breakfast in the country at ten tomorrow. Can you make it?"

"Can you stop me? Delighted, old boy – see they haven't locked you up yet."

"Crooky?"

"Yes?"

"I hear they're looking for you," he laughed.

"Ah, see you in the morning." They enjoyed the banter.

"Then that's agreed, our three targets will be taken from insider-traders, who recommended purchases to third-parties before the companies collapsed," Digby affirmed his aims.

"What's our reasoning, to pick this cadre?" Rupert asked.

"Chuck, explain the effect it had on some of your friends; but first I'll spell out the basics, for Rupert's benefit. Quite simply, it's like a run on a bank, and those who get there first, get the best deal, while other members of the public who put their faith in the Directors, go bust. It's rather like the men on the 'Titanic', who dressed as women, to escape in life boats and save themselves; but in these cases, the CEO of a company is dressed as an ordinary shareholder, and sneaks share sales to save himself, before the company 'sinks in icy water'. You follow Crooky?"

"Oh! Put simply like that, of course I do. So where are these people now?"

"Chuck is here, especially to help identify such scum, but his prime duty will be to recruit the shooters."

"May I interrupt?" Chuck interjected.

"Sure, go ahead Chuck."

"I have a personal score to settle for a friend of mine—my golfing partner. He was sold over a million shares in Enron the day before it collapsed. And the guy, who sold the shares to him, has been allowed to keep his profits. In those days, the Judiciary regarded such a felony as minor, but that's not how my partner sees it, and neither do I. This crook's dealings, affected thousands of small punters to an extent we'll never know; whole lifestyles were ruined by him. And his position today; I'm told he's living like a king after a few hundred hours of community service, and he's probably back in corporate business."

"Okay Chuck, name him, and we'll take that one on board. So now, we're looking to you to recruit a shooter, who is mean enough to kill to make a statement, against the practices of a person like the one you just mentioned. In fact, I'll put your guy's difficulties at the top of our hit list, and link him to the shooter you come up with, but without one we can't go forward. So, over to you Chuck, and in the meantime Rupert and I, will pick the balance of the targets from that report," he pointed his finger in Chuck's direction. "Shooters Chuck, a few more shooter recruits is what we need."

"Right! I rest my case," Chuck acknowledged his assignment.

"Rupert, we need two more examples of community service dished out to thieving executives, to make up our total of three. You know the types: convicted and awarded petty sentences, before the judges got sterner directives from the Fraud Task Force in 2003. In particular, look for those who returned to business after their paltry convictions. And how are we going to find them you may ask?" Digby posed the question, and waited. At that point he would have welcomed a comment from Rupert, but perhaps just as well it wasn't forthcoming, because in the face of its absence, Digby, found himself possessed by a genius idea. The American 'invasion' was about to take off at a tangent, with the abandonment of Chuck and the shooters. It would solve itself, within itself, if fed with the right ingredients.

"Hold everything! I need time to think... Eureka! Eureka! I have it!" Digby shouted excitedly, and Rupert recoiled in shock.

"Tell me! Tell me!" Rupert shouted back—I hate such surprises.

Digby's facial expression remained frozen, as though nothing noteworthy had occurred to him, and he began to reveal his plan...

"When my dear Mildred passed on," he referred to his wife, who had departed this earth some ten years earlier. "I employed Scraggs and Scratchit, the private investigators, and they yielded positive results in the States when they traced her beneficiaries; so I think we could give them this tracing job with confidence. Obviously, we couldn't give them all the details, but just a few innocuous pointers, for them to locate the type of people we want to trace. Those crooks, who are laughing all the way to the bank-- the ones who have started new businesses. You know the types I mean Rupert; give me your comments, input, whatever?"

"You're still a bit vague Diggers. I don't know exactly what you're getting at. Why do we need them, and what precisely, would they be tracing for us. One thing more, how confidential are they?"

"I must admit I have only a limited experience of them, which is based on the one good tracing job they did for me; but unless you have any other ideas, I suggest we engage them."

"That's fine, so we engage them to trace the crooks. I'm with you now, I think." Crooky was still not absolutely sure.

"Then that's settled," Digby accepted.

"But Diggers, if they're to trace the crooks and we've already given that job to Chuck, there's duplication and he becomes redundant."

"I don't see it that way." Digby countered. "I agree, he volunteered a person to get the list started, but we've no need to accept his contribution. He was supposed to be looking for shooters. Now if my new plan works out, we aren't going to need any shooters at all."

"Digby, all you've mentioned to me so far, is crooks, and you say we don't need shooters. So, where's the retribution?"

"I'm getting around to that, bear with me. We'll cover one thing at a time if you don't mind?"

"Well, whatever you're thinking I'm telling you this-- we must drop Chuck, from our plans. He's a close friend of yours, and that's just one more reason to drop him."

"What on earth are you talking about? We've already settled the matter, and he's joining us. We can always find something for him to do to make him feel wanted, even with my change of plan."

"Look at it this way Diggers. Chuck is ten years our junior and he's an American. If he gets caught, or we get caught for that matter, he won't be able to wriggle off the hook like us. Your best friend could go down for years, and that's not what you would wish for him…is it?"

"But he was so hurt when I left him out of the African plan. I want to make it up to him, and he already knows about the risks."

"You know about the risks, he doesn't…think about it?"

"So what do I do now? He'll be so disappointed, and he knows our plans."

"I don't think so, well… not entirely. With your new idea of employing private detectives, there's a different concept about which he is not aware, and neither am I if it comes to that. Quite frankly, I can't see how you can do battle with only one side. You find the crooks and then what?" Rupert wanted to know.

"Ah, that's the brilliance of my plan, and all will be revealed as it unfolds. Just, be patient." Digby, was in charge, and perceived Rupert, as a well-hooked trout on the end of his intriguing line. He would play him along for a little while longer, and enjoy the game, before he reeled him in and disclosed the second part of his plan.

"Diggers, I know you don't often take my advice, because you're a stubborn old bastard who always knows best, but for just this once hear me; and if you value the future of your good friend, let him go. He's too vulnerable to the system, and a life of misery is not what you'd wish for him, if we're caught."

"He'll be very disappointed, you know."

"But he's not a fool, and he'll see sense when it's all over; and you'll tell him the 'mother' of all stories," Rupert offered, the 'mother' of all stories as compensation, and pitched in a pleading smile for good measure.

"I'll do it," Digby accepted, "but I'll have to blame you."

"You do what you have to do; it'll be cheap at the price."

"Chuck, I'm really very sorry not to have enlisted your services," Digby was seeing his friend off at Gatwick airport, "but Rupert refused your participation, for reasons better known to him, and as he and I work as a team I had to accept his decision. I tried my best to push him on your behalf, but he wouldn't budge. I'm so very sorry..."

"I'm here, Goddamn it. I came when you called, and now I'm being rejected. Why for Christ's sake? At least, you owe me an explanation."

"Of course I do Chuck, and I would confide in you, and explain our new plan, if your further ignorance of this whole business was not to be your salvation. The position is this, if we haven't learned a lesson from the African affair we'll be in court in the US, and the last thing I want for you, is to be in the line-up with us. Why you may ask? It's really rather simple; you're much younger than we are, and your justice department would have no mercy on you. Fifteen years between us makes a hell of a lot of difference, and neither can you claim to be an English Lord, if it comes to that. If we are prosecuted for our crimes, our standing as English Lords will introduce immeasurable mysticism, which can only be in our favor, and that's something you just don't have. Whatever you may think, I'm your friend, and the consequences don't favour you joining the fray. So Chuck, dear chap," Digby's hand was on Chuck's shoulder as they walked toward departures, "back down gracefully, and wish us luck."

"Diggers, your explanation I accept, and it goes without saying I wish you luck, but whatever the pending consequences, I remain disappointed."

"Diggers...?"

"Tell me?"

"I expect you in Texas in November. No hard feelings. Bring Crooky along too. Strangely enough, I somehow knew from the beginning, he would throw a spanner in the works," he offered a knowing smile.

50

"Mr. Scraggs, Lord Banks speaking."

"Yes my Lord, how can I be of service?"

"Can we meet at my club in St James this evening, for a bite to eat?"

"Delighted, my Lord. Shall I be required to bring anything with me?"

"A notepad, perhaps. Shall we say around seven?"

"I look forward to seeing you again, my Lord." It wasn't often Scraggs dined with a real Lord of the Realm, and unfortunately for him, his wife was the only person in whom he could confide about his elevated eating habits. No matter how fleeting the encounter, his profession demanded the utmost privacy.

"Rupert, get your arse over to the club at 6.30 tonight, for our first planning session. I'll do most of the talking, but I need your ear to the ground to give me a second opinion on Scraggs. He's a wily old bird."

William Scraggs was a diminutive figure; a character of Dickensian fashion. In dark-brown tweed, his matching waistcoat was adorned with a pocket watch and chain. The crimson tie he wore, seemed to be the only exciting element about him, and lifted his absolute dullness. His spectacles, were 'John Lennon' fashion from the 1940s… and the small circular lenses were held in position by a finely crafted tortoiseshell frame. They comfortably nestled on the bridge of his pointed nose, looked exactly right, and matched his sharp intelligence, which was about to be revealed in his replies to Digby's questions.

"Scraggs my dear fellow, it's a pleasure to meet you again after all these years," Digby stood to greet him, and then pointed to the empty chair opposite, as Rupert waited for Digby to cover the void in the introductions. "My associate, Lord Rupert Crook-Smith," Digby gestured in the direction of Rupert. Scraggs stood to shake hands, but Rupert remained rudely seated in the course of their contact. "I'm honoured Lord Rupert," Scraggs said, before he sat down for a second time, with Rupert's discourtesy behind him, and a thought of how impressed his wife would be, when he told her he'd actually met two Lords, and not one, during the course of the evening.

"Mr. Scraggs, there is a distinct possibility, that we may have a commission for you in the 'New World'. Are your associates over there as good as they were ten years ago?" Scraggs cast his mind back to his last commission, which had been a tremendous success.

"Lord Banks, my investigative ability in the States has expanded enormously since I last worked for you, and the crimes we come across seem to getting more heinous by the day; something to do with the state of the world we live in, I rather suspect. Did you realize, detective work is one of the largest growth industries after Information Technology? In-depth investigations are now an everyday event for us, and we've grown beyond recognition. Now, I'm not saying bigger is better, but the bigger we are the more resources we have at your disposal. So I say this to you Lord Banks, with the greatest of respect," his punch line was about to be delivered. "Award your commission to us, and I'm confident you will be pleased with our endeavors on your behalf."

"Scraggs, be a good chap; select what you wish to eat and excuse us a moment?"

"Crooky I need to take a leak, join me," Crooky knew the score but made light of the situation.

"You want me to hold your hand, Diggers?"

"Yes, if you put it that way." Digby was annoyed; his engineered situation was so transparently obvious anyway, he could have done without censure from Rupert.

"So what do you think Rupert, first impressions; he gets the job or not?"

"Did you have anyone else in mind?"

"No. But we could make enquires and someone else might be cheaper?"

"I say, better the devil we know, and you tell me he did a good job before-- finding your wife's relatives."

"Then that's settled, he gets the job," They returned to the lounge and Digby warmed to Scraggs old-fashioned demeanour, which in truth was very similar to their own.

"So what have you decided on Scraggs, the steaks are always rather good?"

"In that case I'll switch from the fish and take your advice Lord Banks; I'll have the sirloin."

"And you Rupert?"

"Same here."

"Three sirloins with vegetables in season," Digby told the waiter, "and a bottle of the Chateau Neuf du Pape '48."

"Now, let's get down to business. As you've most probably read in the news just recently Scraggs, several prominent business people were sentenced to Community Service under the Bush legislation of 2002, enacted to combat corporate fraud."

"Our problem is this: Rupert and I feel sorry for some of these people who did community service years ago," he kicked Rupert under the table to keep him in check as he switched to inventive territory on the spur of the moment, "and we're worried they have fallen on hard times, so we want to trace them to offer our assistance. Quite honestly, we as some of the more fortunate members in society, feel we owe it to them, if you follow? It's something Rupert and I have always been talking about, and now we want to act. We'll judge their circumstances on the reports we get from you, about their lives after Community Service-- and if our comrades are struggling, we want to know about it. May be we can help them anonymously, to get back on their feet."

"I know exactly what you mean Lord Banks, and I must say I commend you on your generosity. They're lucky to have such caring people like you around."

"It's nothing really; we'll just be looking after some of the less fortunate people in our society, who have strayed by the way. We feel they deserve some kind of support from the likes of us." Scraggs had to admit to himself, he'd never heard of anything quite like Lord Bank's proposal in all of his considerable life, but he'd handled idiosyncrasies before, and this was just one more notch in his 'belt of knowledge', so to speak.

"Mmm... This steak's delicious; I appreciate your recommendation Lord Banks." It was the first time for Scraggs to be in the Blue room at the club, and its ambiance had somehow added to the juices of his steak. "May I ask, how you would like to instruct Scraggs and Scratchit? If I presume rightly, you're engaging us to seek out these people?"

"Yes, yes, of course. We will give you a list of twenty companies in which there was insider trading several years ago, and we want to know everything about the people involved, the CEOs, before they were sentenced to Community Service. Why they were sentenced, for how long, and what they are doing now? That last question, what they are doing now is really very important and most confidential, because it will determine how much help if any, they receive from us." His brow wrinkled in creative thought and he kicked Rupert under the table again to ensure his silence, as the type of 'help' he was considering continued to form in his mind. But whatever idea eventually dawned, it wasn't going to be the charitable perception that Scraggs was entertaining.

"To recap Scraggs, we need their life story up to the time of the crime, and then from the time of their release to the present day. It will enable us to gauge the level of their distress." The widest spectrum on each individual was intentionally requested by Digby to disguise his true intentions, and mystify Scraggs.

"I see what you mean Lord Banks," Scraggs didn't really see any such thing, but played along in the interests of his recently accepted assignment. "They're certainly very lucky to have such caring souls like you around," he repeated his admiration.

"Rupert, have you anything to add?"

"No, no. You've said it all. I'd only be echoing your words."

"So that's it Scraggs. It's just a matter of getting our list of the companies to you—and your retainer of course."

51

"Why change the plan Diggers? I felt a bit foolish when you kicked me under the table and rambled on, with new ideas off the top of your head."

"Look Crooky;" he sought a soft spot in Rupert's make-up, to enlighten him on what he was doing. "Sometimes I'm inspired for just a few minutes with mind-blowing ideas, and that was just such an occasion. As I now, perceive the overall picture, we'll need another private detective agency with connections in the States, completely separate from our Mr. Scraggs."

"Why, what's wrong with Scraggs?"

"There's nothing wrong with Scraggs. We've engaged him, haven't we? But now we have to tie up the other end of the spectrum, which involves those who came a cropper to insider trading. We have to find out who they were, and whether they've rebuilt their lives. In particular, we want to know how bitter they still feel about their losses. Perhaps we can't answer that last question, but we'll make an assessment from the reports we get from our second investigator. These are the people, we really care about, and not the others we would have Scraggs believe. Once Scraggs has supplied the information, his job description will change from investigation to observation. He doesn't know this yet, but whatever we do, the other side of the coin must always remain hidden from him, which is the reason for the other investigating agency.

The task of the second agency will be to locate the victims, of those sentenced to minimal Community Service for crimes committed against them. We're employing two very different investigators, because we can't afford to have any one company comparing notes within, when the aggrieved who have fallen on bad times, decide to settle their scores."

"What scores?"

"Oh, dear me…I thought I had explained all that! Community Service was a soft option dished out by the judiciary prior to the harsher guidelines now in force. Previously, white-collar crime was sentenced with a nod and a wink from judges, who believed such acts to be naughty, but not very criminal, in spite of the hardships suffered by their victims-- the small shareholders. According to the report Chuck read when he was here, the felons learned no lessons from the light sentences imposed, and now they're back in business.

So I can't help but wonder, and you might also too, how many of the victims of these earlier crimes lost track of those who affected their lives so drastically. And this is what we'll determine, from the information supplied by our second agency. Now do you follow?"

"Not really… Where do we get the second agency from?"

"We start looking, and if I'd had any sense, I would have asked Chuck before he left for the States, but on second thoughts perhaps its better we find our own. My most recent lawyer could be suitable for our cause. You've met him— the one I asked to appeal on Jesse's behalf. He confided in me at that time, he's interested in a seat in the House of Lords, and is prepared to make the right donations. He also mentioned in the course of conversation that he pays for his London rent by specializing in US divorce cases, which has to be in his favour as far as we are concerned. He's bound to have a brace of detectives on-tap in the States.

All we really need from him, is a list of the small shareholders with the addresses, where they were living at the time their company went bust. Then we'll ask him to trace where they've ended up, and give us their up-to-date addresses. After that, we check out their change of neighborhoods, and those who moved down market from their original addresses on the share registers, are the ones we're really interested in. They will receive our latest information package that

Scraggs has compiled, with the data about the CEOs who caused their ruin."

"What exactly do you mean?"

"Well, the only way I can explain it is this. We will have engineered a situation for human nature to take over, and it'll make an interesting study as we sit back and let Scraggs' men observe the outcome. I suspect, the ones with the run down addresses will respond to our information, and react against those who caused them financial ruin, but how they respond is anyone's guess. Now are you with me?"

"Masterful Diggers, absolutely brilliant. So we'll put the cat among the pigeons, sit back and wait for the fireworks! I bet those who lost small fortunes at the time, have been generating evil ever since. We make it easy for them to find their tormentors; now I'm with you."

"Why thank you Rupert, I thought it was rather brilliant myself, and that's the nicest thing you've said in many a year."

"Well to tell you the truth, it's the nicest thing you've come up with in many a year."

"Enough, enough, I can't bear it," a hearty laugh followed and he steadied his stomach with both hands.

"But Diggers, our actions could lead to murder in extreme cases, I mean..."

"Who knows?" Digby, feigned surprise, that his intentions had been exposed so quickly.

"I think the wiser of them will employ lawyers, on a no-fee-no-award basis, if there isn't a statute of limitations. But now that you mention it," he of course, knew all the time; "it might be a good idea to recommend in our package that they take legal action-- though in reality, a few hotheads are required to deliver a statement to corporate fraudsters. Of course, their actions are their own responsibility, but I must confess I prefer the violent African option, to convey, an attention-grabbing message. Now all we have to do is pray that Cassini-Brown, gets his assessments correct, and those that never recovered in life, erupt in a newsworthy manner."

"Lord Banks; it's Mr. Scraggs here," the voice at the other end of the line carefully stated its gender using the 'mister', but Diggers knew he had balls by the depth of his voice.

"Yes Scraggs, are you offering a progress report?"

"Err...not exactly my Lord. I was wondering if you wanted photographs to fit the names in the reports, because if you do, it'll entail sending manpower to the addresses that would otherwise only be written down."

"And it's going to cost more than you quoted to me?"

"Yes my Lord, that's why I'm phoning."

"Scraggs, I have to have up-to-date ones, not news cuttings from the time of the trials. It'll be good for personal relations, when one of my agents approaches the unfortunate individual with an offer of assistance, poor souls," 'the bastards' he mumbled under his breath. "So hang the expense, and get me the latest mug-shots to match your report. Do I make myself clear?"

"Absolutely. I'll make sure you get up-to-date mug-shots, thank you my Lord."

52

"Ah, here it is," a tone of triumph resounded in his voice, as he picked out the visiting card of Cassini-Brown, from the handkerchief pocket of his jacket. "Toni, Digby Banks here; I need a favour from you."

"Just name it, Diggers, and I'll see what I can do," Toni knew, that his entrance into the House of Lords required friendly gestures, to endorse his application to the Appointments Committee, and Diggers, could be the one to fire his future ambitions.

"I need some footwork from your organization in the States. Tell you what..." a thought crossed Digby's mind. "Can you make it tonight at St James, around seven for a drink?"

"Delighted Diggers. I'll see you then," he wasn't the one seeking favours so his acceptance was brief-- but it did cross his mind that the time was ripe, to revive the matter of his peerage. The only issue that now remained was Digby's invite to Rupert, or should he be informed of the *fait accompli*? He chose the latter.

"Great to see you Toni," Diggers pumped Toni's hand in welcome, as they moved toward the sherry bar with the spectacular brass fittings, polished to perfection over the years. "We must meet like this for a drink more often," Digby suggested.

"I'll second that, Diggers. So, tell me how I can be of assistance to you in the 'New World'?"

Digby paused for thought; he was still trying to work out how he would tackle his requirement, and at the same time give away as little information as possible, thereby putting distance between the footwork, information gathered, and most of all his intentions. He decided against offering a benevolent reason, as he had done with Scraggs. Only hard lists, financial ratings, and addresses were required.

"I suppose you could classify what I require, as corporate footwork; slogging," he opened the description of his operation cautiously, forming ideas as he proceeded. "Because, I'm looking for the names and addresses of shareholders in twenty companies, that went belly-up, some years ago. It happened when the 'insiders' sold-off their shares, before the public was aware of their internal problems. Actually, I have a list here for your people to work on," he produced a copy of the same list of companies he had given to Scraggs, and handed it over to Toni, who put it aside without a glance to concentrate on Digby's conversation.

"In those days," Digby continued, "insider-trading was very much in vogue, and regarded as a Community Service sentence, that is-- when you were caught. And this mild attitude to the crime, encouraged the same people to use their experience, and work the same ploy, over and over again. I want nothing to do with them-- I don't even need to know their names. What I want, is the names and addresses of their victims, those who lost $100,000 or thereabouts in these companies," he tapped the list on the table, "all due to these Community Service freaks. The figure of 100,000 I mention is the value of their shares at the time of the collapse. And it's your expertise that I seek, to find out who they were, and where they live now after all these years," Digby sensed, it was time to justify in some small way his requirements, for the benefit of his listener.

"Toni, many lives were ruined by such collapses, and Rupert and I want to do our own personal survey to see how things worked out; did they lose their lifestyles or not? We might even make personal contact to collect statistics." He didn't offer any further explanation, and Toni, ever a good lawyer, didn't question his motives. "But without names and addresses our task becomes almost impossible," Digby's plight became a plea, just short of a begging bowl.

"I fully understand, but what you're asking will require accountants, corporate lawyers, and it's much more complicated than I expected; even detectives, on the beat. It's mammoth." Toni grimaced at the prospect, and offered an indecisive smile as he balanced the cost of the favour, against the odds of Digby and Rupert sponsoring his peerage. The sponsorship won. "But it can be done," he accepted the challenge with a sanguine smile, much to Digby's relief. "However, on this one you'll be talking to one of my specialists, whom I'll send over to meet you at a sensible hour. 11 AM tomorrow suit you?"

"Thank you Toni; I really appreciate your support. Strange as it may seem-- Rupert and I already regard you as one of 'us'. Rest assured, you'll not regret your generosity, and interestingly enough, I was only speaking to the Home Secretary last month in the company of the Lord Speaker," he left out the police presence, "and he thought most highly of your assistance to the Party. He also praised your charitable works. You know Toni, I think this could be your year."

"Straight up, Diggers."

"Straight up. Drink for the road, Lord Cassini-Brown?"

53

"Rupert, I need you at the club. This investigating fellow from Toni, is due here around eleven, and I want you to hear what he has to say."

"I'll be with you by 10:30."

"Okay Crooky, but just in case you aren't, let me tell you the story so far…Toni's an international lawyer... English with Italian ancestry, and as you know my friendship with him goes back a long way. He tells me, he met you yonks ago, before this most recent effort about Jesse's appeal. Anyway, he's in line for a peerage, and to get on the right side of us he's going to do a tremendous amount of work in the States, for free, I hope. In return, we back his application to the peerage when it eventually surfaces, with a nod and a wink to the PM. You know, the usual routine; I don't quite know why I'm spelling it out, but I expect you to play along with me during the interview if his investigator chap arrives before you do, and we don't get the opportunity to talk earlier. Don't be late if you can help it."

"Lord Banks, there is a gentleman at reception asking for you; appears to be an American." The waiter offered a card on a silver salver. "Are you expecting him Sir, or shall I inform him you're not in?"

"I'm at home, Hubert, please show him in," a few seconds later, Rupert and Digby, stood to greet their new arrival."

"My Lords, I'm Kevin Robertson." He thrust out a hand.

"Take a pew young man. Can I offer you coffee?"

"Thanks."

"As you know, I spoke with Cassini-Brown yesterday, and he told me you were just the person to do what I wanted. I gather you're an American through and through from your accent, so I suspect you'll be more familiar with the 'over-there', than us Limeys, over here," Kevin laughed politely, at Digby's rhetoric, not yet sure of his ground. Rupert as usual over reacted, to the displeasure of another club member, who coughed to show his objection.

"Well Mr. Robertson," he referred to his card to jog his memory, "I'll call you Kevin if you don't mind. Your starting point will be the share registers of those companies that went under to insider trading. Did Cassini-Brown explain it to you?"

"He sure did, I got your list first thing this morning, so my being here is really only a formality, for you to get to know me and connect the sound of my voice to my face, in case we need to phone. I have also to warn you, to be circumspect when you talk to me over the phone. Spell nothing out in detail, because whatever you say these days is on record; I can't emphasize security enough."

"You hear that Rupert? We must be circumspect when we communicate with Kevin. Is there anything else you wish to tell us?"

"I can't give you an exact time frame, but I estimate, I'll need about a month. It's the onward addresses you want, that are likely to cause delays. I was told you need twenty shareholders, one from each company, provided they lost at least a hundred grand. Is that correct?"

"Spot on. But whether the companies are functioning now is of no concern. As I said, it's the records from that time that we expect you to use, to trace the present addresses of the victims."

"Precisely; plus any local observations I find on the ground, quality of areas etc. So my Lords, if there's nothing else I'll be on my way, and thanks for the coffee. I'm on the plane to NY this evening. As we say in the States, 'have a good day'." He was out of their sight before they could blink.

Spring was on the horizon, the overcast skies of winter were in the past, and Digby was gazing toward the distant hills that rose from the riverbanks. The pale morning light on the water threw him back years, and kindled memories; sweet memories of rainbow trout and tasty suppers, as he recalled, how he lifted the flesh from the bones to savoir its freshness. The sound from bedside phone brought him back to reality. "Yes?"

"Good morning, Lord Digby," it was his secretary Jean.

"Sorry to disturb you so early Sir, but Mr. Scraggs from Scraggs and Scratchit is on the line. Can I put him through?"

Digby sighed, took a deep breath, exhaled, and mentally thanked God for the quality of the life he was living… "I'll take it."

"Lord Banks?"

"Ah, Scratchit, there you are," he addressed Scraggs as Scratchit and enjoyed his roguish error. "I'd given you up for lost."

"You can't be serious, my Lord."

"So, what's the news?"

"I've completed your task and wish to hand over my report."

"Capital, capital, shall we say seven this evening. You'll dine with us at the club of course; suit you 'old boy'?" Digby's spirits were soaring.

"I'll be there, my Lord."

"And bring your account, there's a good chap; don't want to keep you waiting for funds… all things being equal," he added, just in case the report wasn't up to 'Scratchit'. He enjoyed his mental nuance. The weather and the news augured well for the day, and the untrained voice from the shower, deceived its owner, and sounded melodious. Diggers, was excited. The first part of his exclusive plan was ready for examination, and seven o'clock that evening couldn't come too soon, but in the shower, he'd changed his mind about inviting Rupert. He would keep him in the dark until phase two arrived from Toni, and things really began to hot up. 'A one on one, is all that is necessary tonight,' he reassured himself.

"Scraggs, come sit over here; I thought you'd never arrive." It was only two minutes past seven but seemed far too long for Digby, whose impatience urged on by excitement, was getting the better of him by the time Scraggs arrived.

"It's there?" He pointed to Scraggs briefcase.

"Yes. Would you like to see it?"

"Yes, I would," he held out his hand in readiness, and flicked his fingers to physically hurry it up. The pale green file that emerged from Scraggs case was blank on the outside. Digby opened it, and read the first few lines to confirm it was actually his, before he shuffled through the pages and his eyes came to rest on three asterisks at the end. Consequences, and counter consequences, would be reviewed in the comfort of his home

"Your account Scraggs," he flicked his fingers again, and Scraggs responded by producing a substantial envelope from his inside pocket.

"I'll see you next week and settle this," he held up the envelope. "It'll be cash, so perhaps you should take the wife on an illicit cruise?" Digby grinned, and Scraggs, somewhat taken aback, coughed at the thought of the immoral suggestion, but nevertheless, lamely thanked Digby, for his suggestion.

"Now that's behind us, what would you like to drink? Damned bad manners on my part; should have asked you sooner. Tell you what Scraggs – we'll have champagne by way of an apology."

"With the greatest of respect my Lord, I don't need champagne; you've done more than enough for me by the award of your patronage."

"Nonsense Scraggs, I insist. Steward!"

54

"It's exciting, damned exciting," was how Digby, explained the report to Rupert. "Yes, most definitely," he could come over and examine it himself the following morning; even have breakfast if he made it before nine. Rupert, as always, a stickler for punctuality where food was concerned, made it with five minutes to spare.

"Come, we'll go into the study and look at this properly." Digby downed the last of his vitamin pills with a mouthful of Kenyan coffee and was on his feet.

"Read it out loud Diggers; I'm listening."

"I'm not reading out the whole damn thing, just because you're too lazy to put your glasses on your nose. The meat of it is this… we have a list of twenty directors who received Community Service sentences for commercial fraud in the nineties, when the businesses they ran collapsed. Each has an address, there's also a mug shot, credit ratings, and even a valuation of the property in which they are now living. Ah… now listen to this! Besides these people having criminal records, the report supposes their actions plunged many losers into despair over the years, and it winds up by stating some of their victims committed suicide as the only way out.

Which I suppose could mean, that the victims we seek are not around. Anyway, we'll cross that bridge when we get to it. Toni's investigators aren't going to give us dead leads. But bear these suicides in mind, if ever you start feeling sorry for the crooks as we proceed; they're already directly linked to death and suffering. Another point to remember is, that those who profited from their crimes are now doing very well, according to this list. And, we must presume, without a care in the world for those they wronged.

Digby needed to think-- he had chosen his favourite chair at the club, on a slightly raised dais, which gave him an unhindered view of the room, and the passing trade as he chose to call the members, when he cared to lower his paper. He was in the process of pouring his second coffee, when the waiter approached.

"An international call for you, me lord, from America," he added. "It's a man's voice, but he wouldn't give his name." He leaned over the back of the armchair in a confidential manner, "cubicle three Sir."

"Thank you Hubert, I'll get it." Digby made his way toward the line of boxes and slipped into the one with the red light over the door, which he closed behind him as he recalled the words 'to be circumspect' – it had to be Kevin.

"Hallo?"

"I'm with you tomorrow, same place as before, at the same time you met Toni, if that's okay with you?" Kevin asked.

"That's fine," Digby replied, and was going to say something more as the dial tone cut in. 'Circumspect to the extreme' he mumbled under his breath, but he supposed one couldn't be too careful. Nevertheless, it was nice to know he'd have the other report before tomorrow night was out. If he recalled Toni's time correctly, it had to be 7pm, and then another breakfast with Rupert would follow to explain the ins and outs. He ordered another coffee, assessed the five-hour difference between New York and London, and concluded it was early morning over there.

Robertson looked as though he had stepped out for an evening stroll rather than off the New York plane, as he breezed into the club with a confidence inspired by a second visit. "Yes Sir, this way Sir," he was acknowledged as soon as his visiting card settled on the porter's desk. "Lord Banks is expecting you Sir."

"Good to see you Kevin," Digby was in expectant mood, and noticed with satisfaction a document case in Kevin's hand as he sat down.

"Before we proceed, what can I offer you?"

"Scotch on the rocks will hit the spot."

"Make that two," Digby instructed the waiter, "and plenty of ice."

"Relax Kevin, first we get the drinks in, and then we can look at your report in relative comfort…Good flight?"

"I suppose so," he didn't enthuse. "The usual champagne and lobster, and as for the movie-- I can't even remember, what it was?" They chuckled, as their drinks were placed in front of them.

"Cheers!"

"I think this is what you've been waiting for," the file was black and spiral bound, and like the Scraggs report the cover was blank, but the greater thickness promised greater expectations.

"Take your time, Lord Banks, I'm quite content to enjoy my whiskey." Kevin eased back into his chair and soaked up the ambience of the room. It was the pristine Victorian moldings in the subdued light that fascinated him at first, and then it was the gilt framed English landscapes in their own strip lighting, that infused his pleasure and devoured his stress, as he examined them, one by one. Half an hour passed before Digby looked up, and nodded approval. He placed the file on the table, and smiled his first question in the direction of Kevin.

"Tell me, why is it that most of the victims live in the deprived areas of New York State? Is it because they relocated due to their losses, or were they not well off at the time they invested their money in these bogus companies?"

"That's a difficult question to answer after all these years. But when the victims relocated, even outside New York in the New York State counties, it didn't necessarily mean they were scaling down. As you know, every State has its good and bad regions, and quite naturally the same applies to good and bad areas in towns. I'm sure you noticed any change of address is either written in red or green ink. Red is a downgrade in my opinion, and green is an upgrade. I hope these markings helped. Those who didn't shift status, I've left unmarked in black."

"From my initial glance, I see that nearly 75% of those who lost money, also lost status. Would you agree that's a fair assessment?" Digby asked.

"I think that's about right, and perhaps another indicator of the hardship is the time lapse between the losses and the move. The sooner they moved, the more they were affected. But you did make another pertinent point, as they lost money they usually lost status by down- sizing. Are you happy with the overall report?"

"Yes, yes I am… I'll be phoning Toni later this evening to express my appreciation, and it goes without saying I'm particularly grateful to you."

"I wish you a good evening Lord Banks…"

"Toni, Diggers here. Your man Robertson has just left my club after giving me his report. It's good, very good. I just wanted to thank you, and let you know how much I appreciate your efforts. When do we meet for a drink?"

"You tell me Diggers. Perhaps the sooner the better if we're going to discuss my 'housing' business – if you get my meaning?"

"Toni, buzz me next week-- and thanks again."

55

"Rupert, you've read both reports; now it's up to us to fit them together."

"Diggers, after our African campaign you're now an expert in covert operations– what do you recommend? How many on that list do we pit against each other? The full twenty or just a few of the more deserving?"

"Guide lines Rupert, that what it's all about. We will select ten of the most aggrieved, definitely not the full list. Only the most prominent victims; those who lost the most money in the companies that went under, which led to foreclosure by the banks as their collateral collapsed, for their properties. Such people have good cause to demand redress, and Kevin agrees with me-- it's the ones who relocated almost immediately, who were the hardest hit. So they must be the first, to receive information about the crooks that caused their distress. Something, which will always remain a mystery to me, is why they didn't do something about these cheats at the time, and smack them with civil suits. Surely, they must have known who they were."

"I wouldn't be too sure about that Diggers. Information as we know it today, was not invented then, and it's quite possible that these humble people took the loss, moaned about it, and that's as far as it went. True?"

"You're most probably right, but now with our planning, I hope they'll set the record straight. Our very expensive package, I might add, is about to land on their doorsteps and give them a second chance in life. I'm betting, and I hope I'm right, it'll wake them up after all these years of agonizing, and it's their reactions to our package, that we expect to deliver our message, and send a warning to future transgressors."

"I like it Diggers, but what will our package contain?"

"To kick-off, I suggest a credit rating of the person in question, a passport picture, name and address and present occupation, and also an estimated income, place of work, family status and telephone numbers. Have I missed something?"

"A covering letter?"

"Well of course, that's the medium we'll use to convey the information, but it has to be anonymous, because it could be dangerous if we identify ourselves. Don't forget, it might incite murder and violence, and in truth-- that's the point entirely. This card we're playing comes with warnings to impress and deter any future insider tactics— similar to our African venture. Again, the key to our success will be Press reporting, to publicize the message, as the drama unfolds.

"My letter will read something like this..." Digby studied his rough draft.

Dear ... whoever?

I am a friend, who has watched your decline over the years, since the value of your shares collapsed and the bank foreclosed on your property.

It must have been a painful personal experience to lose your house and life savings and move away from your neighbours. I offer my belated sympathy.

The purpose of this letter, with the attached details, is to inform you about the present circumstances of the person who caused you such suffering, and to give you the opportunity to redress your grief.

The perpetrator of your poverty was sentenced to minimal Community Service, and you were sentenced to a lifetime of misery.

How you propose to act on this information is entirely up to you, but it has been researched at great expense. So use it to your satisfaction.

The culprit responsible for your agony has risen from the ashes, and might wish to compensate you for the crime that cost you so dear."

Good luck, good hunting…

"Diggers, is that enough… shouldn't there be something more?"

"I don't think so. It serves its purpose, so why say any more?"

"Perhaps you're right; so what's next?"

"Preparation of the ten letters, to send to the victims we assess to be the most suitable; those who will serve our purpose and yield the most publicity, when we give them the means to plan their nemesis. And if logic prevails, their actions will be in proportion to their hurt over the years; the direr their circumstances the worse their revenge will be. Whether their actions are legal or illegal, we won't know until after our monitors report back. It's then up to the news media, to exploit these stories for all they're worth, and I'm sure you agree, they never need much encouragement to do that. I think we should congratulate ourselves. This whole plan is developing rather nicely, and after we've posted these letters, Scraggs observation teams will serve our curiosity."

"Isn't this whole thing illegal?"

"Well of course it's illegal! Tell me what isn't illegal, if we use our own initiative to balance an unjust law from the past. In truth the law is changing, but far too slowly, and people will continue to suffer if our message to deter, doesn't serve to impress potential corporate criminals."

"But Diggers, it's called incitement to violence and reaps heavy penalties."

"I have already admitted as much, and now we're into it up to our necks—you want out?"

"No, no, I was just making an observation."

"So pack your bags and we'll be on that plane tomorrow afternoon. Let's post these letters in New York."

"Is that safe?"

"Depends on how you see it, but since 9/11, New York has never been safer. Just fart and you're surrounded by cops; so you'd better stop taking those garlic pills." Digby enjoyed his ribaldry, and Rupert guffawed, to acknowledge his guilt.

"Tomorrow afternoon we'll be airborne with a selection of ten letters from our list."

"That's it?"

"Yes."

"And who's going to type the letters?"

"There's only one, and that's the covering letter which I'll do. Then I'll make ten copies with ten different addresses at the top, and the information from the reports I'll photocopy and attach them to the covering letter with a photograph. We'll send the original photo of the crook, but there's no reason why the rest of the material can't be copied. Anything else?"

"Diggers, you're brilliant."

"Why, thank you Rupert. That's the second time you've said that in as many days. It should be a good trip and don't worry about a search at JFK. The Yanks still hold the British aristocracy in awe, or what's left of it; and that's us, believe it or not."

56

"Rupert, we'll take the limo to the Chelsea Savoy; sixty-five bucks and worth every penny. New York, New York... it's fantaaastic! As Chuck would say."

"Rupert, say something?"

"I'm tired."

"We'll eat at the Irish pub next door tonight, and tomorrow we'll invade China town and see the sights-- after we finish what we came to do. On day three, we get the hell out of here and back to Blighty."

"Hey Diggers, where the hell's breakfast?"

"Oh, didn't I tell you? We have to go around the corner to the coffee shop; it's the same place we dined at last night."

"What! Some more of those bloody paper cups. No class, whatever else is buzzing in this city, it lacks class."

"But the coffee's good?"

"Yeah, I suppose so," Rupert, reluctantly agreed, "and after the coffee in paper cups. Tell me!"

"We go to Grand Central Station, to do the business in the Post Office there. And that's why we're wearing our Panama hats and shades, to fox the cameras. And please Rupert, remember-- when they say, 'hey Mac-- what's with the hats?' ignore the cheeky blighters."

The Post Office, just down from Times Square was not particularly busy; only one person stood between Digby and the counter, before he offered his letters to the clerk, who took his money and stuffed them into the sack behind him. Certainly, not an inspiring job, and not of the category Digby was likely to vie for. Rupert, in the meantime, had joined the queue at the far end of the hall and had cleared his five envelopes without a hitch.

"If you like," Digby volunteered as they exited the building, "we can go to the 'Top of the Rock', and view the city."

"And what about Ground Zero?"

"We'll do that after the Center, and at the same time we can take in the stock exchange and eat some fantastic Chinese. We must take this opportunity Crooky, to examine the gastronomic delights of New York, that are here, right under our noses."

In the final stages of their meal, they were sipping jasmine tea when Rupert mentioned his concern in respect of the morning's activities. "Didn't you feel uncomfortable in that post-office?"

"Yes; why of course I did. What are you getting at?"

"Nothing, perhaps I imagined it; but when I think back, the number of CCTV's really surprised me, and then there was that green-eyed monster at JFK that stole my facsimile as it grabbed my prints on the counter. Didn't even bother to take the best side of my face," he joked.

"How many times have I told you— don't even fart near me or I might mistakenly be arrested for you." Digby laughed, they were in buoyant mood; they were on their way home.

57

A sense of relief was noticeable, and Digby stated the obvious. "Thank God we're home; we shouldn't be travelling such distances at our age, but there again, if you want it done properly… Well, now it's up to Scraggs, to monitor the ten we chose from his list, and I rather suspect it'll only be a couple of days before things begin to warm up." The plan, launched from Grand Central, was now in the hands of the postal authorities to deliver; the fuse was lit, and Scraggs' men were being deployed.

The chickens in the yard were scratching dirt and pecking at bits of nothing. The high cost of oil had driven the price of feed beyond his reach. But the connection between oil and feed was a mystery to Jake, who had never really understood figures, and had lost confidence in the government long ago— from the time of the Unicom collapse. That collapse had snatched the sweated legacy of his parents from his grasp and ripped the heart out of his life, reducing him to the status of a lowly farmer scratching a living from the soil; just like the chickens whose eggs he sold for a pittance.

"Martha!" Jake shouted. "There's one of them official envelopes here for us. Open it and read it out; can't find my frigging glasses…"

"Ooh… it looks important," Martha cooed. Aven't saw one of them like this before, not in the whole of my life..."

"Marthaaa! Open it, and stop blabbering woman."

"Louder woman, you're mumbling— here give it to me! I'll do it myself. Always have to do it myself when I want some sense out of life." He grabbed the letter from Martha and held it at full arms length under the light, and read it silently to himself.

"Shit! I don't believe it."

"You don't believe what?"

"After all these years, I see satisfaction... It's a miracle just waiting to happen, to ease my mind. I'll sleep tonight, you'll see." He strode over to the cupboard in the hall, and almost disappeared inside it before he emerged with a pump-action shotgun, which hadn't seen the light of day since his inherited land was sold to pay his debts, as his stocks collapsed.

"Jake, what are you doing with that gun? Put it back in the cupboard where it belongs. You killed defenseless animals with it before, and now there's nothing to kill anyway."

"I remember you enjoyed cooking and eating such defenseless animals. So just watch it go back to work on animals... that's just what they are— fucking animals!"

"See this!" he waved the letter in the air and cast it aside, "it's the answer to all my worrying over the years. I'm going to nail this motherfucker, whose living it up on my mother's sweat in the fields."

"Leave it be Jake! Put that gun back in the cupboard. There're times to forgive and forget."

"Never! Never!" He checked the pump action to make sure it was loaded, and strode with purpose toward the battered utility. Standing the gun upright between the seats, he slid in beside it and cranked the engine.

Martha picked up the discarded letter and studied the details.

"'My God!" she raised her free hand to her forehead, "he's going to kill someone."

"Emergency control Syracuse P.D, how can we assist?"

"It's my husband! He's going to kill someone! You've got to stop him!"

"Can I have your address, ma'am?" the voice was calm.

"There's no time, you'll be too late."

"Where is your husband now?"

"He's on his way across town!"

"Ma'am, stay calm. Now give me the address he's heading for."

"It's in the letter."

"Is it there with you?"

"It's somewhere here, yes, yes! I've got it!"

"Right, now read the address to me slowly."

"It's in the Armory Square neighbourhood, 4, Lexington Gardens."

"Now can you give me your address?" the line was silent. "Can you do that?" he coaxed.

"South Salina. 34, Bridge Road."

"We'll be in touch. Now you leave everything to us."

The sirens on the black and whites were heard before they were anywhere near Armory Square, and they drowned out the sound of the single-shot on the perimeter fence as they swerved to a halt. It was an accurate shot, and the body fell forward to offer the macabre of a sizzling steak, as the brains of the host cooked next to the sausages, and the fork he was holding was stuck in the grass like a bolt from the heavens. Screams, shouts, and the pandemonium that followed were to no avail— the police had arrived too late.

"Hands-on-head: now! Do it!" the policeman shouted, steadying his pistol with two hands and pointing it at Jake. Jake instantly dropped his gun. "Down, face down!" he was pushed to the ground.

"Hands behind back," the officer shouted. "Now! Do it!" Jake obeyed without another thought in his head. He was cuffed, dragged to his feet, and ducked into the cruiser. By now the 'cooking cook' had been pulled off the flames, with melted sausage like features. A hardened policeman dived for the fence to vomit, and then returned to the scene to cover the hideous mask with a barbecue apron.

"No, no! I tried so hard to save him and I failed him." Martha wailed. Her head was buried in her hands after receiving a personal call from the area Police Chief to commiserate, and praise her for her prompt civic action. When they did eventually meet, he laid a comforting hand on her shoulder and promised a meeting with Jake before he was transferred."

"I haven't felt so good in years," declared Jake, to his free legal counsel.

"Jake, hear me. This could be first degree murder," his counsel warned.

"I feel great. I'll sleep well tonight, wherever I am."

58

Scraggs' man hadn't been prepared for the instant eruption that followed the mailing, and was not on the spot when Jake 'exploded'. In fact, he'd just booked into the motel and was about to start his survey in the area, when he heard the police sirens that quickly faded into the posh part of town. If only he had known what they were trying to tell him, his report might have been the first to reach Digby, in England, but when it did eventually arrive, another fatality was already in Digby's hands.

And that had only arrived sooner, because of the close proximity between the victim and the aggrieved; they lived in adjoining streets and were similarly wealthy. The victim of the corporate crime, who had been informed by one of the letters, had neither, a red nor green mark against his name. He was one of the few neutral assessments, who had been luckily cushioned by a win on the state lottery around the same time as his loss. Nevertheless, he felt cheated, the pressure had built up over years, and Digby's information was the match, to light the fuse. He also genuinely believed, he could murder with impunity, and his latent hatred spurred him on to take revenge. On the same day that he received his letter, he had waited for darkness to fall, before he ventured into the night like a common thief. He would surely have gone undetected, had Scraggs second man-on-spot, not been observing the victim's residence. When the shot rang out, Rockford quietly climbed out of his vehicle and slipped into the shadows of the telephone shelter, to observe the house more closely. Only seconds passed before a man emerged in a nonchalant manner from the place of the shooting, and strolled toward a house in the adjoining street. The sequence of events, keenly followed by Rockford, was then telephoned into the police anonymously, and served to soothe his civic conscience.

Basking in a glow of good citizenry, he then returned to his car to relax. But the shock of a knock on his window jerked him out of his mood—the helmeted cop silhouetted against the sky was most unexpected. He powered down his window for a closer look and the figure saluted his effort. "May I see your license, Sir?" Rockford handed it over, and the beam of the flashlight told the story. "I see you don't live in this area, Sir. Why are you here, Mr. Rockford?"

"I've been on the road for the past six hours, and have just pulled out of the traffic for a rest. I'm sure you understand, I don't want to fall asleep at the wheel."

"Would you mind stepping out of the car, Mr. Rockford?"

"Is there a problem Officer?"

"Put your hands on the roof." Rockford obeyed, and stretched over his own car to be frisked for the first time in his life—his weapon was found.

"You're licensed to carry, Mr. Rockford?"

"I work for Scraggs and Scratchit International detective agency, and to answer your question—yes, I'm licensed to carry. It's all here in my billfold." Rockford took out the appropriate legalization and also offered his business card. "Just a couple of questions, Mr. Rockford. Did you use the public telephone at the corner?" He pointed to the booth. "And how long have you been here?"

"No, I didn't even know it was there," he lied; he didn't want to be involved. "About twenty minutes," he lied again, to make sure he wasn't on 'the spot' when he reported the matter.

"I suggest you go on your way Mr. Rockford. There's been a murder in this area and we're checking everyone out. Someone tipped us off using that phone over there, and whoever it was left the receiver hanging off the hook, to make sure the call was traced to this area. Strangely enough, it was also a man's voice that called in and gave us the addresses," he insinuated the source, but didn't press further.

"Well, I've no need to explain it to you Mr. Rockford, you're in the business; but you tell me why a murderer would want to tip off the police? That's who the lieutenant thinks it was, but I personally think it had to be a passer by; the strangest things always occur when you least expect it. No matter, we're still looking, and we'll eventually find our witness. Good night, Sir." He offered a casual salute, and Rockford cursed his stupidity at having left the phone off the hook as a second lead to the scene of the crime.

"What did he have to say for himself?" the lieutenant at the telephone booth asked the motorcycle cop as he pulled up and remained seated on his bike. "His name's Rockford, a private dick from out of town. He gave me some bullshit story about pulling off the highway for a rest. He was legally carrying a .38 S & M. But the true reason why he was here on the spot, remains a mystery. Anyway, we can always haul him in. He said he didn't use this phone, and he had only been here in his car for the last twenty minutes, which places him out of the time frame."

"The set of prints on this receiver is going to tell the tale," he waved one of his men over from the sidewalk. "John, see if you can get a match on these." He handed over the telephone receiver cut from the booth, which had been placed in the usual specimen bag. "Let's see what that turns up," he confided to the helmeted cop, who was the only other person on the spot, showing any interest. The real manpower had gravitated to the address reported by the caller, and had made an arrest of the number one suspect after a preliminary search.

"I have it!" declared the forensic man in triumph, as he flicked open the top of the writing bureau, and saw the letter, open full page. A portrait picture was stapled in the top corner.

"Look at this," he left it in place and read the details.

"It's absolute poison!"

"Get the photographer here, and everyone out. And chase that bloody cat out of here. I don't want it shitting on the evidence." The cat was the only resident left.

As the phone booth detective headed for his transport, he confided to the motorcycle cop who was standing beside his bike.

"By the way, we already have a suspect in custody from the address we got from the caller. He's down at the station with his lawyer right now. No weapon has been found so far, but it's bound to turn up; it always does."

59

"Rupert, please come over and spend the night. Things are getting a bit out of hand, but I'll explain when I see you." Digby, in his own estimation, had entirely misjudged the operation. Scraggs' monitoring of the ten addressees had so far reported three deaths, as a result of his letters; perhaps it was time to inform the police of the remaining few on the list.

Urgent counseling with Rupert, to stop the slaughter without incriminating themselves, needed discussion, if lives were to be saved, now that they were assured of the right publicity. Of course, he had known all along when the plans were originally thought out, that there were going to be a few hot heads, and perhaps, one or two deaths. But at this moment the bomb was ticking for others to die, where revenge had yet to respond, and his dilemma was, the reaction of the police. If he reported the full extent of the operation to save more lives, where would it leave him and Rupert?

"Rupert, disaster-- bloody disaster! We have to act now before any more die." Digby was frazzled.

"What?"

"We need to talk."

"Diggers, from the way you're acting, not only do we need to talk, but you need a double whiskey to steady your nerves. And if it's as bad as you are making out, I think I'll join you." He placed the bottle on the table between them.

"Ten letters and five deaths, so far... God only knows, where it's all going to end. We can tell Scraggs to warn the other potential victims by phone and they can take precautions, but it's the other side of the equation that points directly at us, that worries me. And that Scraggs, could also shop us, when he finds out he's been used as a conduit to commit murder; because that's what he is, if we look at it truthfully: a conduit."

"Have the police Stateside, found any of the letters we posted?"

"How would I know that? If they've got any of the suspects in custody they're bound to have found something that'll lead them to Scraggs, or worse still, to us. It's then that Scraggs' organization will realize we're somehow connected to the crimes; and so I suppose, is he."

"It seems there's nothing much we can do without incriminating ourselves, other than telling Scraggs to warn those potential victims that are not yet dead. On the other hand, if we keep quiet, surely there's a chance no more will get killed; perhaps this is the lot, and the others are not interested— maybe they're considering legal action? But whichever way you look at it, it's a bit late in the day to be applying the brakes now." Rupert finished his analysis.

"I'm inclined to agree with you Crooky, if we can't do something without incriminating ourselves, we keep quiet, and hope the whole thing blows over."

"Another thought just occurred to me."

"What?" Digby was agitated.

"Well, if they find some of our letters they're also going to find our finger prints on them. We should have worn those rubber gloves you see on TV."

"So now you tell me-- thanks a lot, Rupert Crook."

"I say we lie low and say nothing, and see what happens. Neither do we say anything to Robertson.

"Tell me Rupert, why are you suddenly full of ideas; it's so unlike you? Let the matter rest for now-- I don't want to hear another word." Fingerprints, and rubber gloves, were not of Digby's choosing.

60

"Interesting, very interesting; that's what I like to see." Detective Captain Dwight Billings was looking at two almost identical letters, found at the homes of the murderers; both of whom were in custody. "Have you anything else Lieutenant?"

"The people who wrote those letters are of English origin. I base my theory on the fact that they spelt 'neighbours' with a 'u', which to me is a sure giveaway. Another most extraordinary thing is the fingerprints on the letters that I double-checked myself. I find it hard to believe, but they belong to Lord Banks and Lord Crook-Smith of the British House of Lords; and about that there's no doubt. I have positive ID from the recent immigration forms they filled in at JFK a couple of weeks back, plus one of the envelopes dated and stamped, that circumstantially ties them to Times Square Post Office at the time of their visit."

"So, tell me about the CCTV footage at Times Square?"

"I've called for it, and if I was a betting man I'd put all my money on the chances that these English Lords will show up on the footage. Either inside the post office, or going into it at around the time stamped on the recovered envelope."

"I'd bet on that too. Now what about the prints on the phone-booth receiver?"

"Ah, that's another piece of good or bad news, depending on how you see it. The Private Investigator, we found at the scene of the first crime, apparently lied to the patrolman. We matched his prints from his license to those on the phone receiver. He isn't the killer, but he needs to explain why he hung around after he phoned in the message about what had occurred. He knew something was going on in that area, and I want to know how."

"Thanks Lieutenant. I have a strange feeling it's these Brits that are going to screw me, because if it's true they were around the post office at all the right times, it's big shit. I'll have to inform the FBI and the State Governor's office. I need those CCTV's a.s.a.p. on this desk."

"We hear you Captain, an' you got it."

"Wait one! First, get that Private Dick in here, and kick ass! I want everything he knows, and promise him immunity from aiding and abetting etc., providing he offers you something useful. Got that?"

"Rockford! Either you come down here to the station pronto or I put out an APB and you come here in cuffs." The Sergeant was kicking ass, and five minutes later Rockford appeared at the front desk.

"What's with you Rockford, you tell shit to the patrolman and you're compounding a felony—that's how I see it. You want to keep your license?"

"Am I supposed to be shitting myself? You don't scare me. What do you allege I've done?" He pointed a finger at his accuser.

"It's what you didn't do... that you should be worrying about. Your prints were all over that phone...why?"

"Okay, okay, I admit I knew something was likely to happen in the area over the next couple of days, because that was my assignment– to observe and report. But in truth, I didn't know what to expect while I was waiting there. I was one of two, in a 24-hour stake out, when I heard the shot and investigated the scene. Then I informed you where the killer was living as my civic duty, and that's about it.

"How did you know where the killer was living, when you were parked around the corner in your car?"

"I got out of the car when I heard the shot, didn't I? And it may come as a surprise to you, but that's what trained observers do. It was my diligence that located that address, and you guys should be bloody grateful." Irritation showed in his voice. "Only an idiot policeman would park directly outside a house under surveillance, but why should I tell you what you already know."

"I'm listening." The interviewing policeman refused to be baited.

"I had the victim's address, and that's the place I was staking out. I didn't know what was going to occur until I heard that single shot, and saw a man casually walking by, whom I judged to be the killer. I didn't know where he lived before that time, and I didn't even care. But after the event I had two addresses: the house of the homicide and that of the killer. But I didn't want to get involved with you and all your forms, since I was also reporting to my boss, and I can do without parallels."

"Very noble of you, Mr. Rockford. So where did you get this person's address from, before he was killed? Let me guess the answer to that. You knew all the time he was going to be killed; didn't you?"

"No, I didn't. My instructions were to observe and report on this person's pattern of activities for the next ten days. That was the maximum of my budget from Scraggs and Scratchit."

"Holy cow! What type of name is that? Scratchit and what?"

"Scraggs. It's an old English firm based in London, but they have registered offices here in town."

"Okay, you walk for now Rockford. But I'll check your story out, and if just one word doesn't fit, you're in big shit, and next time you'll be staying over. Got it?" Rockford didn't look back.

It was bold and true to life; the big black lettering on the frosted glass door was prominently painted in the up-market building. "Scraggs and Scratchit," specialized in almost everything under the sun, or so it seemed to Billings, as he ran his eye down a list so long, he found it impossible to memorize anything. He followed through his knock on the door, leaving the torrent of confusion behind him.

"How can I be of assistance to you Captain?" His presence was of no surprise; the prospect had already been conveyed to him by Rockford. "Tea, or perhaps you prefer coffee?"

"Mr. Scraggs, I presume?" Captain Billings wasn't quite sure whom he was addressing.

"Yes, that's right Captain, you're rather lucky to catch me. I'm only in the States for a week at a time. So how can I be of assistance?"

The Captain coughed and cleared his throat, feeling slightly uncomfortable; he found himself in a nineteenth century room full of eccentricities. A large world-globe stood on the floor in the corner next to a roller topped desk. A quill and a silver inkwell also caught his eye and added to the unusual. He accepted the delicate china cup of English tea with a certain amount of apprehension.

"Actually Mr. Scraggs, I was going to send my deputy, but I have made the effort to come myself because I regard this case as extra sensitive. It involves Lord Banks, and Lord Crook-Smith, whom I assume are your clients."

"Why do you say that?"

"Mr. Scraggs, this is bigger than both of us, and I was rather hoping to hear your side of the story, detective to detective, before I brief the FBI who will, no doubt, forward my findings to the AG."

"Captain, put your cards on the table, spell it out, and if it is to the benefit of whom ever you mentioned, I can pass on a message, and I'll do just that." He didn't actually admit he was representing anyone.

"Well, for starters, your man Rockford has been caught with his pants down— staking out from his car on your behalf. And what's more, he gave false information to a police officer at the scene of a crime. His fingerprints gave him away in the end— very amateurish of him, and you have my sympathy Mr. Scraggs. I know how difficult it is to get good staff these days. It appears we're bearing a common cross, in that respect."

Scraggs was noticeably softened by his remarks, and offered an involuntary smile, to show he wasn't devoid of the problems they both faced.

"I'm here because he led me to you, and I'm grateful we have the murderer in custody because of him. However, what we can't understand is why he lied to us in the first place. He denied he was the person who called into the station reporting the incident, and then he went on to defend his action by quoting the numerous forms he would have had to complete down at the station."

"I don't understand, Captain. Why would he do that?"

"Possibly to protect his surveillance project?" the Captain queried, "and the good reputation of your firm. I believe his intentions were good as a law-abiding citizen and a loyal employee, and I know for sure, he had nothing to do with the murder. But in the end he led me to you, which brings me to the conclusion, you're the right man to confirm what instructions these English Lords gave to you."

"Captain, you know I can't do that— client confidentiality. I can't even admit, I'm employed by these English Lords."

"Mr. Scraggs, the circumstantial evidence tells me you are, but I am a reasonable man and that's why I'm here. So please hear this, and pass it on to the clients you're 'not representing'." He put his index finger to the side of his nose in a conspiratorial sign they both understood, and smiled for the first time, since he entered the room.

"The house of the murderer was searched and a letter was found from the Lords, giving the name and address of a past CEO, who had scammed the murderer of a considerable amount of money some years ago. This letter is not an isolated one, there are others followed by homicides, and the chain of irrefutable evidence leads me to believe your clients will eventually have to answer to the US Justice Department."

"Captain, I'll make a deal with you. You tell me what evidence you have and I'll tell you what my instructions were. What do you say that?"

"First, you tell me what instructions you received, and then I'll give you the proof we have for a case."

"Captain, the other way around if you please." he smiled and received a smile in return.

"Mr. Scraggs, please… someone has to begin or we'll be here all night! Okay, I'll concede, because I want you on that phone to your Lords in England without further delay. They don't yet know it, but I've got them by the balls."

"Ah, that remains to be seen." Scraggs was used to tough language and gave nothing away.

"From my side, Mr. Scraggs— a letter written by your Lords was recovered at the crime scene with their fingerprints all over it, identical to their entry prints at JFK. Also, an envelope was recovered, dated and timed, that matched the CCTV footage of the Lords in person outside the Post Office, Times Square. We also have some more shots of them queuing inside handing in letters for posting. They wore crummy Panama hats and sunglasses, and stood out like freaks, but the horizontal cameras looked them straight in the eye. It was them all right. That's as far as I go for now Mr. Scraggs, but we're working on charges to indict them."

"Captain, if what you're saying is correct, this has to be incitement to murder, but the only instruction I received from the Lords was to trace twenty people, who had served community service time, for insider trading. Lord Banks, told me, he wanted to be sure they hadn't fallen on hard times after their convictions for creaming-off shares. And he further described to me, the rap on the knuckles these people received from your judiciary, with a few months' community service, but by this time Lord Digby was rambling on and I didn't really get the drift; other than his primary instructions. Interestingly enough, nothing was said to me about the poor devils on the other side. Those who had lost their property, houses, lifestyles, and most of all their savings, weren't mentioned at all. But with your latest information, I rather suspect they set up the 'community servers' as victims, for those who sought revenge. How exactly it was done, I cannot say, but from what you tell me, and from what I know, there must be ten pitted against ten, because that's the size of my stake out, and we have five deaths so far."

"Mr. Scraggs, where are your men staked out for the other five."

"They're still out there, but they haven't reported any movement. This is the list; please use it." He pushed one of the photocopies across the desk. "Hang on, I'll try to contact the Lords for the other side of the equation. Give me five minutes." The phone rang twice before it was answered. "Hallo," it was Digby on the end of the line and Scraggs recognized the 'hello' despite its brevity.

"Lord Banks, this is Mr. Scraggs, calling from New York. I'll come straight to the point. There are five people out there, who could get killed, if I don't get the addresses of the victims of the Community Servers, to whom I now believe, you dispatched ten letters. It's gone too far and people are dying. I beg of you my Lord! We have to save the others."

Digby couldn't believe his ears. Only the night before he had discussed his concern at the outcome of his plans with Rupert. They had even debated how the situation could be contained, and now the answer had fallen into his lap. He didn't think twice about the possible consequences to himself. "The names are as follows," he read out ten names and addresses for Scraggs to take his pick, of those still outstanding. "Is there anything else I can assist you with?"

"No my Lord, but I thank you profoundly." Scraggs, remained civil, it was in his nature even though he felt duped.

"Thank you Mr. Scraggs, I owe you one." Captain Billings dashed for the door with the information, time was of essence, and he needed men on the ground.

"I want you, you, and you, and you Sergeant will lead the team. Your instructions are to find and detain these people," he handed out Scraggs' list that by then had been copied several times over. "Divide the areas you're familiar with among yourselves and tell me when these people are apprehended. Remember, you're dealing with disturbed people, so I want you to do the job hands on. No screaming sirens and high profile arrests; do it quietly and with understanding, and hold them under the Homeland Security Act until I tell you what to do with them. I'll inform the FBI later, but for the present, I'm sure you can handle the emergency more quickly. Spare no extremes; this is a national disaster. Seek, find, detain, and be careful. Treat them as dangerous. Do I make myself clear?"

"Yes Captain," they chorused.

"Okay. Move out!"

61

"Conrad Black?"

"Yes?"

"It's Special Agent 'Ginge' O'Hara FBI. We met at the Washington conference last year. He used 'Ginge', in spite of him being an 'Irish Patrick' through and through, because Conrad could more easily identify with the nickname they'd used at that time. I'm contacting you on behalf of my Director, to speak on a delicate subject."

"Delicate, is it that bad?"

"Could be. We're seeking extradition papers for a couple of your members of the House of Lords."

"Don't tell me, they've got themselves into some more trouble. Refresh my memory?" He acted as though he couldn't guess their names, even before he heard them.

"Lord Digby Banks and Lord Rupert Crook-Smith." O'Hara, read out from the heavy subject print at the top of the letter bearing the facts.

"I thought so. What have they done this time?"

"Incitement to murder is how I see it."

"Jesus! I know these two old dodderers. How the hell did they manage it again?"

"They've done it before?"

"Not incitement, but they've made an international nuisance of themselves before, and I was on the case. Lucky for them, the other government judged it to be a good thing; they weren't exactly heroes-- but they got away with it."

"Come over and see me if you like. Better still; come with your legal man. But I'll tell you now, if you press charges where these two are concerned, you'll make fools of yourselves. They're doing these things all the time, and past evidence from other cases has never been filed. Be assured; they'll make monkeys out of you. By all means come over Ginge, if you want to talk, but it's they who'll have the last word. The end of next week is good for me, but let me know when you decide and I'll book a hotel and pick you up at the airport— it'll be my pleasure to shake your hand again."

"I've got it. American Airlines, landing at around midnight Terminal 3, Heathrow. See you then, Ginge."

"Hi there!" Conrad stepped forward wearing his best smile.

"Hi! Good to see you Conrad." Hands were duly pumped between friends before the second member of the party was introduced. "Conrad, meet my legal counselor Russell Stanton; call him Rusty."

"Rusty, my pleasure, welcome to England. Shall we…" Conrad gestured toward the black police Jaguar that was sitting on the tarmac with the engine running. You're at the Bedford in Russell Square. No clash with your name intended Rusty," they laughed.

"Ten tomorrow. A meeting is scheduled with the Home Secretary, so I'll send a car to pick you up at around 9.30, if that's okay with you?"

"Sure thing Conrad, see you then. Good night, or perhaps I should say good morning."

"Sleep well— and a good morning to you too."

62

"Rusty. Isn't this a hell of a city-- everything's so quaint? When did you last see Big Ben?"

"Some ten years ago, I guess, it was either '97 or '98. I was with my present wife at the time, and she's been nagging me ever since to get back here. And I'll tell you this for free: it's going to get worse after this trip—the nagging I mean."

"Why don't we make it a foursome in the autumn and sort out the nagging?"

"Good thinking Ginge, I'll hold you to that: it'll also be good to take a vacation before the dollar collapses."

Home Secretary Gilmore, may I introduce two colleagues from Washington: Special Agent Patrick O'Hara, F.B.I., and Legal Counsel Russell Stanton. Their Director wants them to have a quiet word with us about the Lords. As I briefly explained, they've been misbehaving again."

"Yeah, yeah… Digby and Rupert, for God's sake."

"Yes Sir, the *enfants-terribles.*"

"What's it now, for crying out loud? Oh, Agent O'Hara, I do apologize for ranting on like this; I seem to have forgotten my manners. Gentlemen, take a seat, I'm all ears...So now, what seems to be the trouble?"

"Mister Home Secretary, to put it in a nutshell, two of your Lords have incited criminal acts in the United States to commit murder and we seek their extradition. But, before we do that, my

Director thinks a quiet word in your ear is the best way forward, to prepare for eventualities. On the surface of it, these two are jerking our country around. They think our judiciary doesn't take corporate fraud seriously enough, and they're bearing a cross for the under-dog in a fiendish way. Rusty, take over."

"Well, it's like this, Home Secretary. The Lords opened old wounds, when they informed ten victims about the present day lifestyles of the cheating executives, who had impoverished them by insider trading. On getting the news, the victims went berserk and killed five of the ex-CEOs. After the Lords saw what was happening, they supplied information to us to arrest the balance of the ten before they could do any harm. But that really doesn't solve the problem: the charge to incite remains."

"Mr. Stanton, have you caught any of those incited to kill?"

"Yes. We have two in custody on homicide charges and three turned their guns on themselves after they killed their victims— an extraordinary pattern by any standards. I've never witnessed such behavior before."

"You're saying you have eight deaths to date, and five former CEOs are out there, who don't even know they could be targets."

"That's about it Mr. Minister, and we're in the process of hauling in the other five, who haven't responded to date."

"Mr. Stanton, tell me, how did you find out who was on the hit list, and how did you discover it in the first place?"

"Well, that's the strange thing about it. As I've already said...the Lords gave the New York State Police their full list when they heard how their plans had misfired. Mind you, I'm only guessing their plans had misfired, and they are the only persons who would know that for sure. But one thing I'm damn sure about is, they didn't expect to have blood on their hands to this extent. In my assessment, they didn't intend to kill at all, but they recognized the potential of people getting hurt from the information they supplied. Otherwise, why the stake out, and what was their reason behind it?"

"Mr. Stanton, what is the oldest person you know of to have been extradited to stand trial in any country in the world? Seventy, eighty, perhaps ninety, but I regard the extradition of Eichmann and Pinochet as exceptions, and one of a kind."

"I can't recall offhand, but I would say eighty, is top of the shop for America."

"Don't get me wrong, Mr. Stanton. I hold no briefs for criminals. I'm a lawyer myself by training, but I prefer the excitement of a political career. These Lords, quite frankly, are a pain in my butt, but they are charismatic figures and likeable rogues. I would think their lineage, comes from the times of smuggling barrels of rum on the south coast of England, to avoid excise duties. Both of them, inherited peerages rather late in life, after their fathers passed on--to God only knows, where. They're the types, who are quite capable of swaying any jury in their favour, using their bearing, and charm, whatever the charges. I've met them, and I know them, and they have an aura about them. By the way, I used the American expression 'butt', to be understood." A lighter moment filtered into the meeting, and Gilmore even detected a smile from Rusty, unlike the others, who actually laughed.

"Minister, I believe you're trying to tell us something?"

"I am indeed: if you follow the law and have these fellows extradited, which I think is entirely possible, you shouldn't be surprised if you don't get a conviction; even if they're as guilty as hell in the eyes of the law. And it will be because corporate frauds are in the spotlight in America today, and most of your citizens, including members of the jury, have been touched by share manipulation, monopolization, price fixing and cartelism— all part of the broader picture. It therefore follows, as well you know, all the sympathy is on their side. And, by the way, the two old men you're after are in their eighty-sixth year. They call them 'the terrible twins' in the Lords--so I hear."

"Can we meet them face to face?"

"Mr. Stanton, Agent O'Hara, they are not under arrest, and if you would like to contact them, I'm sure Conrad, here, can arrange it. How about it Conrad?"

"Delighted Minister! I always seem to learn something from them, and I'm sure our American friends, will also—learn something from them."

"Thank you for your time, gentlemen. I wish you a pleasant stay while you're over here." The Minister passed through the door into his main office and left them to their discussions in his anti-chamber.

"What do you think Rusty?" Ginge posed the question.

"I don't know what to make of the Minister's comments. What do you think?"

"Well, one thing's certain, we have to meet the Lords before we go any further," he turned toward Conrad, and offered a questionable glance. "Please Conrad, we need help?"

"I want to speak to Lord Banks, and would you please come back on this extension," the secretary would know where to find him. "In the meantime gentlemen, can I offer you a coffee?"

"Yes Sir?" a head appeared around the door in answer to the button.

"Three coffees, and some of those chocolate biscuits the Minister favors, if you're still handing them out?"

"Right you are, Sir, give me five minutes."

The phone rang; "Lord Banks on the line three, Sir."

"Lord Banks! Detective Chief Inspector Conrad Black, speaking Sir. Perhaps you recall the interview with the Lord Speaker and the Home Secretary, not so long ago."

"Yes, yes I do indeed, ended in bloody turmoil, what… eh? So how can I help you? Don't want to raise a private army by chance, do you?" He guffawed into the phone, and Conrad entered into the spirit with a slight titter.

"Not today thank you Sir, but I do have a couple of American gentlemen with me, who are dying to meet an English Lord. They also want to talk to you about your American activities. Is it possible to fix a time tomorrow Sir, and sign us into the members' lounge?"

"Delighted young man. One o'clock in the dining room. We'll see you there."

"Thank you, Sir."

"Well done Conrad. Did I hear one o'clock?"

"You did, and you are invited to lunch by their Lordships. What's more, I'm convinced you made the right decision to meet them before you go any further."

"Rusty, did you hear that, lunch with a real live Lord; wait till the wife hears about this." A certain amount of excitement could be detected in Ginger's voice, which was normal routine for the course, and expected by their Lordships, who would in turn manipulate this human weakness to their advantage.

Back at the precinct, Captain Billings was far from impressed, on seeing the dregs of humanity, detained under the Home Securities Act. He was only sorry he'd been too late to save another victim before his men had acted. A short study of the histories of those in custody, clearly explained why they had stopped short of murder, if indeed the letter could have fired their hate, had they troubled to read it. They were all old men-- suffering from the ravages of time.

"What the hell is this, Sergeant? Who are these people?" Billings didn't like what he saw.

"We collected them from the addresses you gave us—their ID's fit the names on the list."

"And the letters-- did they have the letters?"

"I've got them all here." He offered four envelopes that hadn't been opened, that were recovered from the standard tin mailboxes on the post beside the sidewalk-- none had been emptied for weeks.

"They disgust me, get rid of them."

"But Captain, we've charged them," the Sergeant didn't want to let go.

"With what?"

"Vagrancy."

"Holy cow! That's all I need. They're stinking the place out—give them a meal and fifty bucks from the benevolent fund, but get them the hell out of my sight!"

"Sergeant?"

"Captain?"

"These letters haven't yet been opened, so they don't know what's going on, and neither do you. And that's how it's going to stay. Got it?" He opened one of the four identical envelopes, and checked the contents, to make absolutely sure he had the extra evidence he believed to be there. Once confirmed, he locked all four in his safe for the Federal authorities to examine on their return from England.

63

The Lords walked in single file from the restaurant threshold toward the two strangers seated in the company of Conrad, all of whom stood as they approached the table that had been laid for six on Rupert's instructions.

"Gentlemen, the waiter will take your orders," Rupert announced as they reseated themselves.

"Then I'll tell you my side of the story," Digby, quickly chipped in, before anyone else could utter a word. "Conrad," Digby, looked in the direction of the police presence, "from now on you'll be plain Conrad to me; we're almost old friends with our regular meetings in this house-- and all that."

"Whatever you say, my lord."

"You call me Lord Digby, and my partner in crime," he chuckled, "won't mind if you call him Lord Rupert. Now please introduce us to your friends from New York. Times Square, Broadway, Madison Gardens— all fascinating spots, even if their history began around the time I was born." He laughed out loud, and received a couple of tolerant smiles in return.

"My Lords," Conrad took over. "May I introduce Special Agent Patrick O'Hara and his Legal Counsel Russell Stanton from the same organization." Digby remained seated, and reached across the table to shake the Agent's hand, and at the same time observed the strands of ginger hair that were carefully combed up and over, to cover his baldness. He judged him to be in his early fifties, and noticed a glint in his eyes that hinted of humour, as they peered from a pasty face that defined a desk-bound job. His forthright handshake, was nevertheless appreciated, opposition or not. Stanton, by contrast, was more akin to a hawk with his beak-like nose and sharpness of features, and he left Digby, in no doubt, of the challenges that lay ahead. The lizard-like coldness of his handshake also conveyed a stony message, for him to be on his guard.

"Welcome, to this humble house," Digby, spoke for both of them, gesturing with an upward motion of his hand, to the vast expanse of the fan-vaulted ceiling. "I've always wanted to meet a real live Perry Mason," he smiled at Stanton, before he turned to Patrick, "but I'm still curious about your Agent title. Are you perhaps in trade, or even scouting for talent over here?" He deliberately expressed ignorance about the Agent's occupation, to reduce his stature to that of a personage, he felt he could handle.

"Special Agent Federal Bureau of Investigation," Conrad quickly volunteered, to rescue Ginger's dignity, from what he perceived as a touchy position.

"Oh, I do apologize," Digby faked surprise.

"Rupert, do you hear that? A real live policeman— they must be onto us at last," he said in a low confidential voice, and then laughed.

"Could be, could be," was all Rupert could muster.

"Agent O'Hara, are you on duty or can we speak freely?" Digby, chuckled, and Agent O'Hara looked uncomfortable.

"Oh, it's really of no consequence Agent O'Hara, don't worry too much about it, and feel free, because in this House we say all sorts of scurrilous things about each other, since slander under this roof, doesn't exist." Digby was in his element, dispensing a touch of tradition. "Anyway, even if you are on duty we'll be delighted to answer your questions. Didn't Conrad tell you, we're really rather good at answering questions." He cast his mind back to the last session in the Lord Speaker's Chambers.

"Who's having the partridge?" Rupert changed the subject and the Legal Counsel volunteered to try it.

"We've been wondering all week what that partridge was like: isn't that right, Diggers? One can't be too careful with bird flu flying around. Diggers, get it? Bird-flu, 'flying around'." Stanton was deliberately made to feel uncomfortable, but refused to change his order; an action that was duly noted and acknowledged by a mischievous twinkle in Rupert's eye, followed by a wink in Digby's direction, when no one was looking.

"Yes, yes, we did Crooky. And now we'll find out from Perry Mason. Excuse me... I've forgotten your name."

"Stanton. ... Russell Stanton," he veiled his annoyance.

"Ah, I've got it now; won't forget it again; so sorry Mr. Stanton."

"Now where is this man Humphrey?" Digby asked, and the eyes of the whole table looked in the direction of the empty chair. "Rupert, are you sure he was invited?"

"Of course I am, I personally invited him."

"He's the Lord Speaker." Digby explained for the benefit of his guests, "and today he appears to be most unreliable– if Rupert really did invite him. No matter-- we start without him."

"I believe you were in New York just recently, Lord Digby?" Special Agent O'Hara posed his first question.

"Yes, yes indeed. We attended a book launch and did a little business; the weather was fabulous. Mind you, three days was far too short, but the House was sitting at the time and bills had to be put to the vote. Majorities, quorums, and all that sort of stuff, and quite honestly, it's lucky we were here; some only scraped through by a whisker."

"And at that time you posted ten letters to victims of corporate fraud?"

"Patrick, I'll call you Pat if you don't mind. The only reason you took some of the recipients into custody so quickly, was because of my information to Scraggs, my private eye, who was with one of your Police Captains when our plans had gone terribly awry, and people were dying at the drop of a hat. So, in all decency, it just had to stop. Perhaps I should give you some of our background if you're to appreciate the bigger picture. We, that is Rupert and I, have already fought an anti-corruption campaign in Africa, and made an impression. In fact, our small contribution to a highly respected

African nation, was recognized by their refusal to apply for our extradition." He conveniently overlooked the technicalities of the law that prevented it.

"So after that success, we trained our sights on Corporate America, when we saw how President Bush, had originally legislated against Corporate Fraud in 2002 and how derisory the sentences were, before revision of the law in 2003. For instance, 600 million dollars of insider dealing received a sentence of just six months Community Service – hellish unfair to those who lost their shirts-- don't you think? In those days, the insiders also tended to keep their ill-gotten gains.

We believed when we launched our plan, that if the victims knew the present day bloatedness of those responsible for their ruin, they would take legal action to redress the imbalance." He stated what he would have them believe, though he and Rupert had doubted from inception, that nicety would follow their information package on reaching the victims.

"Unfortunately, we misjudged their anger," Digby lied, "we really had no idea of the festering hate that existed," he lied again… and this time Rupert supported his lie with a nod of his head. "We couldn't imagine people would end up getting killed, but now that it's happened there's nothing much we can do about it. Perhaps we should look on the brighter side of our action, since it's now water under the bridge, so to speak..."

"Hold it right there!" Stanton was far from happy. "Consequences have to be accepted by those responsible for such actions, and both of you are in the 'food chain'." He pointed rudely at Digby, and Rupert.

"Forget the 'food chain' and get to the facts Mr. Legal Counsel." Digby was also annoyed. "There's no going back, so we must look to the future, and what does that tell us? Corporate thieves are now on notice from the warning shot we fired across their bows, and future thefts are going to attract dire consequences. Surely that's a good thing – it must deter, and save both of you the trouble of having to deal with such burgeoning cases in the future."

"If that's what you think-- I feel sorry for you. In my book, murderers are jailed for life."

"On the contrary Mr. Stanton, none will be jailed for life. It just won't happen with your present judicial system as we now stand, and the failure of a prosecution will be a double warning to crooks in the future. The relatives of those who were killed by our scheme will blame you, and not us, when you fail in your prosecutions … you know why?"

"You tell me: you seem to know so much about American law," a note of sarcasm was matched by a smirk.

"I only know what I read, and as I see it, those who killed will survive, whether or not you risk your reputation and put them on trial."

"Risk what?"

"Your reputation, of course. If this rookie lawyer understands the law as it works in America today," he pointed to himself. "I'll be brief: I don't know of anyone in America, with or without a friend or relative, not touched by corporate fraud. Look at Enron, World. Com, Dynegy, Morgan Stanley and hundreds more."

"What do you think Pat?" Digby asked.

"Leave me out of this; I'm just a simple policeman."

"Russell, you carry on," the Agent told his subordinate.

"Here's another point to consider..." Digby ploughed on. "Where will you find an unbiased jury, composed of jurors not influenced by the plight of the victims, and who cares about the villains who died as my plan went awry?"

"I'm sure that…" Russell began...

"Let me finish," Digby rudely insisted. "These so-called killers were only seeking true justice, because of the leniency shown by judges to white-collar crimes in the past. Am I right?"

"You listen to me;" Stanton, pointed at Digby. "I let you have your say; now it's my turn." Digby gave way. "The courts passed sentences based on the facts they possessed at that time, and neither you nor I know what these facts were." He defended the judiciary.

"Come on Rusty, the truth of the matter is, the sentences didn't match the crimes whatever the facts. But today, juries will interpret these killings for what they are, justifiable homicide, a backlash of pent-up emotions attempting to cleanse the corporate system of fraudsters!"

"Never heard such garbage in my life, you're crazy!" Rusty seethed, as he thought of Digby's cleansing theory, to justify homicide.

"You think I'm crazy, do you?" Digby's bucolic nose began to glow; it always glowed more deeply when he got angry. "If I'm crazy, you have to be insane! Clearly, these killers were deranged before my letters reached them. Why…? Because they couldn't afford legal counsel to redress their grievances at the time they happened, and my information only served to rekindle, the hate for their suffering, building up over the years. That's the truth… so you calm down."

"I won't calm down! Just you listen to me!"

"Hold it! Hold it!" Agent O'Hara held up his hands. "We're getting nowhere. Why don't we wrap it up for today, and think things out more slowly. There's absolutely no need for this aggravation."

"Okay okay, sorry I blew my top." Russell generously apologized.

Digby, was going into a sulk, but surprisingly changed his mind. "I too apologize unreservedly, but I would like to drag an opinion out of Pat, before we retire to the lounge-- if I may?" Digby coaxed a response, with a grimacing smile.

"Ask away." Agent O'Hara was trapped.

"Pat—do you think I'm crazy?"

"Well of course I don't, I believe you've made your point."

"Thank you Pat, and as far as I'm concerned your opinion just about wraps it up. You've confirmed what I wanted to hear." Agent O'Hara frowned, and Digby leaned forward to impart a word on a more intimate note, to both of them. "Of course you know, you have a hopeless task, and I pity you your jobs in the nicest way if you'll pardon me for saying so. But, have I got news for you!"

"For us, Lord Digby, you have news?" Pat asked, and offered an expectant smile.

"I don't know if it's that much of a surprise to you Pat, but Rupert and I won't be coming to New York, and we won't be standing trial."

"Oh, why's that?"

"As I see it, I gave information to your Captain to prevent further murders when I saw what was happening. So first and foremost, you owe it to me, to hold off your 'hounds' until some of the murderers have passed through the legal system. Now, if by some fluke, you get a conviction of even one of these people, we'll save you the paper work and come to the States of our own volition. What's more, I'll present myself to a well-informed jury sympathetic to the little man, who in their eyes, tried to tackle corporate thieves. I assure you, they will be the types who have lost to corporate greed, and the pain they bear will be reflected in the anguish of their relatives and friends. They are the ones who will be judging my actions-- they are the ones who'll create your own worst nightmare. Remember the New York subway vigilante; he was as guilty as hell, and he walked free. We've moved on since then, but the legal system continues to fail the public, victimized by big business. Even this morning, the BBC reported another corporate scam. CEOs back dating share bonuses, to cash in on higher share prices."

"Let me give you a few more imponderables to digest. Congress isn't about to change the federal law to fit our crime. Your failure to assemble an untainted jury means we'll walk free, just like the train vigilante did, some years back. Opposing counsels can question the jurors for all they're worth before they're appointed, but in the end expediency will do the appointing, to get the show on the road. None of the prospective jurors are going to admit to being fooled by poor investment advice, but secretly, they'll welcome the opportunity to use the system to acquit the accused, which is us, and the two murderers you have in custody. What's more, psychiatrists say, the hiding of such secrets is bound to affect the verdict in our favour, so we can afford to take the chances. Now, if you're wise, the only good to come out of this business will be the lack of our presence. But, if you have other ideas and insist on pressing ahead with our extradition, there's another obstacle in your way. I'll call it 'domestic fear' for want of a better name. Your Attorney General, who is burdened by internal political pressures, will turn you down, and then you'll be forced to drop all charges before the law makes an ass out of you. In fact, the only thing that could possibly be in your favour, is for us to meet our maker before we meet you in court." He laughed, relaxed, turned on the charm, and the bush fire spread to the visitors faces.

"Who wants apple pie and ice cream? It's the best dish north of the Thames," Digby declared.

"If I've left anything out Rusty, feel free to ask questions."

Conrad sat back bemused, not having heard anything like it before in the whole of his chequered career. Somehow, he felt proud to be British; the presentation was so well made-- with or without the murders.

"Lord Digby," Pat spoke in place of Rusty, after a pause to reflect. "I admire your guts, but we have no questions to ask at this point, and we can't comment on your proposals right now, but I'm sure they'll be considered. If it's any consolation to you, I see merit in what you say, and I know many people in America who think like you do. And I'll say this...if they found out about your concern for those who lost money to corporate greed, they'd be praising your efforts and demanding a tickertape-parade down Broadway. What say you Rusty?"

"Sure thing Ginge," his smile, melted the harshness of his face.

64

The adjacent Club class seats of O'Hara and Stanton on the Washington bound flight, offered the opportunity for them to chew over the 'ifs' and 'buts' of the law 'biting-ass'. In life, they had always been on the up and up, and weren't about to deal from the same deck of cards, used in the subway-case, to make monkeys out of themselves.

Stanton opened two miniature bottles of Chivas, and held them together as he poured their contents onto the ice in the crystal glass, specially acquired by the steward from the first class cabin. He didn't drink whiskey out of plastic in the City, and wasn't prepared to lower his standards at 30,000 feet. O'Hara was on juice for a change and wasn't that fastidious, he had only asked to retain the whole carton – hydration being the enemy.

"Pat, this nightmare isn't going to go away with my whiskey, or your juice if it comes to that. The more I think about it, the more ammunition the Lords seem to have, and they'll blast us out of the water if we let them."

"So we don't let them."

"Then we must look for damage control and not an all-out prosecution; but how?"

"I suggest, we propose to these guys in our custody, on second degree charges, that they plead guilty to something minor, and we let them off lightly." Pat suggested.

"But if we do that, we have to get them to plead guilty, to a minor offence, before we offer a lesser sentence. And why should they plead guilty to anything, when the odds are in favor of acquittal?"

"What would you do in their shoes?" Pat sought legal expertise

"I'd do what I had to do, to keep me out of prison, and a suspended sentence is the best sure option. You know something, whatever happens, they're going to make a fortune out of the literary rights after their case. They've never been anything in life and would have died paupers, if the English Lords hadn't poured gas on their 'flames'. It boils down to one thing– we must avoid becoming the butt of jokes in the press, and we shouldn't lose sight of the fact that we're in this together..."

"Good thinking Russ: you want to take me down with you."

"Call it a joint effort," Stanton laughed.

"So how do we save our skins?"

"It all depends on whether we think these cases will make or break our careers, and there's no reason to prosecute because we went to London. There are other people out there– for instance, the newly qualified with no reputation to lose– whose careers are less settled than ours. They can take on these cases."

"I don't think that's smart Russ. Give a complicated case to a guy fresh out of law school, and we'll get the blame anyway. That's a definite no-no."

"It was just a thought, on the spur of the moment." Russell offered.

"What about someone near retirement, who isn't aware of the forceful case put to us by Lord Digby. Or the whole business has to be politicized and taken out of our hands, which is probably the best solution?"

"That's it'! Stanton shouted. "We drop it into the AG's lap because of the prominent people involved, Lords from the House of Lords of England, required as prosecution witnesses before they stand trial themselves. Supposing Lord Digby is right, and the AG turns us down; then we'll have no basis to prosecute these murderers. Which means, they're off the hook, and so are we. Only if the Lords are friendly key prosecution witnesses, can we win anyway, and why should they be friendly when they want us to lose. On the other hand it's just possible, some screwball counsel might not consider them essential witnesses at all, believing the case is strong enough without them."

"Surely we'd have to offer immunity to the Lords from the 'accessory before the fact charge', if we want their co-operation. But in my opinion that's a poor exchange, and they won't be coming over here anyway– according to them. You're the expert Russ, I bow to your superior knowledge."

"My superior knowledge is it? Even if we offered immunity, are they going to bear witness against those who must be considered as part of their team– I don't think so?" Russell declared.

"Rusty, they're most probably the only people who could sway the jury in favour of the prosecution, but to do that, they would have to admit their principles that drove them forward were wrong, and so was their assessment of the pussy-footing sentences the Insiders received. And that's something they wouldn't do without huge inducement."

"Don't lose sight Pat, of the fact that we're up against old-type Lords, with firm principles, which means they could suddenly turn into hostile witnesses if they don't like our procedures. Who knows what they would say when cross-examined, and there's no earthly reason for them to co-operate; they hold most of the cards."

"Possibilities…distinct possibilities, we have to think– how long to touch down?"

"Two hours. So let's get some rest and think. Wake me up if lightning strikes." O'Hara joked.

"You do realize this could go as far as the President, and we could even get medals if we put these killers behind bars. But if we lose, we have to wonder at what price, and for how long we would have to pay?"

"Till we retire and even after that; bet your bottom dollar on it!"

"Sweet dreams…." Russell turned on his side, and faced toward the blonde, a double bed width in front of his face.

65

"Mr. Attorney General," Special Agent O'Hara was about the same age as the AG. and felt comfortable in his company. He had called on him in his chambers to brief him on the London encounter. And those in the know, always used Mr. Attorney General before they broke into more personal vocatives, which allowed conversation to flow.

"Pat, good to see you, how was it over there?"

"It was that good, we want to go back but not on business, if you know what I mean. Good people. It's the subject we discussed that nearly killed us."

"Recommendations Pat? Where do we go from here, and how do you see our way forward? Do we drag these guys over here squealing, or what?"

"Well, to begin with, they told us that they will not be coming, and extradition won't be necessary if we can win just one of our homicide cases. Which they challenged us to do if we want them here on a voluntary basis."

"The law is the law, and I assume our indictment is sufficiently strong to compel them to come over here?"

"That's what I thought, before I met them."

"And now?"

"We have to rethink the whole issue of extradition, and the whole policy of prosecuting these people. I doubt we can succeed even if they have committed murder. The jury sympathy factor is against us, and the longer the case goes on the more likely the acquittal. That's something I learned from the O.J. Simpson debacle."

"Won't it make us look bad, if we let them go?"

"Whichever way, we're going to look bad. It's just a matter of preference."

"Stanton– what does he think?"

"The same as I do. They would be difficult cases to win, and to lose such celebrated cases at this stage in our careers could be a disaster. And perhaps you, should also consider the elections at the end of this year."

"Well... someone has to take them on. They're in violation of our laws, and we have an extradition treaty between our two countries."

"We also thought we should take them on, originally. But that was before the Lords lectured us in London, about what they intended to do if we insisted on extradition."

"Oh, tell me about it."

"As I see it Ted... and Stanton agrees with me, high profile figures are involved; Members of the British House of Lords. So whether we like it or not, we have a serious problem on our hands, and I'm inclined to recommend that the case gets bogged down in the system until it's forgotten. Not the best solution, I admit, but that's how we see it from our London visit. Alternatively, perhaps a suspended sentence in absentia could be handed down, if technicalities can be found to accommodate such a verdict. Otherwise, we could appear foolish in court, and lose credibility, coupled with a fanfare from the International press."

"It sounds a hell of a mess to me Pat, and if it puts me in a bad light I'm tempted to follow your recommendations. Incidentally, your Director tells me he agrees with you, and that's why he sent you over here to explain, with your first-hand knowledge from the trip. Again, I appreciate your frankness, and if I want a second term I'm going to have to tread softly. I owe you one Pat, and when I get back in, expect greater things." He smiled, a knowing smile, and Pat understood. "Pass my best wishes on to Stanton, and tell him I admire his diplomacy."

It wasn't to be; the Attorney General and his deputy examined the two files, which had mysteriously appeared in his chambers—nobody else was prepared to touch them. They had filtered through the system slowly at first, before their hot-potato significance was recognized, for what it was worth. Dynamite!

As they jointly absorbed the contents of the two murder charges, they also came across the file to extradite two members of the House of Lords in England, which had 'thoughtfully' been batched in the same time frame as the murder charges; to add to the AG's quandary. Without too much examination, they knew an extradition charge against two Members of the British House of Lords was completely out of the question, considering the British and Americans were fighting side-by-side in Iraq and Afghanistan. But to be quite safe with this strange and isolated case, they would solicit a second opinion. Ted picked up the red phone and punched in a secure number.

"Rod, can you spare a moment? I need your opinion on a delicate matter that affects your portfolio." Rodney Johnson, the Secretary of State for Foreign Affairs, was appointed during the President's first term, and was thoroughly qualified by a wealth of previous overseas appointments.

"Sure Ted, let's meet for lunch at the Capitol, but I should warn you I fly out to the Middle - East this the evening. Is twelve noon okay?"

"Sounds good to me."

"See you then-- and I look forward to it."

"You want my advice?" Rod asked, sharing his voice with a partly filled mouth of steak.

"I know what I would do with these files Rod, but your opinion could help me quicken my steps in the direction of the shredder. You get my point?"

"Look, as I see it Ted, everyone is peeing down the leg of the guy in front. Our foreign policy is in shreds, and the only friend we have in the world is the new British Prime Minister, and the Lords are part of his establishment. I say, you leave the Lords where they are; and whether you prosecute the homicides with or without them as witnesses, is up to you. But at least with the homicides we're on home ground, and if we go down we go down. I suggest you get rid of that extradition file, and for God's sake forget it ever existed. Do the destruction yourself and make sure you have all the copies."

After the luncheon meeting, classification of the homicide files was upgraded to secret, and Stanton was informed that the AG would take decisions on 'everything' at a national level. Whatever happened to the extradition file was never acknowledged, and although he had his suspicions, Stanton could only sigh with relief in the company of O'Hara, as the Lords slipped off the hook for a second time, in their criminal careers.

The AG was about to appoint his own prosecutor. "I believe this one stands the best chance of a conviction." Ted handed his choice to his deputy.

"Yes, that's what I thought; you think we should go ahead?"

"Well, we can't back off because we might lose, and it could be a plus for the elections if we win, or even lose with a popular verdict. Either way, I see it as a win-win situation. But, I think we should exercise caution, and only prosecute one case at a time; feel the temperature of the water so to speak-- see what happens."

Three months, almost to the day, the first test case agreed by the AG for prosecution had finally been heard, and in the Judge's mind, only one verdict could be reached at the end of his summing up. All that now remained was the length of the sentence to fit the crime, as the verdict of guilty was handed down.

After four days of deliberations, and separation from their loved ones in the service of their country, the jurors were anxious to go home, and a weekend behind closed doors was the only cloud on the horizon. An expeditious, unanimous decision was in the seeking.

Many a juror with less personal involvement would have thrown in the towel long ago, in return for a verdict of guilty. The evidence overwhelmingly favoured conviction, no matter how extenuating the circumstances were, but it was the Foreman who had led the rebellion as he addressed the other eleven. He recounted the moment of his father's fatal heart attack, when he heard that insider-traders had flushed his life savings down the pan. Two other members then stated their problems, when they had experienced deaths in their families, about the time of their losses, but in truth, they'd found it difficult to connect them to their financial ruin. Another tearful juror, then stated the case of her miscarriage on hearing of her financial undoing, and as the inexperienced visualized the emotional scene they were swayed in favour of a not guilty verdict. She had skillfully massaged the chords of sympathy to which they could relate, albeit, in another time zone and circumstance.

Another day passed, and the to-ing and fro-ing continued, but by Thursday lunch the atmosphere was claustrophobic, and the pressures demanded a decision. Thursday, therefore, became the penultimate day, as the weekend loomed like a thundercloud over their heads.

It was three in the afternoon when the jury finally ceased discussion, and filed back into the courtroom. A unanimous verdict had been reached, and the Judge had a sentence in mind to justify guilty, in the second degree, with mitigating circumstances.

"Have you reached a unanimous verdict?" he enquired of the Foreman.

"We have, your Honour."

"In the case of the State versus Leonard Olshosky, to the charge of second degree murder. What say you?"

The Foreman already knew what was written on the half-folded piece of paper as he opened it with a certain amount of reverence, and willed his hands to stop shaking. Furthermore, he recognized that legal history would be made with his declaration, to contradict a sentence of twenty-five, fifty, or even one hundred years, that was clearly within the judge's reckoning.

"How do you find the accused-- to the count of second-degree murder-- guilty or not guilty?" the judge urged him on, and the hush in the court was almost unbearable. It went on...and on...until the foremen announced, "not guilty," which was followed by instant applause to shatter the court's demeanour.

"Silence in the Court!" The Judge hammered his desk in disbelief, and steeled himself to control his shaking head, and nervous twitches, that fought to undermine the supremacy of his image. It was an irrational verdict, he found difficult to accept, but he acknowledged the system. The law was the law, and he had no intention of intervening, even though on occasion, it proved to be an ass. He also regarded himself as lucky, to have the majority of the country behind such a popular verdict, over which he had presided. It would serve him well, if he decided to stand for the State Legislature, at the end of his term.

If the AG wanted to grab hold of the not-guilty verdict with all the 'thorns' attached, and declare a miss-trial during an election year, it was up to him. There was no public outcry in the press to do anything about the result, so what had appeared as a crisis initially, had turned up trumps for the incumbent political party. Now the only problem that remained was the second character in custody, and a decision on that score was about to be taken by the Prosecuting Counsel, assisted by a document shredder, and loop-hole, about to be found in the law.

"Mr. Leonard Olshosky, you have been found not guilty to the charge of second degree murder; you are free to leave this court." A strike of the gavel announced dismissal.

+ + +

"I'm glad we settled our debt with Cassini-Brown. He phoned to thank me for our endorsements; said he was looking for a second-hand ermine cape...Don't suppose you have an extra?"

"You know Diggers, he saved us a cool quarter million with his free services in the States, and he could have had my spare with pleasure if the moths hadn't got there first. A mangy alley cat has a better pelt than my spare. Think I'll donate it to the British museum for a cleaning cloth," he laughed.

"Did you see that column in the 'Times' about the murder that never was. Old Scraggs telephoned, and pointed it out. He seemed rather pleased– God knows why?"

"Well, wouldn't you be if you were privy to the details behind it?"

"Ah, didn't think of it that way."

"You never do: are you in the House tomorrow Diggers?"

"For my usual afternoon kip, and tea… yes, how about you?"

"I suppose you know the cream-teas on the terrace have been discontinued?"

"What! Who told you that?"

"Don't you ever read your circulars?"

"Sometimes... so now we have to go to Wimbledon for cream-teas, I tell you… this place is going to the dogs. Surely a man is entitled to his cream-tea, if he attends the afternoon sessions? That's the least he can expect– a cream-tea." The hot scones and thick clotted Devon cream had been the norm as far back as Diggers could remember, and the thrill of picking out whole strawberries from the conserve-jar was his pleasure, compared to searching in muddy fields. The ultimate scone in the house, had become a personal creation over the years, offering a mouthful of pastry and cream sweetened by strawberries, to yield a spiritual experience. As the seeds are crushed and the juices flirt with the cream, the scone is moistened, and slips down the throat with the ease of a herring from Holland.

A motion to reverse the decision on cream teas was about to be tabled in the house as a matter of urgency; it was of national importance to those who were steeped in tradition, whatever the cost to global warming.

"Diggers, I'm tired. Do you really think our actions made a difference?"

"Will we ever know...?"

+ + +

Epilogue

"Crooky, I spoke to Chuck, and he wanted to know how things had developed, and could I confirm we had something to do with that recent Olshosky acquittal."

"What did you tell him?"

"The truth of course– we got him acquitted."

"Did we?"

"Why are you challenging me like this? Of course we did. We broke their determination in London and they didn't have the backbone to do anything about it, when they got home. That's how I see it. Chuck says he's 'mighty proud of us'. He asked, what happened to the case of his friend, Henry Legg, who is still complaining about the fellow that screwed him, and how his new business is growing by the day. He finally wound up by inviting us to stay on his ranch. It's a difficult invitation to accept, eh? Told him to come over here of course. We have to be on their most wanted list over there, and I didn't think it worth the hassle. You'll be pleased to here, he arrives next week."

"Then you'll get down to telling him the 'mother of all stories', if I know you."

"How well you know me Crooky, and that's the least I can do... seeing how we bundled him onto that plane like so much baggage."

"Did I tell you, Jessie and Brian are at home?" Crooky mentioned the thought casually, as though it had just occurred to him.

"What's that? Why on earth didn't you tell me?"

"They've only served six months, and it's the last thing I expected, but good for them and good for us. Think of the petrol we'll save, travelling down to see them.

"Thought you'd like to hear what they had to say."

"Tell me."

"Apparently, the 'slammer' was overcrowded, and they've been tagged with these new fangled electronic bracelets."

"A good thing too. They're not the usual run-of-the-mill criminals that blow things up. Did they say anything about wanting to see us now they're out?"

"Didn't mention it old boy... suggest we let sleeping dogs lie. If they want our help with an appeal, I'm sure they'll ask us."

+ + +

"Conrad, guess who?" It was Simon on the line from Nairobi.

"Don't tell me, you have a new development?"

"No, no, nothing like that, but I was wondering if you could give me the contact of one of those Lords, who got so involved in the activities I was investigating. It's really just for the records, but it could also prove useful if we need some advice."

"Simon, I don't know what you're up to, but just leave me out of it."

"Conrad, you know me. Why would I involve you in anything? It's all in the past. I thought the matter was closed."

"Yes it's closed; so why do you want to open it again by contacting some of the players?"

"Please Conrad... I'm not involving you. So what about it?"

"I'll call you tomorrow." Conrad hung up, leaving Simon to his thoughts. The number Simon required was obtained from Gilmore's secretary, who had such things at her fingertips since Conrad had solicited a meeting with their Lordships, which had ended in lunch with the 'Hawks' from America.

"Take this down Simon;" he read out a number, "and do me a favour, keep out of trouble. These Lords always seem to attract it, and those around them are the ones who get hurt." Conrad hung up, left with a thought. 'What on earth is he up to, should I have asked?'

"Are you sure they will pass us onto Jesse Holt and Brian Stewart?" Major General James Uku asked Simon.

"Would you like me to make the call?"

"Do that."

"Lord Banks, please excuse me for troubling you." Simon didn't explain how he had got his number, and Digby didn't ask. "I'm trying to get hold of Jesse Holt. I served with him in the forces and we lost contact when he retired," he easily lied.

Strange thought Digby, he's just been released and something's in the wind already. How this fellow had connected him to Jesse was a mystery, but he saw no harm in doing Jesse a favour by passing on his number. After all, the debt he owed Jesse, could never ever be repaid in full. It was likely to go on forever.

"Thank you Lord Banks. I really appreciate your assistance." Simon handed his scribbled note across the desk to General Uku.

"I'll take it from here." Uku said, as he slipped the paper into the back of his diary to meet the agenda he had in mind.

"Colonel Holt," Uku opened the telephone conversation. "I owe your number to a mutual friend of ours, and shall be exceedingly grateful, if you will agree to meet me next week at your convenience. If you can spare the time I have a proposition to put to you, that you may well find, to your liking."

"Who are you?"

"My name is Uku, I come from Kenya, and all I ask is a chance, to explain myself to you in person. I can assure you, you won't be disappointed. What do you say?"

Jessie was intrigued... was it all happening over again? He liked what he heard, and his bracelet enforced, little or no restriction.

"Telephone me before nine on Tuesday. It's a date. We'll meet in the city." he replied.

"Simon I'm off to London this weekend to learn a few tricks of our future trade from Colonel Holt. While I'm away, take some time out with your new bride, and Kamba can mind the shop. Because when I return, there won't be much free time for any of us, and the recent oil strike in the North adds to our load of rip-offs and abuse of office by greedy officials. Re-negotiation, and naming of the corrupt, will be the penalty to retain their concessions. We have a huge backlog to clear. Crooks, with 'constitutional rights'. 'Rough Justice,'" he laughed.

+ + +

"It's good to be rich, but it's the means to this end that counts."

CPSIA information can be obtained
at www.ICGtesting.com
Printed in the USA
FFOW01n0516090217
32211FF